# GIRL ACT

Kristina Shook

Kristina Shook Publishing
Copyright 2013

# ACKNOWLEDGEMENTS

*This novel is dedicated to my dearly departed Sarah Lawrence College professor Dale Harris—whose attention and detail to educating me was AMAZING—he taught me the art of 'pausing' and he boldly told me what I needed to do in order to hone my craft—I am forever in his debt and his spirit is always with me when I sit down to write.*

*And to my lovely, dear friends, you know who you are—a zillion thanks!*

# CONTENTS

"Rated G is nobody gets the girl. PG is the good guy gets the girl.

R is the bad guy gets the girl. XXX is everybody gets the girl."

AUTHOR UNKNOWN

# GIRL ACT

# 1

## ACTORS

I was naked on a sandy beach, just at the crest of it—with the frothy, white foamy tide coming in slowly, past my feet, up my ankles, across my thighs, and in between my spread out legs. All the while I was orgasming noisily, in rhythm with the sound of the waves crashing.

Buzz, buzz, buzz went the alarm clock loudly—before the actor shut it off. He was the dirty blond I had met at the Verizon commercial callback, that typical commercial-style actor, the kind that looks smart, but can also drive a Chevy Blazer or grab a beer with a group of blue-collar guys in a Miller commercial. He looked at me with his classic blue eyes—going cross-wise, trying to act funny; he could never stop putting it on. I knew the drill: the morning after sex shower, and then the tennis shorts, t-shirt, sneakers, and tennis racket in his hand.

"How'd you sleep, babe?" he asked.

"Another wet dream!" I said, loud and proud.

"About me?" he asked.

"Oh, yeah," I answered.

He laughed and got out of my bed, turning so I could watch his very cute, firm ass walk towards the bathroom.

It was a tiny Los Feliz studio apartment—that housed a full size mattress, an upright Ikea desk covered with acting paraphernalia, a black Ikea futon couch with two pillows; one that had the word LOVE embroidered across it, a 5x8 richly woven Navajo rug that hung on the far wall, a small bathroom, a petite kitchen and a roof deck that housed a picnic table, four plastic Ikea chairs and thirty-two potted plants. It was surrounded by a white lacquered fence covered with purple bougainvillea. The low rent kept me from worrying if I booked an acting job or not.

I got up, not wanting to shower; hoping the people at Starbucks would smell last night's dirty sex all over me and be jealous. I had become a typical LA transplant, wanting to be noticed at any cost and in any which way.

He was my fifth actor, and the sex had been fair, not like the Charles Bronson look-alike I had gone with after booking a Domino Pizza commercial. Incidentally, the earlier part of my 'wet dream' had been about the 'Bronson' actor—chasing me across the sandy dunes, pulling me onto an inflated raft and sexing me up with his enjoyably rough tongue, but when you're an actress, you use white lies to please everybody. I had heard the shower go on and just stood there, thinking about that Bronson look-alike, a TV actor who hadn't booked a job in a long, long while. He had once been on General Hospital for a year as a stud-muffin character, the kind that married women use as an unkempt lover, and he had played a bit-part as a cop on a hit TV show. But at the time I met him, he was having to grab odd jobs as a grip. When we met, I had had my own small dressing room and the overhead light didn't work. Being a lead actress, I got to complain, and he, being the grip/electrician, was sent into fix it.

He strode in, wearing form-fitting blue jeans, a Gap shirt, with a handsome amount of stubble on his very attractive chin. And to top it off, his thin lips were parted. There's always that kind of first meeting, which I crave experiencing—it's where I go, "Oh, My God!!! I have to go to bed with this guy," and that's just what I had with the actor/grip. He had dark brown neatly cut hair, dark intense eyes, a fit body and muscular legs.

Yeah, I knew he was worth a climb on. I guess the meaning of a bad-boy to me is the kind of guy who is so sexual that he just can't be ignored. And being an actress, I wanted to experience everything. So we flirted—it was so easy. And he asked for my number and I counted, "One, two, three, four, five, six, seven," and then, "Here it is." And he called me that night.

"Hey, Vivien, you want to go out tonight?" And I said, "It's eleven already," and he said, "Yeah, I know, the night's just starting to pop."

So I said yes. I was going to say yes, no matter what. Not being a 'hitch-hiker' type girl, a girl who goes out with strange guys with hard-ons, I should explain that the redheaded nine-year-old, the real star of the pizza commercial, his mother was a screenwriter who knew the actor/grip from a Monday night workshop created and run by Tommy Moretti, the co-writer of an Oscar winning film, and she told me how amazing the actor/grip's work was whenever he hit the stage. So it was, in away, like meeting his 'stage mother'.

We met on the corner of Hillhurst and Hollywood Boulevard, at the King-King bar, and he was already sucking on a draft beer when I sat next to him. He was washed and smelling like he had a bar of Dove under each armpit. He licked his lips and I held onto my stool as he ordered me a Bud Light. His profile was GQ, but with a Montana twist, which incidentally was where he was from.

We babbled about booking acting work and how impossible it usually was. He was on the outs with acting and trying to make up his next plan; I was still thinking that my big movie break was due any day. My agent Ray had huge plans for me and I believed the hype.

The actor/grip talked about his stint on GH and the popular cop show, and about the once-steady paychecks. Booking acting jobs is all about freedom, opportunity, and living in the moment of becoming a new character. But when there are no bookings, it's all about apprehension topped off with boredom at having to be just yourself.

"Are you a free spirit?" he asked.

"I think so, but what's your definition?" I asked.

He said, "Having sex on the first date."

I nodded, and then tried not to smile as I asked "Is this considered a first date?" and he nodded yes.

Then he asked me if I had ever done one of those 'trust' exercises.

"The kind where you fall backwards and let other people catch you, and you trust that they won't drop you?" I asked (FYI, it's taught in most beginner acting classes).

"Yup," he said.

"Okay, then yes, and more than once. Why?" I asked.

That's when he told me how he wanted to blindfold me and drive me to his place over near Melrose Avenue, and how he wanted to have sex the whole time with the blindfold kept on. And I slid off the soft bar stool and pulled my black Chanel bag over my shoulder and said, "This free bird is standing; grab her while she's up."

Outside I got into his vintage black VW-beetle and once I was in the tattered leather passenger seat, he pulled out a conservative necktie, a leftover from some insurance commercial audition. It had been in the back seat with his other audition clothes, crumpled up, but ready. He put it over my eyes, tying it tight and when I told him I couldn't see anything but darkness, he started the engine and off we went. It was cool, I sort of guessed he was taking Hollywood Boulevard and cutting down maybe La Brea, but I was just guessing and the passenger window was blowing air in and we didn't talk. Like when you're falling backwards, no one says a thing, because you have to just 'trust' that they will catch you—even the breath gets held and the silence lingers.

He helped me out of the VW-beetle and onto the sidewalk. It was like a blind character role that I had just been cast in, or maybe it was just 'Method' acting. There were three thick steps and then he unlocked two locks, held the door open and led me in. Then he relocked the locks, took my hand, and led me up twelve carpeted steps. Wow, I was walking up a flight of stairs in the dark. At one point, I touched the wall and felt a frame covered in glass, but I let go of it.

We turned left, then right, and I knew I was in his bedroom. He put me on the side of his bed, and then came in front of me and began undressing me while I just sat there, moving my arms so he could take off my top, and then my bra and then my favorite blue jeans with my slogan 'WHAT IF' sewn on the back of them.

Then he stood in front of me, parting my legs, and had me help him take off his t-shirt and his jeans and his flannel boxer shorts. Feeling that flannel reminded me of one of those kids' books filled with touchy-feely fabric. All I can say is that I knew it was flannel.

He was already at attention and his penis size matched his feet, which meant he'd be an excellent fit inside of me. He slid me back on the bed and pulled the blanket from under me, and then he put his mouth near mine and we kissed for a while. Then he spread my legs really wide and he licked me like I was thirty-one flavors or more.

Oh, wow! He was inside of me for hours. When he was in—he was fast, like a baby seal swimming upstream. Okay, so I'm corny sometimes. My hips moved back and forth and he glided us all over his king size bed, and all the while, it was sheer black before my eyes.

At some point, I just let myself feel everything, and I wondered about what we looked like. He begged me to sleep with his tie across my eyes so I did, and then in the morning, he took it off and I saw the room. It was plain; a bed boxed in a wooden frame, a nondescript dresser, and a wall-to-wall closet with clothes that looked like any guy would have. He didn't have any photos or plants, or anything that might have belonged to an ex-girlfriend.

We exited through the hall and that's when I saw the framed glass—it was a movie poster from a Sundance flick that had gone on to gross a ton of money, and there was his grinning mug on it. So I'd screwed a real working actor, or at least a has-been. A few feet from it was his framed glossy 8x10 soap opera picture, the kind that gets signed and given to fans. And then there was his cop shot from the popular TV drama show; that one turned me on the most.

"I'd like to do it with a cop," I said, feeling like anything was possible after the necktie.

"That can be arranged," he said in a very matter-of-fact tone. He dropped me off in front of my brick apartment building and watched me walk into the courtyard, I didn't turn around, but I heard him drive off.

It was two weeks later when I heard from the actor/grip. He left a sexy message about seeing a car wreck off the 101 Freeway, and how he'd like to bang me in the back seat. Later he called just before eleven and asked if I'd do him inside of it. I said, "Sure," and he picked me up at midnight and we found the totaled silver Mercedes near Woodland Hills. We parked a few feet away and walked to it.

"No one died, did they?" I asked.

"Nah, I saw it happen, just a mega lawsuit."

We got in. The black leather backseat was still intact; the car reeked of fragrant air freshener. He sat down and I got on top of him. This time I got to lead us in the in-an-out game. We did fifteen minutes of serious humping and then left.

He dropped me back at my apartment. I smelled like sex and the inside of the crushed Mercedes. The last time I saw him, he had asked me to meet him in Griffith Park, in the open field area where the park rangers have arranged several really large rocks and a few picnic tables; it's been used as a backdrop a ton of times for commercials. I was in my favorite jeans again, the "WHAT IF" ones, a clingy black top—that clung to my red bra, creating size 34 C mountains, and my faithful neon Nike sneakers. I had hiked halfway up when a cop yelled at me.

"You're trespassing!!!"

"No, I'm not?!!!" My mind was so focused on finding the actor/grip that it took me a minute or more to recognize the cop's smirk. He was dressed to the nines. His cop pants were snug and he had cuffs dangling from his left middle finger.

"Where's your gun?" I asked.

"In here." He gestured with his right hand in the shape of a gun at his zipper.

"Is it loaded?" I asked.

When you screw an actor and you're an actress, you can go on for hours with trashy, over-the-top dialogue, because unknown/semi-working actors never ever get enough lines.

"Why don't you find out," he said, as he took me by my arm and yanked me off the trail and in the direction of the mountainside that didn't face the Hollywood Hills houses.

"I'll have to search you, Miss," he said.

"Sure, Officer, you have to follow police procedure."

He faced me against a tree, pressing the side of my face into the thick bark as he spread my legs apart, the way they do on all cop TV shows and in the movies.

"You better not be packing," he said.

"Just a kumquat, Officer," I replied, innocently.

He slid his hand up my right thigh, then my left and gradually into my crotch, where he dug like he was planning to bury something deep. My face still touching the tree, I played the tough girl part, not the victim. "Go ahead cuff me." And he did cuff my hands behind my back. Then he unzipped my jeans and yanked them down to my knees, gripping my butt with too much force, but still I kept my moans silent. And then he unzipped himself with one hand, slid a condom on and put his erect fleshy gun inside me.

The actor/grip/cop discharged enough seeds to fertilize a troupe of wanna-be actors or politicians on my ass and down my thighs. When we finished, he pulled back up my jeans and un-cuffed me. Then he spun me around—my face checkered from the imprint of the bark, my lips puckered and my eyes beaming.

"Stay out of trouble, or next time I'll arrest you," he said.

"Uh, uh," I stammered, feeling sticky, smelly and oh-so-human. He left the condom on the ground. I know it wasn't environmentally correct to litter, but it was erotically exciting to see it.

Off I went back down the trail and onto Commonwealth Avenue again, over to Prospect Avenue and onto Rodney Drive, leaving him to exit the park on his own, as every good cop should do. A month later he booked a movie in New York, and dropped by to give me his cop uniform, as a memento—I had to keep it.

The very last time I ever heard his voice was from LAX; he left a message on my machine just before his plane took off.

"Vivien saw a broken down school bus in Torrance and thought of screwing you seat-by-seat, finishing you off against the steering wheel." I had to smile, and I saved the message. When I got lonely, I'd play it over and over. The crappy thing is that when you use the phone company's voice mail system, it only lasts a little over two weeks and I went on to be single way longer than that.

The shower was off and the Tennis Actor was standing in front of me, just staring at me.

"I'm hurrying up, don't worry," I said, as I slipped on a cotton dress and then reached into my closet where I still kept the cop uniform on the top shelf and grabbed my yoga clothes. I followed the Tennis Actor out the door with my trusty rescue dog, Shadow. No one really noticed us at Starbucks; the morning crowd had dispersed.

The Tennis Actor drove to the public tennis courts in Griffith Park, taking Shadow with him—which was one of those sweet things I dug about him—while I walked up to Yoga Vibe over on Hillhurst. The morning group was in and we did our sunrise salutations, our downward dogs, and while I lay in meditation I realized that I, the 'official callback actress,' was finished with Los Angeles, AKA Hollywood, with all its hype, propaganda and buildup of 'maybe gonna make it BS' and all the actors, producers, directors and studio heads.

Afterwards, I talked to Carol, the yoga goddess, whose broad boned body was extra fit, and I said, "I'm done with LA, I need to move away." She grinned at me, not saying a word. I stood there, thinking, and then I said just as if it was common news to everyone but me, "I'm not amounting to anything here. Not even sure I have a purpose anymore."

She took a deep breath in and out and then said, "Sometimes, we have to go home to begin again."

Carol proceeded to tell me how she had been a Wells Fargo Bank teller for five years, and then spent a year as a co-manager at a finance company with her then husband, but one day, she stumbled in the middle of a supermarket aisle, and while lying on the linoleum floor had a panic attack, where she couldn't stop shaking, trembling and sobbing. By chance or luck, the man, who sat down next to her on the supermarket floor trying to help her, was a yoga teacher, and he taught her how to breathe, how to steady her heart rate and calm her racing mind, right there while other shoppers looked on. Within three months she was divorced, living with her sister and studying various types of yoga.

"Look for the signs, they will appear," she said.

"Really, will they?" I asked.

"Hold your thoughts up to the sky to have the answers shown," she explained. I left her and the Yoga Vibe feeling hopeful, but still a bit bewildered.

I met the Tennis Actor back at my studio apartment; he was off to an audition for Crest Whitestrips. I had watched him place the strips across his upper and lower teeth—maybe he was trying 'Method' commercial acting.

"They work, don't they?" he asked as he held up the Polaroid 'before' shot he had taken. I said, "I'm buying!"

He washed his mouth and smacked on some aftershave that smelled expensive. I counted to ten in my head and then I said, "I'm tired of LA."

He just nodded in agreement as he put on his brand new khakis and his new pale blue button-down shirt. He never wore the same outfit to an audition unless it was a callback. He had new clothes at my place and at his, and at his best friend Aaron's house—a hard-nose screenwriter who claimed to have used my 'weirdness' for two of his screenplay characters. I gave Shadow a dog chew and took off my clothes, at last ready for a hot shower. He ignored that I was twisting my nipples for sensation, understanding my continual need for pleasure.

I had heard all about body piercing and had once met a British guy (who looked as if he could double for the actor Tom Hardy) at the bar over on Cahuenga Boulevard that used to be called the Burgundy Room—he had just gotten a cock ring.

And when I asked, "Does it look cool?" He unzipped his pants and pulled out a firm cock with a silver ring through the tip of it.

And I had to admit it looked really attractive and not at all strange. Everything sooner or later appears normal. At least, in Los Angeles.

"Bled for two frigging days, now it's all right; thanks for asking to see it. Luv," he said proudly. It's cute how the Brit's use the word 'luv' instead of 'babe' or 'honey'.

And I said, "Looks totally cool," and then we continued drinking our beers til the bar closed, and no, he didn't ask me over to his place. So how it feels to touch or how a condom fits over it, I still don't know.

"Wish me luck!" the Tennis Actor hollered.

"Luck!" I yelled, and then stood by my window watching him walk away. He wasn't in love with me, nor I with him, just a good, good guy. And yes, he would make it just fine without me.

# 2

## YES

I had gotten tired of the East Coast years and years before. At that time, I was living half a block from Chinatown in Manhattan, and had decided that I needed to go out to Hollywood, California, and be in the movies. It was either New York or Los Angeles and I had already done NYC, and my best friend Paloma had said, "You need to chill out from NYC for a couple of years. Maybe Hollywood is the right place for you."

It was my Aunt Helen who had suggested that I go out to Los Angeles as an adventure.

She said, "If you live by palm trees, you'll feel something new. Los Angeles has palm trees, rows of them."

Paloma added, "Go for it!"

And fortunately, Aunt Helen had given me the four thousand dollars to fly across the country with, money that allowed me to rent a single studio apartment (as in the one on Rodney Drive) and even to buy an eight-hundred-dollar

Toyota hatchback, circa 1975, and, boy, did it look dated. Coincidentally, classic/vintage is in in LA.

I waited tables at Universal's cafeteria on the studio lot (yucky if you're an actress, because you feel invisible and horribly obscure). I would have done temp jobs but I'm a one handed typist—(I'll explain why later on). Anyway, a year later I quit, because I met an art model named McKenna from Memphis, who suggested that I become an art model like her. Number one reason; the flexibility of hours would allow me to go out on more auditions. Number two; I had curvy hips, shapely thighs, and even a soft belly (not a camera-thin/anorexic actress body, but the really fleshy, rounded butt kind).

"You have an hourglass figure, the painters will go nuts over you. You have to become an art model," McKenna informed me.

She was tall and thin; she had the 'Egon Schiele' artist-type body and had made a fantastic career of it.

So I said yes, which normally is what I say, because my best friend Paloma had once told me a story of how John Lennon had gone to see some art at an apartment in Manhattan and he had seen a carved sculpture on the wall that said "yes," and, as he went out on the rooftop—there stood Yoko Ono. She had made that work of art.

Okay, so who knows if the story was or is true, but when in doubt, act 'as if'. Even if it wasn't, it had worked for me. Starting out saying "yes" just made life easier than saying "no". No is a two-letter word that every actor, director, producer, or screenwriter hates to hear.

The phone rang, pulling me away from the window and out of my deep thoughts. It was the painter, Kenneth. He needed me to pose for a few of his friends in Venice; his other model had unexpectedly canceled, leaving them stranded for a muse.

"How fast can you get here?" he asked.

"I'll be there in twenty minutes. Unless I fly, and then, well, that's a minute or two," I said.

He liked my wry, okay, really dumb, humor. Everyone knows in Los Angeles, that to get to the West Side (Santa Monica/Venice/Marina Del Ray), it takes less than an hour when there is no traffic and up to two hours when there's traffic. The key is going when there's no traffic and taking the 10 Freeway or Sunset Boulevard all the way there. So I dried off from a quick warm shower and put on my black DKNY dress and gave Shadow an extra dog treat. I had already done the art schools from Pasadena to Brentwood, and after just a year, I was only working for private artists.

It was then that I decided to see if I could borrow some extra paint from Kenneth to paint my own "YES". Maybe if I hung it up, I'd get the answer to where I was to go after I left LA.

Kenneth is one of those realist painters, where everything looks as if you could snatch it off the canvas. There were two other painters, a guy, older than Kenneth, originally from somewhere in Russia, who did charcoal drawing that blurred real images with an imaginative bent and a local California artist Kenneth had known for years, who laughed a lot and told jokes when everyone took breaks.

Kenneth's studio was the quintessential artist studio, the kind a set decorator would die to use as a movie location: enormous open space, museum white walls, a model block in the middle with several old easels set around it, a lengthy steel counter with a stainless steel industrial sink against the far wall, a very used and trusted coffee maker brewing for the billionth time, a slouchy, worn out leather couch with a Mexican blanket draped over it, a black leather club chair, a single metal bookshelf with stacks of art books, a stereo, and no TV. The tiled bathroom had a shower, a toilet, a cobalt glass sink and gray bath towels.

Large finished painted canvases were stacked against the walls close to the door. A wooden table with four heavy ornate chairs was where I'd sit with Kenneth and the Russian artist, while the California guy moved around us, never standing still. It had always gone that way.

I arrived to a warm bear hug from the 6'2", sweet-faced Kenneth. To win him over to using me as his art model, I had had to prove myself. The key to being an art model is simple and challenging at the same time. A set of three B's: Being able to contort the body. Being able to hold the pose fifteen to twenty minutes without moving. Being able to go right back into the same pose after a short break, without changing the level or position of any part of the body. I had first posed for one of his ex-wives, also an artist, who told him about me, and that's how I started posing for him and attaining all three B's for twenty-minute stretches at a time.

There's that thing I like so much, when you meet someone new—and it just doesn't take long to feel a kind of closeness, as if you knew him/her for years. Kenneth and I had that; we just dug each other as subject and artist. He liked my curvy hips, my breasts and my imperfections, which incidentally make an art model worth drawing. Supermodels need not apply, imperfections rule on canvas every time. I trusted him so I had allowed him to take photos of me, for future work.

So there I was, heading into Kenneth's small bathroom to put on my Chinatown-bought silk robe while the artists took their positions behind easels. A crimson velvet chair stood on the raised model platform, otherwise known as the model block. A minute later I walked toward it, taking off my robe and letting it fall to the floor.

Being naked in an artist's studio or art classroom is a thousand times different from pole dancing at Cheetah's on Hollywood Boulevard or any other 'live nude girls' place. No one is there to get horny. Artists see beyond the T&A; in fact, they notice the color of the areola, the size of the nipples, the contour of the thighs, the outline of the veins, the nape of the neck, the slope of the shoulders, and the hair that sprouts in whatever shape, length and color above the vagina. An art model doesn't jiggle, she stays motionless, and that's what I did as I faced the chair, and twisted my wide hips out so my breasts showed and my neck arched. I held one hand on the chair where I was pivoted and the other above my head, my fingers curled toward the painters. I heard Kenneth's guttural noises of approval, since, I knew what type of poses he liked and tailored them for him. "Ahhhhhhhhhh," he said. That's probably the fourth unspoken key to art modeling: being able to anticipate the pose an artist wants.

Someone once asked me what I did while they were drawing or painting me. I remember liking the question, because it made me think, "If I'm posing, looking at the ground, after a while I begin to see images; a shape, a face, or a creature. Of course, this is only possible if the floor has texture."

Modeling is the quietest I've ever gotten, and the closest to meditation that I'll ever get. Being so wrapped up in the stillness, without forcing myself to not think and to just stare is how it happens for me. Sometimes I daydream, but not a sexual daydream, because then naturally my hips and lips would move.

Also, art modeling is the way I got over the 'drilled in' idea that it's necessary to have super-skinny thighs and the 'perfect' actress body. Once you have artists tell you how exquisite, beautiful and unique you are—you're free.

Every time I've met one of those "Help I'm trying to become a skinny twit" actresses at an audition, I've told them to art model at least once. I'll say, "It's the quickest way to body self acceptance and you'll be comfortable if you ever have to shoot a nude scene in front of a film crew." Hey, I'm not a shrink, and taking care of myself is enough of a task, why add to it?

There I was, facing the window that funneled in the bright California sunlight, when I thought about the "yes" and decided to imagine polished silver metal 24" x 24" letters spelling out "YES" dangling above my head. Moving like wind chimes by the small hands of three elves dressed in off-white painter pants, matching shirts, and white baseball hats, barefoot and sitting on the high ceiling rafters of Kenneth's studio. The "yes" letters attached to fishing rod lines. I felt this sudden sense that an answer was coming to me in the next day: a map, or a written outline of where I should go.

Later that night, he showed up, the Tennis Actor with his dirty blond hair slicked back, and for the first time I said, "You know what? I can't hang out tonight; I need some alone time, some me time, some un-male time."

In a bitter tone he replied, "I got a callback, thought we could celebrate, but if you're not in the mood, then so what!"

I could have been soft and explained that I needed to be alone only for a few hours, so I could hear my own thoughts and figure out where my life needed to go and where the "yes" was going to come from, but I didn't.

"Congrats on the CB (callback). Talk to you tomorrow," I said and took Shadow and went inside. I used to be the most dumped girl there ever was, til I turned twenty-six (I'm twenty-seven now) and decided to stop waiting by the phone, to stop trying to cross paths with a guy, to stop begging for some guy to let me stay over night, for the whole night, including breakfast, when he really wanted me to leave his place after the sex. To stop screwing him to just fill in the gap between me—and nothingness.

I watched the Tennis Actor amble away, half wanting to run after him and jump on his back and hump his left leg just to prove that I had him, that I could keep him, but I forced myself to close the downstairs screen door and let go. I had never done that, I had always been the one walking away after a guy had asked to me leave or even hinted that I should. I had listened to guys telling me that they "needed their own space for a while" or that they'd "be back in touch, real soon." I walked up the stairs and into my apartment. Shadow raced to his water bowl. I locked the door and sighed. I felt strangely different.

Ugh, I have no plans ever to be a woman without a man, and yet I wasn't lonely. Okay, so I also knew one night was one night and not a thousand. TG (Thank God). I opened my fridge and then made a delicious vegetarian plate of sesame pasta, with huge chunks of tofu and heaps of spinach. Good food calms me down. And tofu rocks! I gave Shadow his Science Diet dinner, and spread my turquoise bed sheet onto the hardwood floor. I took off all my clothes and there I lay naked, just waiting for the sign, the life-size moment of change to appear—the "YES".

# 3

## *EGGS*

Waking up and looking for the sign of "yes" was no picnic. First, I had slept on the wood floor with just a sheet under me—which was fine for Shadow, asleep at my left hip, but my body was stiff in all the wrong places. And from the floor, I saw the used condoms the Tennis Actor had flung nonchalantly when he was ready to ejaculate on top of my belly, face, or against the wall in my little alcove bedroom.

So much for my trying to act 'as if' I could attain Elizabeth Bennet's love success in Jane Austen's *Pride and Prejudice*—which, incidentally Keira Knightley had done a great acting job in the movie version of, and the Mr. Darcy actor (Matthew Macfadyen) was beyond vulnerably perfect for what I had imagined. I read the book in high school and had had the twisted naive thought that I, too, was going to grow up and fall in love with a modern day Mr. Darcy—one who wouldn't toss his used condoms on the floor and who would be in love with me, body and soul. What was I doing? And for how long had I just been doing nothing with my love life? Not that the Tennis Actor wasn't exciting, good looking, and well-built in the area between his legs. But was there really a future?

I sat up as Shadow started licking my thigh. "Is there a Mr. Darcy in LA?" I asked. Shadow barked as if I had said, "Park" and I got up, feeling achy and cramped, turning on the shower in my tiny bathroom covered in pretty blue tiles from wall-to-wall. It was the best feature in the place besides the roof top patio. I stood under the hot shower, thinking over and over about finding out if he (Mr. Darcy) was in Los Angeles, and if I had just been looking in the wrong places.

Then I took Shadow to the Laurel Canyon Dog Park— not just as a bonus for him, but as a way of searching for the hippest, coolest, most real Mr. Darcy. Out of all the dog parks in LA, Laurel Canyon has to have the hottest dudes around. Okay, at least in my limited opinion. I had never thought of myself as a love addict, only because 'addict' has such a negative ring to it. But there I was, at eight in the morning, looking for Mr. Right, Mr. Love, or Mr. Darcy, whoever would be authentic. Meeting 'attached' guys or married guys is no fun (in fact, it's a waste of time and energy).

Anyway I saw a lot of fine looking men in the park as Shadow raced around, barking like the hippest dog ever. I stared at every guy, trying to see what reaction I'd get. Nothing! Ha, ha. I should have grabbed a cardboard box and my red permanent pen and written, "Seeking LOVE, please apply," and put it around my neck. But if my acting coach had seen me, he would have said I 'lacked the balls to command the stage' and he'd have been totally right.

Around that time, because timing at times can be perfectly rotten, the Tennis Actor texted me saying quote unquote, "*24b-up. I'll be in touch soon.*" Ugh! A 24b-up equals a 24-hour break-up, it's not an official ending, it's more like not meeting for breakfast, lunch, or dinner for one whole day until you figure yourself out or screw someone else. I just texted back, *U got it.* And I did. Hey, it's not like I could get snotty or bitchy or throw a hissy-fit. After all I had asked the Tennis Actor to give me last night off and I was in the dog park hunting for a modern day Mr. Darcy-not just any man, of course, but still, facts are facts. So there I was, a few feet from a colossal pile of dog shit, a 24b-up text in my cell phone, and no available men anywhere in the park. "Shadow," I hollered, after cleaning up the poop which, like recycling, I can do with my eyes shut. So much for finding a handsome yes!

I got in my car and drove us down to Sunset Boulevard, with the urge to race up to Zuma Beach in Malibu and watch the surfer dudes. Being afraid of water made it extra exciting to sit and gawk, not to mention that surfer dudes have detailed, killer bodies. But, my cell phone rang. It was Beth asking if I would race over to the Woman's Club of Hollywood to pick up a stack of 8x10's to phone actors for tonight's casting director's workshop. Having a talent agent is great, but it doesn't mean they do everything, especially if they are not 'A-list' agents, and if you're not an 'A-list' actress or actor, yet or ever.

"Sure, give me two minutes," I said putting Malibu on my 'another day' list (along with finding Mr. Darcy/Mr. Right).

I had started attending the workshops as a way to get seen by new casting directors who Ray, my agent, couldn't get me in front of. Yeah, it cost money to be seen, but because I did the phone calls, and solicited other actors to come, I got to do them for free. Okay, so maybe this was a sign that I wasn't yet done with Hollywood, that maybe a really big, amazing stardom break was going to come my way tonight.

Beth was originally from Alabama; she and her actor son had come out West to try their luck, and they'd had some small successes here and there. She was filled with Southern 'gun powder,' and never gave up. I walked into the modest room in the back of a classroom once used for the likes of Myrna Loy, and where actor Charles Laughton taught. Wow, what a Hollywood they had back then! I often think I was meant to be a 1940s or 1950s actress, but still, I can't turn the clock back. Too bad!

Beth was standing by a dark vintage desk with a huge stack of 8x10's and a one sheet pitch 'speech' about the guest casting director. It read blankety-blankety is now casting this year's hottest 'reality show'. Reality TV? I tried not to show my disappointment. Beth was very excited; she wanted a packed house to impress him. The rickety fold-up chairs were already arranged. At night, the parking lot would be used as everyone's rehearsal spot, though I couldn't image what lines anyone would need to rehearse for.

"Mini interviews, just tell them that's all. And they should be themselves," Beth chirped in her sweet, southern voice.

I nodded and scooped up the stack and headed out the door.

"Let's get it full, all right?" Beth called from the doorway.

"You got it!" I hollered as I jumped back into the car where Shadow was waiting, his tongue hanging out.

He's the funniest dog sometimes, the way he'll jump into the passenger seat and act like a human, waiting to be driven somewhere. Without Shadow, I never would have been able to do Hollywood. I would have been too lonely. Because of him and his dog mutt-face, I'd met friends, men, and had somebody to do things with 24/7. In fact, in LA everybody must feel the same way, because there are so many dogs.

I zipped back to my Los Feliz studio apartment and laughed. I had thought "yes" was about moving, not about being suddenly single for 24 hours. I plopped down on my cozy Ikea futon couch. FYI, I always have a spare bed to offer—not that futons are the most comfortable, but when in need, it's there. I put the photo stack in front of me, all color, glossy; gone were the days of black-and-white 8x10's (headshots) that I started out with. Every actor puts a cell phone number on the resume, if his agent isn't 'A-list'. I mean, we're all dying to get that one call where Martin Scorsese, or Quentin Tarantino, or Spike Lee, or Kathryn Bigelow, or the next up-and-coming director says, "Hey, I want to cast you in my motion picture." So, in other words, I was phoning every desperate, wanna-make-it-in-Hollywood actor. I picked up the first photo: cute guy, crew cut, 'army-type'. Think, *Zero Dark Thirty*. He also had powerful dark brown eyes and yummy lips.

I phoned him. "Yeah?" he asked and I rattled off my super, practiced 'reality TV' phone pitch about how this top reality casting director was giving actors the chance to be seen and make money. I added that, after a stint on the hottest reality show on network, he'd be a shoe-in for movie and TV parts. And then I waited, while he cackled loudly.

"So, can you come tonight?" I asked.

"I cum all the time; which picture you got in front of you?" he asked, like only a good-looking, cocky actor can do.

"I don't. I have your name and cell phone number on a sheet with forty others," I lied, because technically I didn't want to say some casting director had dumped his 8x10 along with a thousand others into a reject pile—and that I was recycling it.

"Oh, I'm wearing the grey t-shirt. I can hear it in your voice. Right?" he asked, doubly cocky, probably with a hard-on or with his well-hung cock in his hands.

"Listen, I don't have your acting photo," I said, a bit pissed off, but only a little bit.

"You're East Coast born and raised; you're an actress, probably the dramatic kind; you think I'm cute, but maybe stuck up, but you'd be open to meeting me," he said.

"Yes," I said, because no is for negative, angry, bitter women, which I vowed not to be. Yes, because things like this never happen. I swear I had used a 'business type' voice, and still, he had read my flirty, provocative mind. Oh, well!

"Good, I bet you're something," he said, in a really commanding voice that made me gulp. Gulp.

"FYI, the grey shirt," I added.

And that's how it happened. We agreed to meet on Vermont Avenue at the Figaro Bistro, the French café (it's been used in several commercials), but just to swap books. He said I had to pick a book he hadn't read, as if I knew what the hell he read, or if he could read (ha, ha). I remembered that Kenneth, the painter, had given me his copy of John Forte's *Ask the Dusk* and that it had simply blown me away, and, well, Kenneth knew more than me in so many worldly ways that I figured it was my best bet to impress the actor with.

I decided to play it casual, just regular blue jeans with my patch 'DREAM UP' and my classic snug brown tee (suggesting spunky, yet smart, with some class) and for sexy, my black polka dot thong (not that he was going to see it). And my lime green bra; I'm the type that likes my bra and panties not to match and to be oh-so-bright and colorful. After all, sex is serious enough these days. I wore my brown leather slip-on boots with a slight heel. If I had been in New York, I would have worn my black combat boots for the sheer gorilla-girl look, but Los Angeles is about ease and comfort. I walked; I figured why bring my car when the day was nice.

He was wearing a grey shirt, not the one in the headshot, but a shade lighter, and loose, faded Levi blue jeans and running sneakers. Hell, he could have worn a sleeping bag: he was super striking. He was at a table a few feet from the door. He wasn't hiding. I slid in after feeling his eyes go up and down my body. I think he would have liked a backside view as well, but he'd have to wait. We both smiled and he slid his book over first. Wow—Anais Nin's *Little Birds*, a collection of erotic stories, a book I hadn't read since college that I had figured, or hoped, no man had read because it felt so truly personal. I pushed my Forte book over and he gave me a cocky grin. Maybe he was born that way.

"Read the first story!" he said, like he was my teacher and I was his pupil.

"Yes, instructor," I said.

"Justin!" He reminded me as he opened his book.

Justin, hmm, not a bad name. I told him mine, but he didn't look up, that's how cocky he was. The waitress had been instructed before I arrived. She put two Arnold Palmers and a plateful full of fresh fruit in front of us and left, but not before getting a wink from cocky Justin.

The first story was *Little Birds* from which Nin's book took its title. I wouldn't dare spoil it by giving away any details; it's just a naughty story and it reminded me of how my college years really were all about being the most dominating sexual woman I could be. It wasn't just 'in-and-out' fornication that my college friends and I were after—it was about the greatest orgasm, the longest head banging sex one could have. And I did.

It's like Justin suddenly became a part of my Mr. Darcy plan. Jane Austen wasn't just writing about 'love', she was explaining the attainable feeling when one finds her soul mate. Oh my. Had I found mine? I glanced up; Justin was eating a slice of apple. How Adam and Eve can you get? He was grinning at me, with wet lips and serious eyes.

"Bonus points on the book. Can I keep it?" he asked, as he put his sexy, cute, thin lips over his straw and sucked his drink down. I had plenty of other mementos from Kenneth the famed artist; the book didn't matter.

"Sure," I said.

"Thanks, and that's for you, to get you restarted," he said, as he filled his mouth with blueberries. Oh, so cocky. It's not like I could roll my eyes and ask what the hell he meant by that, because I'd be admitting it. So I just nodded like a card player bluffing. When you're an actress, so much of life is acting 'as if'. Of course you try to figure out your next move, the right line to say, all the while not letting the other person steal your spotlight. Cocky guys, who are actors, are always jockeying for the lead role. The spotlight! He pushed the fruit plate at me, eyeing me in a forceful way, I ate some melon slices, so he could watch me chew. Eating can be so erotic.

"Come on, let's take a walk," he said as he got up, tossing two twenty dollar bills on the table and motioning for the waitress. He had his book in hand. I gulped a quick drink, dabbed my mouth with my napkin, and pulled my book off the table, covering the title with my hand (ever so possessive). He moved quickly out onto the street in the direction of Griffith Park. Walking without Shadow felt like an act of betrayal.

"My truck's up the street. I was checking out a landscaping design I liked, so I parked in front of it," he said.

I nodded like I understood, like it was typical. He stepped back so he was now beside me.

"I like your lips," he said, which made me laugh.

Oh, had he planned that line, because it worked. He hooked his arm into mine and we walked toward his Chevy pickup truck, the kind a hunter or fisherman would own. He opened the passenger door first and, as I got in, he said, "Nice hips," and again I laughed. Maybe he wasn't cocky, just 'weird,' in an appealing and very sexy way. He got in and started the truck, and then looked at me.

"How about we make out at Zuma Beach?" he asked, like it was an everyday question between two strangers.

"Sure," I said, not wanting to sound too excited or horny or both.

"I like your hips, because they swivel," he said as he peeled out and headed onto Sunset Boulevard. I thought he would have asked the usual relationship interview questions, like, "are you single?" and "are you into an LTR?" (long-term relationship), but he didn't.

He played Kid Rock's *Only God Knows Why*. I'd never heard it before and so I said nothing, letting the lyrics fall over me. Justin rocked to it with his hands drumming on steering wheel, as if the song was personal. So odd, I was going to Malibu after all. And to the beach, how weird was that? Really weird, but how could I knock it? I was getting what I had wished for, only I wasn't sure if Justin was really 'genuine,' or if I was going to like kissing him. Zuma is a really beautiful, stunning stretch of beach in Malibu. Since it was a weekday, it wasn't crowded.

The great thing about an actor's schedule is that you can end up with six days of work, followed by nothing. Of course, if you're a bona fide working actor, you make good money and don't care when you have free time.

I hopped out of the truck with Justin staring at my backside. Wow. He pulled out a blanket and a beat-up water proof tote bag and we left our books in the truck; we were done with the reading 'test' part of the date. I had a feeling kissing was 'test' number two.

"So, are you from Colorado, or Maine?" I asked, having studied him long enough. He inched closer to me as we hit the sand.

"Maine," he said.

I glanced at him; he was cute and smart, though I guessed a college dropout, because he seemed to beat to his own drum. The kind of man that doesn't want to blend in or do as other collegiates.

"College dropout, you've had sex with up to 18 women, and you prefer to eat meat over fish any day. Right?" I asked; as we neared the spot he had chosen.

"Applied, got accepted to an Ivy one, but only did a semester. As for women, 5 total, and I prefer cod or halibut over salmon and not meat unless it's organic chicken. I can swallow mussels whole. I like seawater. Anything else?"

I shook my head. I mean, it was fun, and it's not like I had ever just pitched my first impression before. I felt like my art model friend McKenna, who reads astrology charts, and understands people based on their astrological signs. I mean, wow, I was reading him. I suddenly knew that after I kissed him, I'd probably know more, maybe too much.

He spread out a navy cotton blanket and we sat down. He was fast! Like I guessed he would be. He had me pinned under him and was over me, our faces inches apart, just staring into each other's eyes. I felt excited, scared, and a current of sadness rushing through—as if this wasn't real or that it wouldn't last. His lips descended on mine and we began a massive makeout scene. If only it had been filmed, I felt so picture perfect. He tasted like fruit and he had controlling, authoritative lips. His tongue explored my mouth; we were eating each other up, kiss after kiss. I felt his hands sliding under my top, and my lime green bra being pushed up and his hands on my tits, working my nipples. He moved his lips to my ears and began nibbling on them, while I giggled with delight. Then he traced my hips with his hands and we lay there looking at each other.

"You got great eggs," he said.

"EGGS?" I laughed.

"Yeah, you got pretty eggs."

"How do you know?" I asked.

He was quiet and so was I. He didn't answer, but I knew, somehow, I would figure out what he meant on my own over time.

"Listen to that," he said, and we listened to the ocean waves coming in inches from the blanket. We sprang up, and he grabbed the blanket and his water proof tote and we moved up and away from the waves. Once again, we settled onto the blanket. This time he managed to take my bra off, along with my top. We sat up and he put his arm around me. It was the quietest date I had ever been on. I stared at him, and he at me. Again we started making out and this time, his grey shirt came off and we were pressed against each other. He kissed my lips with full force and passion, and from there he went onto to kiss my breasts, tiny kisses, continual, over and over again, as I ran my hands over his 'army' style haircut. Then he stopped and pushed me back from him.

"Should we swap love stories?" he asked.

I was topless, my mouth mashed from kissing and the wetness between my legs had begun to tingle.

"Okay," I said; it was all I could say.

That's when he told me that, aside from acting, he had two other talents: one, growing organic pot and selling it for a hefty profit without ever smoking it, and two, making babies with beautiful women. He had made one son with his first and only wife, now the ex-wife, one boy and a girl with a now former ex-girlfriend. Three kids! And he wanted more. Oh, and he paid taxes and child support, so he wasn't a bum, though it was clear that 'his' dream came first. He was a genuine 'my way or the highway' type guy. Drat!

"Wow, you're not exactly, Mr. Darcy," I said, not thinking that he'd know what the hell I meant.

"I want my fourth with you," he said.

"Why me?" I asked.

"You've got baby-making potential. It's the way your hips are built. Your breasts, they're perfect for breast feeding."

I laughed, I mean, he wasn't joking. There I was, peering down at my own tits, because no other guy had said that about them.

"Perky nipples, which I like. Your breasts would swell up with milk over nine months," he added, like I needed to hear that.

Still, I didn't reach for my top or my bra. I just sat there on Zuma Beach with this eye-catching, cocky, sperm-filled man looking at me like I was a baby making machine.

"How many?" I asked.

"Three, most likely," he said.

"Three?" I asked. He nodded.

Then he traced my face with his fingers and I let him. It felt good, and I knew deep down that I'd probably never see him again. After all, I wasn't going to agree to three babies, let alone one, when there were already three Justin-made kids crawling around.

"Think about it, don't tell me now," he said. I nodded.

"You know, I can picture us having babies. Being happy together. You can still act," he said, as he leaned in and kissed me on the tip of my nose, and then on my cheeks, and forehead. Oh, wow! We locked lips again and kissed for a long, long time.

The temperature changed, it wasn't cold, but I was ready to have my top on, minus my bra, because he said "leave it off for me."

He pulled out a small, fuzzy cream colored blanket—not a baby blanket or I would have screamed. He put it around me. Then he pulled out a cutting board along with provolone cheese, French bread, and black olives. He made a mini sandwich that we shared, then pulled out a bottle of sparking apple juice from Trader Joe's—after all, we weren't going to be drinking wine, what with my potential to produce 'baby' eggs.

The day faded into night and I was still out in Malibu; luckily I had called my faithful dog walker, Sam. Shadow loves Sam because he takes him for super long walks, always in his running gear. He said, "I'm on my way," when I called him from the seafood restaurant on Pacific Coast Highway.

I sat side-by-side with Justin, who wanted my hips as close to him as possible. We shared a large lobster platter. Justin took extreme pleasure, dipping the lobster pieces into hot butter, and putting it in my mouth; everything he did was tender.

We sat in his truck outside my building complex, making out one last time, and then he said, "If you want to share your eggs with me, let me know. I'll do right by you, all the way. I give you my word, and you can meet my ex-wife and ex-girlfriend and my kids, I've got nothing to hide."

"Okay," I said.

Then he held my chin, so my eyes were level with his serious, dark brown eyes. Wow! I couldn't fault him for knowing what he wanted and asking for it. Ugh. I got out and, as I headed away, he whistled. My hips, I knew he was whistling at them like no guy had ever done before.

I looked up at my studio apartment, built over two garages, and noticed that the lights were on. Either Sam, the dog walker, had left them on, or the Tennis Actor was visiting Shadow. I went up, ready for anything, or for nothing but dog licks. There he was in my bed, under my blanket, with his shirt off. "Knock, knock," I said, staring at him.

"I missed you. I sent Sam home, but don't freak out, I paid him for running over here. He had to go see his new girlfriend about something, so it was meant to be." I nodded and sat down in front in my Ikea desk, only a few feet from my bed. Shadow lay on the floor beside him, acting more like his dog then mine.

I checked my cell (I had muted it for the egg-man). Beth had left a ton of messages, wondering where I was and how many actors were coming to meet the 'top rated' reality TV casting director. The last one said thirteen new actors had showed and thanks, and that I have a free workshop any time. Incidentally I had called half the other actors before meeting the egg-man. I clicked my cell phone off, feeling the need for total silence, or no contact, or both. I kicked off my boots and slid out of my jeans and top as the Tennis Actor watched me.

"Hey, no bra." he said. I nodded. Silence filled the room.

"Do you think I'd make great babies?" I asked.

His eyes bulged; I cut him off before he could ask.

"I'm on the pill! And you put the raincoat over your 'Tonka truck' before it goes into my tunnel, dummy," I said, annoyed and suddenly peevish.

He was quiet for a few minutes, and then, as if he had heard it in a movie, "With me?" he asked, adding a slight grin. Which I didn't believe. But on camera it would have appeared sincere.

"Nah, I know you're a career guy; winning an Oscar, you want it, say next week. But do you think I have the potential?" I asked.

"You can do anything, Vivien," he said, and with that, I took off my underpants and got into bed with him. We weren't going to make babies together, but we could have fun practicing, and that's just what we did.

# 4

## AUDITIONS

Auditions are 'it' for actors. There is nothing more thrilling than getting the phone call that you have an audition at 9, or 2 or 5, or any damn time. The Tennis Actor only wanted film auditions, but he always ended up getting more for TV. For me, it was usually commercials, a few TV (small part) auditions and low, low-budget films, but I was fine with that. I just wanted to be seen and heard, any which way. When my landline rang, I was surprised; I was still half asleep. It had been a long night of 'fake' baby making sex (as actors, we really acted 'as if'). Also, I had dreamed that I was having baby-making intercourse with the egg man.

Luckily it was Ray, my Italian-American agent, saying, "Kid, you got a big movie audition. This could make you! Call me back in one minute." Only Ray talked like that; only he had told me that if I was patient, the 'right' role would come for me, and I believed him.

The Tennis Actor was dressed and going over lines when I shouted, "Hey, I got a real movie audition!"

He gave a quick nod. Okay, so actors are competitive! Even when a casting director isn't going to cast a male actor for a female role. Ugh. Someone please remind me not to date anymore actors, ever again. I didn't have time to get pissed-off. I had to call Ray back. He was fast in giving me the location, (Sony Studios), the room, where to park and what to wear. Thank God, the lines were in an email on my cell phone. Before he hung up he said, "Kid, this is the big one we've been waiting for. Do good!"

Those words were fuel for me. I was a skyrocket ready to blast off, still hungry for my Hollywood dream. Maybe the "yes" was about my career. Maybe it was about me landing a movie role. Wow. Being on location with A-list actors. Wow, working with an A-list director.

Acting is all about becoming and being a 'character' unlike myself, but coming from within myself. Okay, so here's where I've got be totally raw, as in nude from my soul—the truth is I'm a hard-core dyslexic. See I've got the emotional life always brimming in me and I can picture a character's history—inner/outer life. It's the damn lines that I have to go over and over, and over—just to memorize. Once I've memorized my lines, I can go in and be it.

I once was up for a really cool PSA (Public Service Announcement), and a top female casting director booked me for the call back. I was so excited, but at the call back they asked me to read new lines off a poster board. I was like, "Oh, shit, I'm going to fail," and I did, because I was too ashamed to tell them that I'm dyslexic and that if they'd let me ad lib, using the same meaning, I could do it justice. The casting director marked me off the list and I've never gotten to audition for her again. It's like having my name written on men's room wall, "VIVIEN'S WORTHLESS!"

Also, I graduated high school at a tenth grade level after being dragged to tutoring four times a week. I gave the tutors hell. I was an original 'Mean Girl'—because I was so angry at being dyslexic. So, now you know why I type with only my right hand. But I love reading. In fact, every time I read I'm utterly thrilled. So, yeah, I'm a Tom Cruise fan, because he had to work really hard to overcome his dyslexia and look where he is! Join me if you want.

I popped out of the shower, dressed, and was heading for the door with two granola bars and a bottle of apple juice, when I spotted Shadow, eyeing me and his leash. I looked at the Tennis Actor and he looked at me. I was about to speed dial Sam when he said he'd walk Shadow, but that I'd owe him a favor. I knew what that meant: a BJ, and not a quick one—the kind where he'd tell me when to stop sucking. Whatever! Why did he always make it seem like I owed him, when all he had to do was ask. Go figure.

All I really knew, as I headed for the Sony Studios, was that I had memorized my lines and that I loved Hollywood, and that I had been happily addicted to movies all my life. Drugs or booze never did anything for me, or to me. It's true! Whenever I felt blue, I watched four or five movies in a row; when I was bored, I watched four or five movies; when I looked at myself in the mirror, I saw an actress. I have a classic nose and high cheekbones, and my hair and eyes are brown. I can look like the best friend, the wife, the mistress, the slithering-shoplifting-backdoor slut, the domestically abused girlfriend, or the stoner.

Just before I found a parking spot, my best friend Paloma, an actress who stayed in NYC, called me. Paloma gets the standard 'Latina' parts on TV, AKA the slut, the bad girl, the thief, the drug dealer's gun-toting girlfriend, or the knocked-up street troll. She doesn't care. Acting is acting in her mind. We both think that acting work is work, no matter how small the part is.

We made a pact years ago not say the name of the show or film we were auditioning for unless we booked the role. The list of rejections is longer for me than her. Rejection sucks. No five-letter word better expresses it than 'sucks'. It's hard seeing pictures of stars in Vanity Fair magazine or reading about the latest projects in Variety or even in the SAG (Screen Actors Guild) magazine, knowing that I didn't get to work with them in some movie, even the ones that went direct to DVD. Sucks. Ugh, I could have been in blah and blah with so and so; is so awful to think, let alone admit it out loud.

So I quickly tell her, "Top movie director, Mr. Oscar winner and the cast is going to have a sexy heartthrob man (Mr. X) and a sexy ingénue (Miss Y), and then me, the unknown, playing the 'bad' girl who's blind in one eye and looks like a model for crack and heroin. But the good news is that Mr. X is romantically attached to my character (there's a make-out scene in the script). Only he dumps me for the sexy-just-over-21-hot- thing (Miss Y), and then there's a car chase and a heist and gun shots, and I either die or wander off with a bullet in my back. Medium budget, but still, my name in lights."

We both laugh, it's so surreal: the story and the thrill of wanting the part.

"Break your ass!" Paloma shouts as we hang up.

I stare at Sony Studios; it's massive, and reeking of cinematic success. My heart beats. I give my name at the gate and the guard marks me in. Wow, I'm on the list. I smile, because I feel important, special, and wanted. Okay, so I live for 'mini highs' like these. I find the building and head upstairs. I've got the sides (lines for the film) in my hands (thanks to my Smartphone). I've been rolling them over my tongue, even though Ray said not to be off book, that this was just a meet-and-greet audition.

I walk in; there are a few other women waiting. We don't look alike, not like at commercial auditions where there are thirty 5'4" to 5'6" brunettes sitting in the waiting area in the same style pants and casual top with the same polished smile and happy faces ready. I sat down. I was so excited; I like audition waiting rooms. Just sitting, knowing that I was going inside the room in a few minutes to meet the Oscar-winning director, felt amazing.

Usually, you only get to meet the director at a callback, but this was a second run- through and I was getting to audition 'as if' I had already auditioned. I couldn't help but glance at the movie posters, half of which the Oscar-winning director had directed. PR in Hollywood is huge, no matter if you're yesterday's 'hot' thing or today's.

I watched a strawberry blonde actress walk out. She held her chin up as she swung her Bottega Veneta bag like she was going places, but really just out the door we had all entered. They don't teach you how to exit in an acting class. Sure, they go over thanking the casting agent, showing no emotion as you leave an audition room, but walking past other actors, your competitors, they skip right over that. How to sit in an audition room and not get wigged out by bigger name talent than yourself, they don't teach that either. One way or another, you teach yourself. Hopefully.

On a scale of 1-10 for self-esteem, ten being the highest, I'm a six. I used to be a four. Probably being dyslexic makes it lower. On a scale of 1-10 in bed, I'm a nine. I started out as five. I mean, I had read about it, and I even sat in a bedroom closet, watching while a thirteen-year-old neighbor went all the way. I was a Peeping Tom. Yeah, she left it ajar, by tossing a pile of dirty clothes in front of it, so the fourteen-year-old boy wouldn't notice me. He was so scared, that he wouldn't have noticed if her mother and stepfather had walked in. How do I know he was scared? Because he sounded like it. He made all the noise; she didn't (which isn't how it is in the teen coming-of-age flicks). Go figure! Oh, and she told me afterwards all about it. She said, "It hurt for a few seconds, and then it didn't. It was smelly."

On a scale of 1-10 about having career success, I'm four-and-a-half at best. So, being less than confident and not wanting to come across like a scared actress, I always tell myself, "You're unaffected, and you're totally emotional. You deserve this role, you're worthy of this role," over and over. I learned this technique thanks to Paloma, who lent me her copy of Shakti Gawain's little book *Creative Visualization*, which she swore by. It's filled with affirmations for getting one's mind to hold powerful thoughts, not fearful or negative ones, and that just made total sense.

Paloma's affirmation is, and has always has been, "Give me the freaking role, cuz' I am the character!" She used to text it to herself before every audition, but now that she's had solid acting work on a cable show shooting in New York, and hasn't needed to. Now her affirmations are just about men.

As for walking in 'owning the room,' which every acting coach suggests, I always wear clothes that make my pear-shaped body come across as natural and desirable. Looking good in Hollywood is no joke. It's not that every director wants to screw every actress or actor—it's just that seeing the clothed-up body has to be as good as if they were seeing it naked. So it's 'tits up,' as Paloma and I figured out back in the early days of auditioning in Manhattan. I always walk in holding my head up, my shoulders back, with a relaxed expression. These rituals, my audition affirmations, poise, and memorization are key. The times I've forgotten my rules or had new lines thrown at me, I was too loud and my reading was off the mark—and they'd just stare me as if I was garbage.

"Vivien!" My name was called and I jumped up.

"Go get him!" I said to myself. "Get this role."

He was at the table with the script in front of him. He looked well-to-do, not larger than life, just a man who dug directing films and who did it really, really well. I sat across from him. I was primed, ready, and my emotions were at my fingertips. He asked me about myself and I told him about art modeling and my dog, Shadow (because he wanted to hear about non-acting stuff). And he asked me what I thought of the 'bad girl' character and I told him. Then we read the scene Ray had emailed me. Then he chose another scene and we read that. I liked my character; she was half-mad, and desperate, too. Then he sat back and looked at me, and I looked at him. I felt self-conscious, but didn't flinch. When you're an art model, every inch of your skin is exposed, so I had nothing to hide. He thanked me and I thanked him, and I walked out, closing the door behind me.

Wow. It was over. As I walked through the lobby and the other actresses stared at me, I gave them that look that showed I felt 'good,' and that my reading had been something 'great,' blah, blah, blah.

When I got outside, I took a long, deep breath. Reading with the Oscar-winning director was exciting, but the waiting to find out if I booked the role was the yucky part.

The Tennis Actor texted me; he needed me to run lines with him because he was up for a part on a top-rated doctor TV show. It was a recurring role, so I headed home. For some reason he liked to use my place to run lines, avoiding his spacious two-bedroom apartment for my cramped homemade style, with a rescue dog to boot.

When I unlocked my car door, I felt a lump in my throat, the kind I always felt when I realized that the guy I was sleeping with wasn't going to fall in love with me—only this time I felt it about the Oscar-winning director, not anything sexual, just that he wasn't going to cast me. He would wind up going with one of the other actresses with stronger credits. I felt gloomy, it had happened too many times before.

"Snap out of it, snap out of it," I told myself.

Ray called to ask how I did and I told him word-for-word what went on inside the audition room.

"That's it, kid!" he said.

I didn't tell him my fears; every actor who hasn't made it big, let alone one-tenth big, has the same set of fears, and every agent or manager has heard it all before.

Later, I ran the TV doctor lines for two hours with the Tennis Actor. I even coached him the way an acting coach would do, which he liked. He even joked about me doing it as a backup career.

"Listen, I came here to make it as an actress, not to become an acting coach. I could have stayed in NYC for that job," I shouted and he told me, "Chill out, I want you to come with me to the audition. Listen, you might get the movie role. Babe, nothing's a done deal just because you're scared."

Wow, he knew what I was thinking and why. Oh, wait, he's an actor, he's done it before. Go figure! I called Sam, the dog walker, to see if he wanted to take Shadow for a dog run, but he wasn't in and I didn't want to leave a message. "Bring Shadow," the Tennis Actor suggested. After all, I could wait in my Volvo with Shadow while he did his TV audition; it wasn't like I needed to sit in another audition waiting room when I wasn't even going into read for a part.

The best thing about my hunter green Volvo station wagon is the size: Shadow could lay his mixed-Shepherd dog body out in comfort and I could load the back with goodies from any store I wanted. I had always bought vintage cars (this was my 4th one). I watched the Tennis Actor stride into the studio lot as I sat in a parking spot across the street. I turned on the radio and listened to Eminem singing, *Not Afraid*, while Shadow chewed on a rawhide bone that the Tennis Actor had bought him (I know, totally sweet giving guy).

I felt sad, even though I shouldn't have. It was like something was going to hurt; like my not getting the movie part, and the Tennis Actor booking the TV role, or that I was just spinning my wheels over and over for nothing. Okay! I think too much. So I muttered out loud "Stop thinking, no more thoughts," causing Shadow to lean over the seat and sniff my ear with his wet nose. His dogface was what I needed to snap me out of my really dark thoughts. And then there was sex. I was looking forward to that; I needed it.

About an hour later, the Tennis Actor came out of the studio and crossed the street smiling; he'd just given "a great read," as he put it. That's when I remembered that I was supposed to water the backyard plants for Becky a location-manager friend who was working on transitioning into a producer. She had a house off of Benedict Canyon, so I zipped us over there. It meant three things: I could turn on the water sprinklers and Shadow could play in the backyard, and I could give the Tennis Actor his requested BJ. And that's just what happened, in that exact order.

# 5

## PAWS

I don't remember oversleeping, but I did. There was nothing to wake up for, except to walk Shadow; I hadn't booked the movie role, and Ray wasn't calling, nor was the commercial agency. I had only a few art modeling gigs and they were at night, and the Tennis Actor had booked the doctor TV show and was already on the studio set. I heard my cell phone ring and picked it up with no amount of jolly in my voice.

"Yeah, what is it?" I asked, like a sulky bitch.

"I think Sam walked your dog, I'm his brother," he said.

I sat up, "What? Wait, what's wrong?!!!" and there was silence on the other end.

"Is Sam in the hospital? Is Sam ok? You're calling me because my dog Shadow and I are his friends. What's happened?" I asked, my heart already racing and my hand out stretched as if I could catch his words.

"Sam fell off a parked tractor at a construction site in Echo Park. It appears that he jumped off." His voice was tender. I was now wide awake and sick to my stomach.

"Damn it!" I said.

Sam and I met in my Los Feliz neighborhood on Hillhurst Avenue; he was walking a pack of dogs of various sizes and breeds. I had seen him around; he was built like a marathon runner (which he was) with a friendly face, and he spoke dog, which translates to 'he loved dogs'. I asked if he could add Shadow to his dog walking route. And he said yes, and it was that easy. I gave him my apartment keys and never asked for a reference, because he was Sam—he was all good.

I cried, and told his brother how Sam felt like my brother, and a part of my family, and that I hadn't ever noticed his sadness—I'd only seen him looking, being, or 'acting' happy. And I didn't know Sam could get depressed.

We hung up and I got dressed without showering and walked Shadow up Hillhurst past the spot where I had first met Sam and up into Griffith Park. Life's strange. One day it's fun and pleasant, the next it's maddening, and the very next it's dreadfully sad, and the next—well, a person just has to wait and see what it will bring. There was going to be a memorial, before his brother took Sam's body back to his parents.

I waited until after the Tennis Actor and I had celebrated his success at booking the doctor TV show. Rumor had it that possibly a 'permanent' TV role offer was due in the coming months. I waited until after we had made out and after I had sat on his lap, looking at his cute actor face. He wasn't Mr. Darcy, but he was mighty attractive and mighty enjoyable to be with. Then I told him about Sam's death. He was upset right away, troubled that he, too, might have overlooked something in Sam's demeanor.

"Should we ask everyone we know if they're faking happiness?" he asked. I was wondering the same thing. Who do you ask first? And when do you ask? We lay in the pitch dark, talking about how long we both imagined we'd live, and about how old age might turn out for each of us. Would we have false teeth? Would we live in nursing homes? Would we die tragically? It was getting really depressing and bleak in my bedroom, as we built our own dark murky sleepless night.

Around four in the morning I said, "I'm going to die screwing, no matter how old I am," figuring why not picture the best way to die.

"How do you know?" he asked.

"It's just a hope," I said.

"Does that exist at the end of life?" he asked.

I sat up. There were only two ways to get us out of our gloomy funk, one was to go to sleep, and the other was putting his Tonka truck in the tunnel between my legs. I opted for number two. So I got up, took off my clothes, pulled a black wig (a mix between wicked-witch/gothic-whore) out of my closet, and put on a mustard colored pair of spiked twenty dollar high heels and returned to the bed room.

"Scene one: woman vampire enters bedroom, sees naked man," I stopped and he quickly stripped, "Man is fast asleep, snoring loudly," I said in the voice of a wanna-be director. He snored loudly, but kept one blue eye open.

"She, the vampire climbs on the bed, straddling him, so he cannot move," and I did just that. "She sucks his neck…" I was interrupted by, "No hickies, I'm on TV," — killing the mood.

"Maybe she was a vampire who kicked ass. Yeah, that sounds better," I said as I dove in for a kiss on his lips and pulled him to the side; now he was on top of me. Wow, with one great, swift movement, I slapped his ass. He felt it. It was war now, the best kind of erotic war there can be, even when…it's not true love.

So funerals/memorials in general are yucky (I know that's a 3$^{rd}$ grade word, but sometimes it says it all) and not something I like to have to go to, but Sam's was the most satisfying memorial I think I'll ever attend in my life. Okay, so I don't know the future, but still, that's what I believe. His army brother stationed in DC, called everyone Sam had ever walked a dog for. He had arrived in LA for one mission only, to take Sam's body back home, but had agreed to a memorial in Griffith Park before.

The Tennis Actor had to meet his acting mentor first, only because he was now really being considered for a regular part on the doctor TV show, but promised to cut out early to meet me at the memorial.

The directions his brother gave were: bring all dogs on leashes and drive up Vermont Avenue, park anywhere possible, and walk over to the gathering. First I raced over to Hollywood Boulevard and into Hollywood Toys & Costumes, the number one shop where I love to buy wigs, and bought a black bandana to go around Shadow's neck for the memorial.

I wore a black dress and black DKNY sneaker heels. I piled my hair up on my head, wore no makeup, except deep blue eye shadow and mascara for a dramatic affect. Yeah, well, I'm into theatrical colors for my eyes. Go figure. And of course I took along a few doggy bags, in case Shadow or some other dog did what they usually do.

The park was packed when I arrived, but I squeezed my Volvo in a space that miraculously appeared and we headed over to the gathering—thirty plus four-legged paws. Dogs were everywhere as if this was a movie. Shadow and I found our way to the top of the pack. A friend of Sam's, who I didn't know, began reflecting on his bigheartedness and loyalty. I recognized Sam's brother, in an army uniform. He and Sam shared the same forehead, and nose, but otherwise looked different.

I'm a crybaby, I just can't help it. I started sobbing, but I wasn't the only one. The dogs barked and that fit so well with who Sam was and how we would all remember him. Barking for Sam! Bow-wow-wow!

I glanced at the girl who had been Sam's girlfriend for a very short time, the last person to kiss him. I didn't know what I would do if I was her or how I would handle the future. She was wearing a long multi-colored skirt and a white-t shirt with Sam's face on it. In the picture he held two scrappy dogs. I liked it. As the ceremony began to wind down, I ambled a few feet away with Shadow, wanting distance. Soon it would be over—everyone and all the furry paws would leave the park. The spot would be empty, without a trace of what had been lost.

I remembered hearing a renowned older actor talking about Katharine Hepburn's memory of her brother's suicide. The story goes that she went to New York City with her fifteen year-old brother, a trip designed to cheer him up and a chance for her to visit family friends. The last thing her brother was quoted as saying to her was, *"You're my girl, aren't you? You're my favorite girl in the whole world."* And then he went upstairs to bed. The next morning, he was found hanging dead.

I don't know why I remember his words quote un-quote; I guess I imagined being with her when it happened. She found him! As an actress, she was powerful. My favorite K-Hep films are *Morning Glory, The Philadelphia Story, Adam's Rib, Suddenly Last Summer* and *On Golden Pond.* She died without Botox or plastic surgery—her face was her original face. Not many actress pass away un-nipped and un-tucked.

Back to suicidal tendencies—I remembered being sixteen and filled with miserable thoughts of self-loathing, feeling like an outcast, a total misfit. If I hadn't found acting, I don't think I would have made it to seventeen, but a chance meeting with a play called *A Streetcar Named Desire* changed that. I read it line-by-line in an hour and then over and over again. I wanted to be the character

Stella, but I felt more like the character Blanche and it haunted me. Would I end up manless and living in the past like Blanche, or would I end up with a man who was an untamed sexual brute, like Stella got with Stanley? Would I be anything? Those kinds of worries, those heavy, heavy feelings; I know them. They are not strangers. Go figure! I guess acting is for those who feel too much everyday, I don't know. I just know that's why I'm an actress.

I looked up and the Tennis Actor was staring down at me. He had arrived. He was wearing a black Nike jogger's outfit, his hair gelled and slicked back. He held out his hand and I grabbed it. Shadow was barking at him, like he always did, as if he had not seen him in months and was overjoyed. The crowd was thinning, people heading back to their homes, to their jobs; it was just after nine-thirty in the morning.

We strolled with Shadow up into the park toward the observatory (the famous location used in the film *Rebel without a Cause*). The Tennis Actor told me about various types of suicide he'd read about, like the male model who took sleeping pills, the pretty European female model who jumped off a balcony (actually he said there had been two who did), and about a well-known songwriter whose music graced several cool films and had allegedly stuck a knife in his own chest. FYI, suicide is not a sexy topic. In my opinion, it's creepy, twisted, and disheartening, but I listened; he had to tell me his morbid stories. In Hollywood, it's hard to tell if a story is just a story, or a rumor made into a story. Anyway, death is like that, it gets you thinking about more death, and so on and so on.

Luckily, being a movie buff and an actress, I knew the one key element that was missing: a scene change. I stopped; he turned and stared at me.

"Hey, want to practice French kissing?" I asked, then added in a breathy voice, "Ooh la la," the only French I know, as I traced the outline of his lips with my fingers.

"Bisous, Ma Poule, Ma Cocotte, Je t'adore, Je ne peux pas vivre sans toi...Mon tresor," he said in the worst French accent possible.

Maybe he watched porn in French? Maybe he had Googled online how to 'woo' a French woman? I don't know. Not understanding French, I had to act 'as if', so in my dictionary it translated to, "hey, baby, let's make out using our tongues," and we did just that, while Shadow sat on the ground by our feet, licking his paws.

# 6

## *ROLE*

I sat in the Tennis Actor's agent's office in a fancy building on Wilshire Boulevard that A-list actors walk in and out of after signing 'crucial' deals or bitching about the lack of work or the kind of roles they want. A really expensive, modern building, with an ultra stylish lobby, where only the top-name directors and producers go in and out, signing 'major' deals or bitching about the lack of work or the kind of work they want.

He was signing his contract for the series regular role he had officially booked on the doctor TV show. I was there to keep his hand steady as he signed his name four or five times (more paperwork when it's a network contract).

To be envious is to be human, in my opinion. There he was, doing what I had come to Hollywood to do—signing to a fat money-paying-contract. I was just a tagalong in the fancy A-list agent's plush office. His older, balding, four-thousand-dollar-suited agent winked at me and offered me a bottle of Smart water and some chocolate from Switzerland.

"Your guy's got talent; the show will last at least five years. Then, it will go into rerun heaven, cha-ching, cha-ching," he said, like I was planning on living off the Tennis Actor. Like I needed to know that a Beverly Hills mansion with an enormous pool was coming, along with other lofty amenities.

The Tennis Actor gave one of those 'acting for the sake of acting' lines: "My character's great, I hope he gets used and abused by the writing team."

I felt the urge to fall out of my stiff grey leather chair and play dead on the carpet in front of them.

"Just you wait. The viewers at home, women and gay men, will tune in every week, just to see what you do next. You're the wild card on that show," his agent said and they both laughed the same laugh.

We wandered outside into the Los Angeles weather, always sunny and warm, give or take a few days of rain. I took several pictures of him in front of the fancy A-list-agent modern building, and he took one of me with my white-rimmed sunglasses, that later I realized made me look like a freak in shades. Drat.

He had been invited to a Hollywood Hills party by one of the leads on the doctor TV show and he wanted us to go. That meant a new dress and his treating me to a half-day at a spa, which included not only a facial and a full body rub, but a waxing of my pubic hair. Bare down there, is the style in LA these days. FYI, it hurts the first time and makes you look like a plucked chicken between your legs, but after you do it once, you go again because growing it back is not worth the hassle—and most LA lovers actually prefer it bare. Go figure.

It was his day/his celebration and he quote unquote wanted to spoil me, but I felt more like my 'messy' self was being over hauled, so I'd look good on his shoulder in front of his new, soon-to-be 'TV friends'. I was too tired to ask him what kind of dress he was shopping for. I mean, it's one thing to buy a dress together; it's another thing for a guy to pre-select it. Oh, well.

Los Angeles is filled with great spas. This one was over in Koreatown, and designed like a hideaway next to a golf course. I walked in and was given a locker key. I promptly stripped, tossed on a robe, and headed for my facial. Who knew I had blackheads and whiteheads? Fortunately, they were removed one-by-one. My face looked blotchy and patchy, but very pure, as if everything—even the emotions—had been lifted. As for the full body massage, front and back, I laid there as a 'pity me' ball of nerves and was gradually rubbed into a 'princess' state of awareness, as if anything I wanted was in reach if I'd just reach for it. Way wonderful!

The last stop was the waxing. I got my legs waxed, armpits, and then my pubic area, which was not overgrown so it only took a quick second for her to pour the wax over all of it, wait for it to dry, and then yank it off. Ouch, but a good ouch!

There I was, spanking new and ready to 'party' into a new role, a new life. Maybe I was becoming his girlfriend and this was how he was going to be treating me. There had never been any talk about the 'boyfriend/girlfriend' thing. We were just hanging out, sleeping together, and no one said "I love you," ever.

I arrived at his Silver Lake apartment. Shadow was staying with my neighbor who had recently broken up with her girlfriend and needed a dog to hang out with—which worked out perfectly. The Tennis Actor/now TV regular money maker was waiting for me with a large Barney's shopping bag. A fancy box was inside, and I didn't even have time to sit down; he wanted it opened right away. The dress was red, not my color, had slits, was tight and required my breasts to be pushed upright. Never mind the designer, it was a 'name' the partygoers would recognize.

He had me strip and put it on. I think he just wanted to see my breasts smashed like the 'red carpet' actresses' are at every award event or movie premiere. He wore a John Varvatos smoking hot charcoal grey suit, looking handsome, and lean. He rented a sleek silver Porsche Panamera, since he was waiting to buy a new car once the checks started arriving. I would say that it was wild, standing in the red dress and slipping on the matching heels, and that I felt a mix of not being myself, but suddenly 'playing' a role—of the sexy girlfriend or lover, depending on which label he was going to use introducing me.

"I'm celebrating booking the TV gig tonight," he said over and over again, as if convincing himself or instructing himself. Go figure. I just smiled and nodded in agreement.

The party was one of those 'Hollywood' parties where the staff has to sign a non-disclosure contract. As in, they never saw drugs of any kind on the property, or in the nose or mouth of any of the 'big name' guests. If I thought drugs were sexy, then I'd probably have enjoyed the party.

Okay, so pot's boring. When I was in high school, I tried it a dozen times, and it made me sleepy and really dim-witted. Cocaine? Oh, I tried it in college, twice, and it just made me want to take off my clothes and screw the end of an umbrella, (which I actually did). Heroin? Never. That stuff's too brainless for words; I'd never try it.

Heroin (Thank God) was absent at the party. Nine thousand dollars worth of marihuana was at the party; an Oscar-winning actor had brought it to share. How cool is that? Beats me! And the cocaine was not spread out on the marble kitchen counter top—but placed in a silver bowl on the marble kitchen countertop, with baby spoons and rolled-up twenties for snorting it. So Hollywood! I only knew the price of the pot, because someone had whispered it to the Tennis Actor and he, in turn, whispered it to me. Coincidentally, I knew no one else to whisper the pot price to. As for the price of the cocaine, probably half a paycheck for the lead TV actor, otherwise known as the host. The staff was made up of three guys in black and white and a funky female chef in all white, who hung around smoking joints in the kitchen.

The music was provided by a female DJ, and pretty-party-people were everywhere, dressed in expensive clothes. I was introduced to blah, blah and the Tennis Actor went off to mingle (actually, he wanted to get high). I didn't stop him. Only in Hollywood can you party like a rock-star, free of the fear of getting caught if you're on private, very private, property. With security at the gates—gotta love that.

I wandered off, searching for a room with books, or art of some kind that I could focus on. He had beat me to it; the movie actor in his late forties, sitting in the den with a book open and bottle of red wine in his powerful hand. The room was over stuffed with teak bookshelves. The walls were antique white, covered with impressionist paintings, a plush couch, etc, etc, you can imagine it all, on top of a large Persian rug.

"Come in and shut the door," he said in his movie star voice. I did.

"Lock it," he added. I turned and stared at him.

"I don't like the noise, 97 percent is bullshit," he said. So I attached the latch, in this circa 1970s house.

"You got enough cleavage hanging out to nurse a litter of stray dogs," he said. I glanced down at my pushed up breasts spilling out of the expensive red dress.

"I'm wearing the newest milk-titty-dress," I said, mocking it and myself.

"Can't blame the dickhead for buying it. You know, it's how we're wired," he said, giving me the impression that he had bought the same type dress for more than one woman.

"Did you see me when I arrived?" I asked, and he grinned. I had caught his eyes on me as I first entered the party with the Tennis Actor. It wasn't a flirting look, just a look of eyes-on-eyes in a crowded room filled with pretty people trying to be noticed.

The party blared behind us, the door locked, I was thinking about it being locked, when he said. "Sit down." I sat across from him, and he passed me the bottle of wine and told me how he used to do drugs; how drugs had been as important to him as banging women, until he almost died of an overdose. I nodded. I had heard the rumors about him. LA is filled with rumors; if you stay long enough and you get lucky, you acquire one of your own.

He went on about the Hollywood machine, the movie business, about greed and about 'sellout' actors—actors who took jobs just to pay the mortgage or to keep their lifestyles, even when they hated the part. I liked his voice; I had always liked it on the screen. He moved his hand, motioning me to come closer.

"I want to read you a poem," he said.

"Okay," I replied. Then he inched over on the couch so I could squeeze next to him, and I wanted to; it was a strange and larger-than-life moment for me and so I sat on the edge of the couch. He grinned as I stared at his manly, well-defined, movie star features. He stammered, unable to read the poem aloud. Maybe it was the wine, maybe it was his nerves, or maybe he just didn't think he could do justice to Pablo Neruda's poem, *I Do Not Love You Except Because*

*I Love You.* He shoved the book forcibly into my cleavage and I took it from him, as his hand fell into my lap.

"Read it," he ordered in the way he might order a roast beef sandwich at a deli. I read it slowly, uncertain of the words, and as I did, tears welled in my eyes. I felt so inexperienced, reading of the deep love that Pablo Neruda must have known.

The movie actor touched the skin on my exposed breasts. His hands were rough, like a construction workers, but I didn't mind.

"Makes you want to find that?" he asked, not waiting for an answer, "It's a risk; screwing is a whole lot easier, give me the book back," he said, and I did.

He tore the poem out of it, discarding the weathered book of selected poems onto the rug. He took the page with Neruda's poem on it, folded it, and stuffed it between my breasts. Then he sat up and kissed me on my lips. I almost blurted, "I'm not on a 24b-up," but I didn't. I kept my silly, inexperienced worries to myself and kissed him back as if I was in a movie.

The incessant banging on the latched door ended our kiss. He got up, unlatched it, and sauntered out. He had that 'walk', that commands attention.

I found the Tennis Actor by the pool under an elaborate 'safari tent' that had been created for the party. He was high as a dustball blowing in a tornado. He grinned at me, as he lifted his leg.

"Vivien, pull off my sock and scratch my foot," he said, and I did.

# 7

## ANSWER

I had to wait a month for the answer to my destiny. It wasn't what I thought it would be, but I accepted it. There's always another shade, when at first it all seems bleak and desolate.

"Your Aunt Helen's dying and she wants you to visit her; she's been asking to see you. To say her goodbye," said my workaholic, academic father. His tone was dry, that of a man used to lots of family deaths, his sister being the last of his siblings.

"Sure, I'll pack up and come East. I needed a reason to leave La-La land," I said.

"I don't think you have to give up your LA life and all that," he said in his usual style of pushing me away.

"I haven't got an LA life worth holding onto, if you want to hear my truth," I said.

He was silent. "Then I guess I'll see you soon," he replied.

"Yes, you will," I said, and hung up.

It didn't take me five minutes to start packing, while Coldplay's *Fix You* song blasted on my portable CD player. It was easy to get moving boxes from Craigslist free section. What hadn't I found, brought or sold off of that mega-classified dot com site? I took digital photos of my very soft bed, my Ikea desk and Ikea futon couch, my porch picnic table and the four chairs. The Tennis Actor showed up when I was halfway done, not a difficult accomplishment in a studio apartment.

"Where are you going? Are you leaving me?" he asked.

"My Aunt Helen's dying; I've got to go to Boston. She needs to see me," I said without looking up.

"I need you, I want you here," he said, as if we were part of a soap opera.

"You just signed a contract for a dream acting job, not everyone gets to do that. Meanwhile I'm doing nothing here. If I leave now, maybe I can become an indie filmmaker back in New York, I don't know. All I do know is that I'm rotting away," I said, without any great emotion.

"I want you with me, doesn't that count?" he asked, as if he wanted to force himself to cry.

"Hollywood has your back covered; they want you. Not me! We've had great sex, but I'm not your soulmate, you and I both know that," I said, speaking the truth out loud for once, without blame. After all, love's a two-way thing.

I had never spoken so straightforwardly; it was as if the words had been packed in the back corners of my mind waiting to pounce, waiting to be let out. Freedom!

"You're my girlfriend," he said, as if that had been a fact all along. But I knew I wasn't that important to him. Sure, I was the only one he was sleeping with and spending every day with, but he had never even suggested that he wanted more with me.

"You wanted friendship with benefits, you said that after we slept together for the first time," I said.

I was trying to remind him about what had happened five months ago. "Things have changed," he answered, as if that was all he could think of. Shadow watched us, making sure we weren't arguing. What a dog! Shadow's very sensitive to loud voices and the tone of anger. Then again, so am I.

"It's okay," I said to Shadow, only the Tennis Actor thought I was talking to him. So he pouted, and then kicked the wall, but not hard. He threw a plastic cup, and then sat down and punched the air and I watched. Good acting is good acting, and a private scene is always a compliment. When he was done, he pulled me onto my bed—which was currently listed for sale online, but I didn't stop him. He was intense, ripping my bra and my 'peace' labeled underwear off, as if the thought of not seeing me again made him extra horny and extra attentive. He was the kind of guy who took to my nipples like a teething newborn.

Sometimes I just give in. I'm easy. I'm a simple slut, and this was one of those times. Hell, I had spent years on-and-off being single, years on-and-off hoping some guy would really want me. A good penis had been, at one time in my life, like looking for *Godot* and my quest hadn't been easy.

There'd been the guy at Vassar College that I met while visiting my friend Leah Bloom in Poughkeepsie. He had curly blonde hair, an open face with kiss-able intellectual lips, and a really academic mind that I wanted to lie next to, that I had wanted to listen to day and night. He had asked Leah for my phone number and she told me he was going to call, I waited and waited; I think I waited two months. Incidentally I never bothered going back up to Poughkeepsie. Pathetic is pathetic, and I once was. Of course, my friend Leah told me it was probably for the best; God's prevention.

And I had had crushes on three no-wins who shall go by commercial titles, as in 'Mister Clean,' the 'Jolly Green Giant', and the dancing 'Dr. Pepper'. Mister C. had been the super cute, Chace Crawford type in high school who I had slam danced with, locked eyes with, and who had caused my hips to move in his direction without my mind knowing what they were doing. I swear my hips moved without me thinking about it. Yeah, I was into punk and he had great introspective eyes. He had been too shy to respond to my failed love letters, handwritten (ha, ha) and left wedged in his locker. FYI, never write a guy a lusty letter, because guys chase girls. So I didn't get to screw him, and out of that 'rejection' I screwed a guy I didn't really know in a closet at a party. Go figure! Yeah, it's possible to screw fast, hard and without love. I learned later, after graduation, that Mister C. had regretted not going out with me. Double Ugh.

Jolly G. G. was a guy who had been at sea, and hadn't been laid in a long, long time (over a year). I met him at a New Year's party at the South Street Seaport in Manhattan and he begged to come home with me, so I let him. He was tall, (a Paul Walker type), and filled with stories of having sailed half the globe. And he was from Martha's Vineyard. Okay, so it's true; don't go to bed with a guy you don't know. The sex was great; it always is with a man who hasn't been laid in a really long time. Let's just say every inch of my flesh was kissed, stroked, and appreciated. He said the usual, "I'll call you, I want to see you again!" and yeah, I waited by the phone. I started daydreaming about weekends going to Martha's Vineyard from Manhattan just to be with him. Three months later 'I got it', as in ONE NIGHT STANDS ARE STUPID!

And last but not least, Dr. Pep, who was my fault; I blew it. Dr. Pep and I met during a college summer program and we danced to Prince's hit song, *Delirious*. He was (a Viggo Mortensen type), rugged in a casual way, and 'true blue,' as in he told the truth, he hadn't been corrupted yet. But I was in one of those 'I don't deserve a good guy' phases and pushed him away. My bad! My mistake! Some girls get lucky: it's one guy and they're set for life, or it's a few and then they're set for life, but for me, it's a total loaded crap shoot.

So here I was with this good-looking Tennis Actor gliding in and out between my legs. There is a God!

But my Aunt Helen had been the one who taught me to believe again, after my manic depressive mom ran away when I turned fifteen. My mom used to be an activities director at a senior center—basically she chose fun things for the seniors to do. She's mildly dyslexic, as in not as much as me. She met a cook at a burrito joint in Porter Square not far from the senior center, who was moving back to Panama to start a coffee plantation, and he invited her to join him. The 'love' story goes that the Panamanian man had started shaking when he sat across from my mother, that he felt his heart pounding and couldn't help but tell her, "My heart beats for you," in broken English. She was so struck by his natural, pure way of speaking, she practically drooled. He had about a year of English under his belt, a slow year, and it moved her to tears. So she packed up her stuff and headed off with him, promising to keep in touch with me and my workaholic, academic, father.

Only a few half-page letters came now and then, and my Aunt Helen said, "You have two choices: number one, blame your mother, get down in the dumps and be a victim of loss, or number two, forgive her, grow up, and create a joyful life of your own."

She was like that, always tossing the coin up. If the toss ended up heads, it was, "I'll volunteer today," tails it was, "I'll make something interesting." Those were her typical choices. My Aunt Helen had sewn words of inspiration across my jeans and on a winter jacket and a raincoat.

"Your mother couldn't spend her whole life with an academic. She had a quest to fulfill herself, and she did her best with the family for as long as she could. And that's all you can judge her on," my Aunt Helen had said, just before I went off to college to be crazy and wild. And it was because of her that I moved to Los Angeles.

I had already graduated from college, only to end up working as a waitress at Dojo's in the East Village and an usher at BAMM, and as a tarot card reader at upscale holiday parties, where I promised the world for a flat fee of a $130.00 per party. I'd always get the females—the confessional types worried about their marriages, their boyfriends, their girlfriends, and their careers. I would just flip the cards and say stuff like, "You're a high priestess and the rods spells out adoring love approaching; get ready for the best passion in bed of your life," if that's what she was worried about. If it was health, I'd turn the coin images up, to show healing and the circle of life, and with career concerns, I'd lay it on thick, "The cards showed hardship and suffering, but now they reveal the rebirth of financial bliss, the promise of continued opportunity, even a Swiss bank account, blah, blah." They would return to the party with their heads high, their shoulders straight and I could tell that they believed me.

I had had Aunt Helen sew the word "BELIEVE" down the right thigh of my favorite pair of black dress pants. I wore a burgundy Indian cloth around my head and a black silk blouse, all because I had met a Gypsy girl named Nancy on 14th Street who told me I had fortune teller eyes, and that party gigs were a quick way to make extra cash and that people always tipped. There was no resume needed, and she and her mother taught me tricks, like how to moan as if a vision was coming up my foot into my eyeballs; how to sigh; how to ask what was wrong without sounding fake.

I made a vow on the flight from New York to Los Angeles to never, ever read tarot cards or tea leaves or palms again. I had kept my promise until the Tennis Actor stared me with that, 'you're abandoning me' look—the one that previously I gave to guys. So I found myself picking up his left hand and rubbing his palm, and saying, "The doctor TV show is going to give you all you want and need, just stay open." And then he said, "Shut up, I'm going to miss you." And a lump came up in my throat. No one ever tells you how to get rid of that kind of a lump, but I tried to swallow it away. FYI, emotional lumps can't be swallowed. Sometimes moments end like this, and there's no movie director around to shout, "CUT, SCENE CHANGE!"

# 8

## *GOING*

Going forward with my decision to leave LA was what I had to do for my Aunt Helen. It wasn't that I couldn't have stored my stuff, what with all the local 'first month free' storage places—it was just that I knew, somewhere inside me, that I was moving away—maybe not permanently, but at least for a few years, or, then again, maybe for good. I felt a mix of excitement along with the fear of leaving my LA friends, my LA acting career, and my LA way of life. Added onto that was guilt, guilt for leaving a guy I wasn't deeply in love with, but whom I had grown fond of being with. Ugh!

Okay not easy to do, but if I was to find my own Mr. Darcy (AKA Romeo) and a career less built on someone else saying, "yes" to me, then I had to go. There were a few days when I wished I could have found an open-24-hours-shrink—maybe they have those in Las Vegas. The trouble was I kept having 'abandonment issues' and pangs in my stomach. The Tennis Actor didn't bring it up, but he looked at me like I was leaving because of him, which I wasn't. At least I don't think I was! So he came over every night to screw the longest goodbye over and over again. Better than the way most movies end. Go figure!

And by the end of week, UPS had shipped all of my boxes to Cambridge, Massachusetts, to my father's cluttered, two-bedroom apartment, which was wall-to-wall books in every room—books he actually had read.

Shadow and I stayed with the Tennis Actor for our last Hollywood night, while he looked over sides for his TV show part. The landlord was relieved that I was moving out because he could now raise the rent. After all, Los Feliz had rapidly become the trendy place to live.

I gave my beat-up Volvo with about a year left on it to a woman who was raising two kids without child support. I had put an ad on Craigslist to drive somebody's car back East and by perfect fate, which is always the case with that site, I got not just any car, but a super stylish red BMW. Hell, Craigslist should have been paying me yearly to do commercials for them, or at least radio spots. The site is amazing. The BMW belonged to an up-an-coming fashion designer who needed it driven to New Haven, Connecticut, to her parents' house. Oh, of course I lied about Shadow and told her, "Yeah, I'm driving across the country all alone." Naturally, I bought a few drop cloths from Home Depot and covered the backseat with them and for all intents and purposes it worked: no mutt hair landed on the seats or in the plush panels.

The morning before I drove off, the Tennis Actor booked his fourth national commercial.

"I'm going to really miss you," he said, with his arms stretched around me like we were in a shampoo commercial.

"Yeah, for maybe a month, until some sexy guest actress arrives and you fall hard for her," I said.

"Vivien, you might not want to believe this, but I like you and if you would stay in LA, I would live with you. We'd rent a new place. You're good luck for me," he said.

Not much you can say when someone wants you and you've always wanted to be wanted. And you also realize that they like you in bed, which just adds 'icing' on the relationship. Maybe sex is a metaphor for icing. I couldn't open my mouth, because it was time to go and that suddenly hurt. I could have borrowed a good-bye movie line, but instead I said, "You'd better become a major, Emmy-winning actor, so I can beat myself up daily with regret." I tried kicking my ass to illustrate my remorse. After a long kiss, a pat on the butt—him patting my butt and then me patting his, I drove over to my agent Ray's office.

Ray was in; he had his back to the door and he was packing boxes.

"So, you're walking out on me? What about my Academy Award?" I asked, with a smirk on my face.

Ray turned, gave me his famous Italian-American hug and started explaining "I'm done here. I gotta get out of show biz, but you, Vivien, got fat talent, fat talent," he said.

I plunked myself down in his desk chair and swiveled around.

"Ray, no worries, I'm going back East, so don't think a thing; I was just teasing you."

Ray had represented, among others, Aldo and his late son, the actor Alonzo, and he liked to talk about it—the story goes that Coppola was seeking Italian-American actors for his Godfather movie. Ray submitted them both, since Aldo was fluent in Italian and Alonzo wasn't. Coppola asked Alonzo all sorts of questions, while Aldo had to watch. Later that day Ray got the call; Alonzo had booked himself a movie part. He shot his scene opposite Robert De Niro. Aldo was ecstatic for his son.

Incidentally Ray no longer managed them, but they stayed friends. The last time I saw them both was a month before Alonzo died. He and his father were in a four-door classic Cadillac. Alonzo was behind the steering wheel, and pulled to the curb, so they could say hello to me. They had that authentic father and son bond, absolute love and respect for each other. Not everyone gets that in life. I felt the urge to jump in and hang out with them for the day; to soak up their affection. To ask for life lessons.

Ray took me to Alonzo's memorial at the Writers Guild Theater on Doheny Drive in Beverly Hills. "That was some memorial, a lot of laughs," Ray said, reading my mind, which was easy because I was staring at photos of Alonzo and Aldo on Ray's wall. "Alonzo knew how to befriend anyone and everyone," I said.

"You're good at friendship, too, Vivien," he said, like he thought I needed validating. All of sudden I felt like crying, like breaking down and sobbing uncontrollably, but fortunately Ray interrupted my thoughts.

"Hey, you're not giving up acting? You better be going into indie filmmaking and weird theater projects. I get it; you're going back to New York City. You're going to make it huge there, right? I'm right, right?"

It was strange because the phrase indie filmmaking made me think—maybe that's what I had been missing out on all along. After all I don't really look like most of the actresses in LA, nor do I get the auditions, jobs and parts they do.

So I said, "I'll never be done with acting. Hollywood's not for me right now, I can't keep on contemplating liposuction," in spite of the fact that Ray probably knew a few plastic surgeons that didn't charge as much as the Beverly Hills kind.

"Yeah, then you have to go back East; you're wonderful the way you are. You don't need plastic stuff done to you," he said, like an agent and father-figure all in one.

"Ray, you need to be singing. Cut a CD and sing in nightclubs; it's time you have your 'Frank Sinatra' night life," I said, knowing Ray was a part-time singer and that he had done it full time before becoming an agent.

"I'm no Sinatra, but I do like to sing. Hey, you know what? My son's living in Arizona and he's got a girlfriend now," Ray beamed.

In my opinion, there is handful of great fathers, and if I had my way of changing the world, I'd rotate them, so that everyone would have one of these great fathers at least every other year, to be adopted even temporarily by these great, loving fathers. Why not! I'd be the first in line, although my father is not on the 'bad' dad list at all. He's just a workaholic, who is emotionally awkward. He can't show mushy love, where dads like Ray and Aldo say things like, "Damn it, you're my kid; you're my flesh and blood and that's the best thing there is in this crazy, messed up, beautiful world. Anything you do right makes me proud." Those kind of corny, cheeseball lines last forever. Being the Italian-American gentleman he is, Ray walked me downstairs, and whistled at the red BMW.

"Not mine. You remember Shadow?" Ray nodded at my dog.

"You gonna be safe enough?" he asked, like an agent/father.

"Yeah, Shadow has a mean stare and a serious bark, and when anyone who is even half crazy approaches this car, he'll snarl like he eats human meat," I said, which was true.

"Vivien, you ever think back to the night you were held at gunpoint?" he asked.

"Not much, because I'm too busy enjoying being alive," I answered.

He gave me one of those pretend knock-out punches on my chin that affectionately means, 'You're good stuff'. Then he knocked on the hood, giving it the official drive- off salutation. I got in and headed toward the 101 Freeway, leaving Hollywood and all the one-liners, all the almost-movie-parts, all the commercial 'smile' auditions behind me. Shadow had taken his last wiz on a patch of grass near Hollywood Boulevard and La Brea. Off and away we went!

# 9

## *FREEWAY*

The freeway is open, wide and designed for screaming at the top of your lungs, for feeling the freedom of adventure and for driving a little bit past the speed limit. Just a little bit. The red BMW came with cruise control and I took full advantage of it. With Shadow in the back, I felt safe and energized. This was my first trip across the country. America had been just a map of names memorized from places in movies. Lots of movies! There were no vegan or vegetarian 'hot spots' on the GPS for going from the West Coast to the East Coast. Something somebody ought to do something about. So I was forced to stop in health food stores and refill my cooler with soy products, tofu and raw vegetables. Might not sound yummy, but it is.

My first state after leaving California was Nevada. Wow. I have to say, there is nothing like driving across a desert landscape. There is a lot of it to see, and it's not just bare, dry land. It's beautiful in an un-lush non-green way. I had

Googled doggy motels before leaving LA and, so far, the Super 8 motel chains were going to be the best place to stay the night.

Heads up, when I first moved to LA I bought a large box of used VHS movies and a small TV that only played VHS at a yard sale in Burbank, near the horse stables. So FYI, the movies that I can quote lines come from that pack—none of them are current movies. So, my drive across country was about to be filled by visiting some of those fantastic film locations. Incidentally, at the yard sale I paid only forty dollars and that included the TV. I felt lucky—go figure!

Las Vegas, to me, looks like it does on all the postcards and in the landscape photo books. You can't help but laugh that some money-making-organized-crime guys got together to create it. Or maybe it was all due to Bugsy Siegel. Who really knows? I felt a rush driving into it, almost a fear, and a giddiness that I could get stuck and become a Las Vegas showgirl, or a high-paid whore with my name monogrammed on thigh high-boots. It was easy to see that if I wanted to, I could create a new life in Las Vegas. The buildings are high and advertising is everywhere. The neon lights are art in themselves, designed to get your attention and it got mine. This was where scenes for *Godfather 1* and *Godfather 2*, *Clear and Present Danger*, *Casino*, and *Top Gun* were filmed.

My overeducated, over-read father (refuses to watch any current movies) he had forced me to watch the black-and-white film *The Misfits*, starring Clark Gable and Marilyn Monroe—the last picture they made before both dying tragically. It was filmed in the desert, too. I guess I just love the idea of being immortalized on film. I guess if I don't go onto make "indie films," (as has been suggested twice), I can always sell my soul and become a reality TV star who creates a sewn-on-words-clothing line, or an organic juice beverage or jars of veggie pet food. Nowadays, actors and actresses have to decide if they should audition for mainstream or break into the reality world; either way, they still have to hope they make it.

But, here I was, in Las Vegas, with two options: to turn back or go forward. Shadow barked, waking me out of my absurd worry, and I pulled over to a tiny green patch while my GPS continued to say, "recalculating," over and over again. Too bad it didn't come with a pause button. Of course, I'm jealous it's not my voice as the GPS guide. Why do all the good parts always go to someone else? Why ask why?

Okay, so thinking like a loser doesn't bring results—that much I learned during three months of therapy at the Y in the heart of Hollywood. I got fortunate and ended up with a young female 'counselor-in-training' for $25.00 an hour (one hour sessions only). She kicked my ass in the right direction, mentally speaking. I was only a year into my new LA life and, well, I was hanging out in various trendy Hollywood bars out of total loneliness and a lack of friends. The bars in LA are the best for finding quick company

and I don't mean for screwing, although that's always an option—but people did just sit and talk while they got drunk and I nursed one beer.

The 'in-training-counselor' got me to enroll in an actors group, to join a yoga class and to go to a café in Venice that held an open mic for poetry and monologue readings. She accomplished this by saying, "I dare you to find two things to do in the next two weeks besides barhopping," and, well, I guess I'm competitive, because I said, "I'll bet you that I can find three things and never go back to Hollywood bar hopping again," and of course I won. Go figure! I don't think a real 'shrink' would have ever said what she did. They just want to poke around in 'loneliness' issues and ask dumb questions about how has my mother's 'abandonment' affected me, and other such crap. That's just my opinion. Anyway, once I was out of the bar scene, I thanked her and quit going to the Y.

"Nothing lasts!" I shouted to Shadow who had parked himself on the grass. I told him to get in and turned the car towards the freeway, glancing at the 'Los Angeles' sign. "Thank you, Hollywood, for Shadow," I called out. Shadow had been just a thirteen-week-old puppy when I saw a man hitting him one afternoon in the Silver Lake Dog Park on Silver Lake Boulevard. I used to do my one-hour exercise walks around the outside of the reservoir and often watched the dogs running and playing, but this time I marched into the park and right up to that man, "I work for the Animal Protection League! Sir, you have two minutes to stop hitting that puppy, or I'll take it away."

Then I strode off and over to the handful of dog owners watching their dogs play and asked, "What the hell's going on?"

"Don't know. That guy keeps hitting it," someone said.

"He shouldn't be allowed," someone else said.

"He's got five minutes to get himself under control, before I yank that dog a way," I warned the group. When a teenager entered the dog park with his Greyhound, the man motioned to him, said something and pointed to me.

"That man down there said you can have the puppy, he doesn't want it," the kid raced up and told me. So I marched right down to the man.

"The Animal Protection League thanks you for giving up this puppy," I said, as any actor would. And the man nodded in relief and quickly left the park. Act 'as if', that's my motto. That's why Shadow is my dog.

On my third visit to the Laurel Canyon Dog Park, with Shadow, I met a black haired, dark-eyed girl sitting on a bench next to a chubby English Bulldog who said, "I'm on my 3rd boyfriend thanks to this dog park." Wow, I was excited. I figured maybe I could have a dog and a cool BF.

"You've really met nice guys here?" I asked.

"Yeah, if you have a dog and the guy has one, it's a connection right away," she informed me, like a total valley girl. Still, I believed her. Why not?

Well, I didn't exactly meet a boyfriend. Instead, I met a one-night stand. Correction, a two-night stand. Instead of becoming his girlfriend, I became his spinning top. Wowie! He had a purebred Shepherd that he had trained, and was, of course, a successful commercial actor. He had a very tight body, and an East Coast stride about him. Oh, and he looked as if he was Robert De Niro's son or a younger twin.

Shadow played with his overly polite Shepherd, so that helped. We talked about acting. What else? He wore a leather brand-name fanny pack, containing a roll of poop bags, treats, a dog whistle—and condoms. Very cleaver! I was ready to tell the whole female population at the Laurel Canyon Dog Park what I'd noticed, "Hey girls, this guy has condoms! He cares!"

My college friends and I had met a bunch of guys who used to say things like, "I can't feel anything or enough with the condom on," or "That thing stops my squirting potential." Well, maybe they didn't say exactly that, but they did complain how a condom took away the 'real' experience for them. Answer: "Herpes and AIDS can take more than that away."

So the dog park actor invited me to have a home-cooked meal at his apartment. "A home-cooked vegetarian meal? Sure, I'm up for that," I said. He gave me his address and explained how to find his house along Mulholland—which is one curvy drive. And yeah, there's a cool movie that borrowed the title from it. Go figure.

The day I went to his place, I left Shadow at home, knowing that four was a crowd. It's like that sometimes with pets. He had the typical 'Hollywood' bungalow house, a brick fireplace, an open back yard, tiled floors and lots of windows. It was easy to find, and I parked next to his FJ Cruiser. When he swung the front door open, he was fresh out of the shower, his hair wet and clean, and he was still buttoning his denim shirt. "Irish Spring, smells yummy," is what I almost sang out, when he gave a hug. Incidentally he hugged me in that way when a guy presses his whole torso into yours and if you don't press yours into his, well, you could be called frigid.

He had two Whole Foods shopping bags on the Spanish-tile countertop. He had the pasta going and had sautéed tofu like a guy who wants to get laid by a vegetarian. He played Billy Holiday singing *The Very Thought of You*, while he tossed the organic salad with homemade dressing. He had 'husband' potential skills that wouldn't really be activated for another ten-to-fifteen years, but the 'set up' was clear. A girl might think this guy would just settle down with her, at least as a steady boyfriend, but I knew different. Another plus was he talked about his mother with affection and fondness, a sign that a guy doesn't have any weird, boxed-up rage against women. But I instinctively knew I was only going to be treated to an erotic experience, so I wasn't thinking about this going anywhere but R-rated.

After dessert, which was chocolate tofu cheesecake (sounds strange, but totally yummy); he made his purebred Shepherd do 'cowboy' tricks with him. He put an orange water gun in a brown vintage leather cowboy holster fastened around his slim waist. "Now, mister, this ain't your lucky day," he said, pretending to shoot—while his Shepherd fell to the floor, rolled over and played dead. They did this seven more times; if I had had some salted peanuts and a box of Cracker Jack, I might have thought I was at a slightly boring circus.

"Let me show you my bedroom," he said, as he took off the holster. It's always funny when a guy says that. It's not like he's a real estate agent. Bedroom equals what it equals—sex. "Buffalo Bill—" Yup, that was the dog's real name. "Go to sleep," he said in a Texan accent and the dog did just that, on top of a fluffy dog bed. Then he took my hand and we walked into his bedroom. His queen sized bed was pushed into a corner and he had a small dresser with an Ansel Adams poster hanging over it. He put new wave type music on—the kind you often hear in a dentist office. Weird, that was warning number one for me, but I didn't pick up on it fast enough.

"Wait a second, I've got a surprise for you," he said proudly, as he disappeared from his bedroom.

So I sat on the bed that was covered by a Western comforter, with cowboy pillows. He came in wearing tight white corduroy short-shorts and nothing else. Weird, warning number two. This time I noticed. He flicked his stereo switch to blast Pink, singing, *Try*. He began to dance across his bedroom, his butt packed into his tight short-shorts. He did what I can only call the '*Spider-Man*' dance, pressing his hands against the wall and then turning quickly and pressing his pelvis against it. Across the wall he went like *Spider-Man*. And I watched, and I watched. No peanuts needed for this.

Later, he jumped onto the queen size mattress, proving that it had box springs under it, and then he helped me take off my Gucci dress, which I wore because I was trying to look like a different type of girl. Go figure. We kissed a few times before he had my bra off and my underwear flung onto the stereo. Then he flipped my legs into the air, with my backside, chest and head against his cowboy pillows. A spinning top was what I was. Weird! He took off his shorts and he was in between my legs like the Sundance Kid. As if he was fishing for gold in a deep stream—he went in and out, and in and out.

Oh, and he had a red condom on: he had pulled it from a cloth pouch between the bed and the wall. He could have taught a Learning Annex workshop on putting a condom on in less than a second. Really, I think a lot of guys would have attended it. Maybe I was remembering him because it was time to swear off going to bed with ACTORS for GOOD and the long drive was giving me the chance to get myself straightened out. Okay, friendship sure, but nothing more. Yup, I was ready to change. Las Vegas was the place to make my vow, once and for all.

# 10

## MOTELS

I pulled across from the famous Flamingo Hotel at 3555 Las Vegas Boulevard where Bugsy Siegel had ruled. I guess he would have been happy with the film version of him played by the hot, ever good-looking Warren Beatty. In that movie, *Bugsy* made me want to be a "gangster" girlfriend for a few weeks. *Ocean's Eleven* was filmed there and it looked so exciting, but I wasn't going in.

"Shadow, we can't afford to stay there on this trip, but maybe one day," I said.

With a Bluetooth in the ear or a dog beside me—I can really get away with talking out loud. I waved to no one and started driving toward our first Super 8 Motel, one that welcomed dogs and was affordable. It was miles away and when we finally got there, it seemed like a movie location; or maybe I just wanted it to be one.

Motels, hotels, are just fancy bedrooms with none of your identity attached to them, and that's why I love them.

If I could, I would live in a hotel for a year, never doing laundry, never cleaning up after myself, and never worrying. It's a rented bedroom with a bed, a TV, an alarm clock, a closet and a bathroom. That's what this one had, along with a small desk. Shadow took the bed right away; he's a creature of comfort and, given that I was suddenly single, he could share it with me.

Motel rooms, hotel rooms, are also the places where, at twenty-seven years old, you realize that in three years you'll be thirty. That's what happened to me. I suddenly found myself adding up the years. I sat down on the super-soft bed and the tears rolled out; it hit me: twenty-seven, not married, not engaged—which technically comes before getting married—and no career. All three! Ugh! Okay, so now I understand potheads. I mean, if ever there was a time I wanted to get stoned, it was in that motel room. Motel rooms, hotel rooms, are also the best places for romance, and here I was, with none to be had. I guess I could have gone guy searching, but with my now red-rimmed eyes, it wasn't worth it.

Afterward, I watched a rerun episode from my dyslexic TV writing hero, the late, great Stephen J. Cannell's *The Rockford Files*. Incidentally he created or co-created 40, or close to 40, television series. I mean he's one of my ultimate favorites. Unlike me, he didn't hide the dyslexia, but maybe he always had enough money to hire a secretary. That's the problem for those of us who have to earn a living with no extra financial cushion. Bummer! Anyway, I just so appreciate the father-son relationship between the James

Rockford character and the dad that he created, maybe he had that in his life, too.

I fell asleep in my clothes, and woke up around 6:00 to walk Shadow and check out early. I was headed to Arizona. I wanted to get far away from Las Vegas—which I'd decided was better as a scene in a movie or on a postcard.

Hello Arizona! In my opinion, Arizona's landscape is red. I couldn't help but notice that right away. The land's burnt red. I pulled into Flagstaff where my bookish father's other favorite black-and-white film *Casablanca*, had been shot. Also, *Easy Rider* and *Midnight Run* had scenes shot there. The town looked undersized. No tall buildings. Wow, the Native American influence was strikingly visible.

I headed into a diner and ordered oatmeal. I felt dejected, as if all the crying had washed away my voice. I watched the families eating together and several truckers drinking coffee. Hey, I was driving myself across America, I had to laugh; there was no time for getting sad or depressed, because I was on an adventure. Correction, Shadow and I were on an adventure and I was driving. The waitress came over and asked about the red BMW, and she told me how she was saving to go to beauty school, and how she planned to move to Texas to become a top hairdresser in Dallas. I told her to go to LA and do hair and make-up for the movies. She suddenly liked my idea better than her plan.

Once outside, I called Paloma in Manhattan to tell her to start focusing on the real guy, the guy she wanted to end up with—the 'Mr. Darcy' husband guy.

"Vivien, when you come here, we'll make a plan," she said.

"All right, let's," I said, and hung up.

I decided to push myself to New Mexico before midnight. On a freeway, a girl in a red car can't drive fast without being pulled over. The truth is I had one of those radar detectors, and so I knew when to slow down, or go— go. The Tennis Actor had given it to me with the promise that I would mail it back. I never drive fast, ever, but I wanted to change—speed felt like a part of it.

Hello New Mexico! I drove past the mountains of New Mexico, cactus and signs for Native handcrafted souvenir shops. I made it into Gallup, way before midnight and booked Shadow and I into an Econo-Lodge. I dropped my Louis Vuitton suitcase and matching bags in the room, washed my face, and grabbed Shadow's leash and off we went for a short walk around the outskirts of the Lodge. I wasn't going to cry anymore, and I wasn't going to think too hard either. So, I tied Shadow's leash to a pole, headed into a food store to buy a Coors—I was going drink my mind numb. Yeah, one beer does the trick for me. Go figure.

I'll admit I felt safe traveling with Shadow, but I was also careful not to glance at guys too long. I just felt that I had to be careful because America is filled with creepy men, and I didn't want a creepy story happening to me. Also, I didn't need a one-night stand. In fact, I was done with those; I had outgrown them.

I drank the beer quickly, while I thought about the two men I had met at the Laurel Canyon Dog Park. One morning I got to chatting with two dog owners. One of them owned a shop on Kings Road and the other was a TV actor. And both were filled with 'female' wisdom.

"You could end up working forever unless you get a money-man," the actor with the Labrador told me.

"You should dress up, let your hair down and go sit at the Ivy; a rich man will fall for you and he'll marry you, and after two years you'll divorce him. And you'll be all set financially," said the shop owner with a Dalmatian.

"Are you guys telling me to use a rich man?" I asked, like this was a joke and I wasn't sure what the punch-line was supposed to be.

"Yeah, I would if I were you," said the actor.

"It's about planning for the future in a smart way," said the shop owner. I laughed!

I mean, they were giving me advice—not some wealthy, matchmaking, reality TV lady, but two guys in the Laurel Canyon Dog Park. Not just 'any' dog park, but one where a lot happens.

Now I was, staying with Shadow in the Econo-Lodge, unmarried, less than twenty- thousand dollars to my name, with no career success and no direction. Ugh! So much for the beer. Now I needed painkillers. My mind was swimming with worry, anxiety and apprehension. Who was I? What was I? What the hell was my purpose? Oh, well, I fell asleep; if I hadn't, I think I would have run out into the

Econo-Lodge parking lot with Shadow on his leash and screamed "MARRY ME, SOMEBODY, MARRY ME."

Texas was next, and I was so curious about that state. I had really noticed it when I saw the movie *Thelma and Louise*. There's a line when the character Louise Sawyer says, *"You get what you settle for,"* and that just hung over me as I drove into the wide-open, ever-green, flourishing, fertile Texas landscape.

Hello Texas! It's a movie location dream. That's for sure. It had been used for *Gas Food Lodging*, *All the Pretty Horses*, *Traffic*, *True Grit*, and *Wyatt Earp* and for my non-emotional father's third favorite black-and-white film, *The Grapes of Wrath*. I found a dog-friendly hotel and crashed. Even with cruise control, it was a lot of driving. The Texas air hung in the room as Shadow and I took an early nap. I just needed to shut my eyes; I had seen so many images flicker past them.

Texas is gigantic, there's just no other way to say it the state is vast. Enormous! And the meals are equally big. The waitress asked, in a voice filled with southern hospitality, "If ya wanting veggie food, well, we don't serve that kind. You're in Texas now! We are about hearty food." And I had to laugh while I ordered toast and a plate of fruit. I mean, it really was a good line, no B.S. about it. And I wondered if she spoke to her man like that. She might say something like, "Now are you gonna service me? Or you gonna leave Texas with your tail between your legs?" I mean, what could any man say to that?

I looked around the restaurant. It was family oriented and had Texas-Americana decor. Much of the land, from what I could see driving through it, was still untamed, and it stretched for miles and miles. You could shoot a Western any day and make it appear circa 1950s. A lanky, 6'1" cowboy tipped his dusty hat at me on his way out the door and I giggled. I mean, he was right out of Central Casting—'oh so Hollywood-ish'. I felt as if he was about to stride out onto the movie set, but no, he was real. It was I who wasn't. I dream movies, think movies, and sometimes everything I do or see feels like a movie. Go figure!

I ordered a well-done steak with nothing on it to-go, which got a wide-eyed grin of approval from Patty, the waitress. I would never have told her that it was for Shadow; I liked her thinking that I was heading back to my hotel to eat in secrecy. I like telling white lies. Okay, so it's a part of show business and it's a part of pleasing people; I'm guilty of both.

People buy into images every day. This actor in a 'straight' marriage, a cover-up for being gay. That actress being naturally 'skinny' when she's had the fat sucked out of her. That's part of the reason some people go up the ladder, as in unknown to 'mega' star. When I first arrived in Hollywood, I was just a year-and-a-half out of college and a non-union actress. Not four weeks later, at my first Hollywood party, I was being offered my Screen Actors Guild card by a powerhouse producer in exchange for sex with him. Sex? I had to laugh; I mean, everyone back in New York had said, "Vivien, look out for the casting couch, for swapping your pussy for a movie part," and I was like "Ha, ha." I mean I thought it was total bullshit. Okay, so I thought about it for a day, sex for a Screen Actor's Guild card, which I really wanted. I mean, being in the union is essential, every actor's goal. But in the end, I flushed his glossy business card down the toilet.

After a morning of yoga and a long Texas style dog stroll, I packed up and headed for Oklahoma. One can't help but want to hear show tunes entering Oklahoma; Richard Rodgers and Oscar Hammerstein had branded it for everyone, and Broadway owned it. Wow, I felt a rush crossing the state line. Hello, Oklahoma! Thank god for CD players. I pulled over, found my Broadway Show of Shows CD with the ten greatest musicals, and blasted it. I can't sing for shit, but with just Shadow with me in the car—it didn't matter.

*The Outsiders, Twister,* and *Near Dark* were filmed in Oklahoma. I was headed for the Big 8 Motel in El Reno, that had been renamed 'Amarillo Motel' during the filming of *Rainman.* I was excited to stay in the real thing.

I don't think anyone can really go back home, and I knew I was returning temporarily to my father's place, that he'd pull out his Ikea sofa in his study and I'd use it for my bedroom until I found another place to dwell. All that I had left behind in his apartment were four boxes filled with childhood; grade school and high school junk, memories of who I was or had planned to be. The open road is the perfect place to think, even with the Oklahoma sound track blaring in the background. The truth was, I was happy that

I was going to see my father; it had been a long time. But I was also slightly unhappy, too.

The Big 8 Motel did not look like it did in *Rainman*, but I didn't care; it was the real location and that was good enough for me. I took a 20-minute hot shower, returned cell phone calls, and sat naked on the motel bed. Motels and hotels are meant for sex. Sleeping alone or with a big dog is okay the first night, but night after night—it gets boring. So I called the Tennis Actor for phone sex. It actually works if two people are horny, only bummer this time; it was just me. He said, "Yeah, I'll get you off, babe," and I waited. I could hear noises in the background from the TV crew. He wasn't in any of the shooting scenes, but he was hanging around, in case the director wanted to shoot him in a scene.

"I'm totally naked," I said. And more silence followed.

Now I'm not the kind who enters a room naked without getting some attention. "I'm ramming a cucumber up my... (fake moans)." More silence.

"See you," I said, and hung up.

He was in the middle of his Hollywood career world and I wasn't. There's a line from the movie, *Elizabethtown*, also filmed in El Reno. The character Claire Colburn says, *"I think I've been asleep most of my life."* And for some unfortunate reason, it seemed to resonate. Maybe that was true of me.

# 11

# COMPASS

Hello Missouri! We reached St. Louis before noon. Some creepy guy in a beat-up Pontiac started tailing me, as in close to my bumper, and I could see his 'evil stare' in my rear-view mirror. Oh God, my panic button went off. Panic as in, "Oh, God, he's a serial killer," I wasn't sure where the police station was, but the airport seemed like the next safest place. He sped up and leered at me through the rolled down car window, not in that 'suck my dirty dick' look but in that "I'm a pure wacko" look. He was cast-able for a *SAW* remake. Incidentally, some of the scenes from the movie *Silence of the Lambs* were shot in Missouri.

I searched for my sunglasses, wanting to cover my eyes that I was sure were already showing my fear. Most times I feel truly fearless, but then there are times where I realize that I live in a world with good guys and really, really terrible ones. This was one of those 'I'm scared' moments.

'St. Louis International Airport' the sign read, like a beacon of light, and as I veered onto the ramp, he disappeared. Ha, I made it. Some of the major movies that were shot there are *Planes, Trains and Automobiles* and, of course, *Up in the Air*. I pulled into the no-loading, no-waiting zone and let out a sigh of relief. I was safe, I felt in control, and I was on solid, protected, highly secured American soil. Okay, I'm on a road trip. This is America, my America, and I want to enjoy it. So I focused my attention on the airport because it's stylish. I had the urge to park and walk around as if waiting for my new Mr. Darcy to exit a plane, any plane, into my open arms. With Shadow in the backseat, I couldn't park.

After ten minutes, I was ready to resume my road trip toward Indiana. I knew if I hauled ass, I would arrive at the Hotel Indigo at 9791 North by Northeast Boulevard. Okay, so besides being a pet-friendly hotel, the address reminded me of another one of my 'forever single' father's favorite old films, Alfred Hitchcock's *North by Northwest*. I'll admit that I like the films my father likes, though I refuse to let him know it. Call it passive aggression on my part, if you want. Whatever!

The freeway drive was trouble-free into Indiana. I couldn't really believe that here I was, twenty-seven years old and finally seeing some of America. Wow. "Better late than never" really rings true for me.

Hello Indiana! Hotel Indigo was modern and glossy; I liked the layout and was beyond happy to check in, as if something really good was going to happen to me during my one night. I'm given to illusions, no doubt, but Hollywood had been all about illusions. Now my mind had to create the perfect scene, the perfect thought of 'what if this happens to me'. It was better than the night before. TG for that. Indiana has had a ton of films shot in it, such as *A Piece of Eden*, *A League of Their Own*, *Natural Born Killers*, *A Night on Elm Street*, *Breaking Away*, *Going All The Way* and *Eight Men Out*. It's just that cool. I liked Indiana right away, I just did. There's a line in the movie *Eight Men Out* that means a lot to me; the character Kid Gleason says, *"People are human."* When you really think that way, it just can't be that bad a world.

I walked Shadow and changed into my yoga pants and leotard top and headed for the gym; I wanted to get into 'Amazon' shape. In college, I told a challenging English professor that I was actually planning on becoming an 'Amazon' after graduation.

"Vivien, you can't become an Amazon. They are women who exist without men," he said, in an overly educated tone of voice.

Wow, how did he know I was guy crazy? How did he know that I suffered from penis envy? Ugh—I still continue to suffer from it. Go figure. Shortly before I graduated, he pulled me aside as he dismissed the class and he said that if I ever found myself in total doubt to seek out counseling/therapy. He just said it as if he really wanted me to know that. I didn't say a word. But later that day, a female student accused me of sleeping with him. I didn't bother to inform her that I wasn't the gender he preferred—

if she wanted to think I was screwing him, let her. A rumor like that is something worth remembering. Ha, ha!

An attractive guy was lifting weights. Salt and pepper hair. Maybe early forties, I thought, but Paloma had also warned me, "Some guys grey early, and it don't match their age." I hopped on the treadmill, pivoted towards him; he could see me in the mirror as I walked my butt into shape. Hotel Indigo scored extra bonus points in my book—the workout room was top rate. Okay, so I'm not the kind to flirt first and, it wasn't like this had a future. He glanced over at me. "Smile now," I ordered myself. I can be so slow sometimes that it freaks me out. Later after a potential 'flirt' scene is over, I look back over it like I'm a director correcting what my character (me) should have done. It's usually a brutal critique, because I messed up the moment and an actress is supposed to be in the moment.

The couple that had been using the rower and stepper left the room, leaving the two of us.

"Where are you from?" he asked.

I told him in five minutes how I had been born in New York City and raised in the West Village, and then lived in Cambridge, Massachusetts, for high school, then college in Bronxville, NY, and then Hollywood and…"SHUT UP," memo to self. I stopped, smiled and got off the treadmill, just as he finished his set of weights and was toweling his neck dry.

"And you?" I asked.

He was in finance, from Washington, just in on business and heading back in the morning. Then I saw it. Damn!

Yup, the gold band on the left hand that says, 'I'm married, get your own.' I nodded. His eyes shifted to his hand and then up at my face, and in the next five seconds, he rattled off three dirty things he wanted to do to my body. I liked the sound of all three, but even if his wife wasn't in Indiana, her essence, her shadow (not as in my dog) would be in the bedroom. Yuck!

"Sorry, I have to go make some important business calls," I said, as I forced myself towards the door.

He touched my arm, and leaned in and kissed me. Just like in those romantic movies, except that those male characters are single and the 'passion' has been smoldering for a lengthy amount of time.

Anyway, I used my hotel key card and there was Shadow on the bed, barking at the sight of me.

"Shhhhhhhh," I said and walked over to pet him. He's one huge baby dog.

"What a relief, just a kiss and I got out of there. Once again, it's only you and me and I'm so glad. We'll find our own compass through life," I said, as if my dog knew what I was talking about. Then I rummaged in my bag, found a rawhide bone for him. Easy to please. And that felt good.

Chicago, Illinois, was next. I had always wanted to see that city because of *Ferris Bueller's Day Off*, as geeky as that sounds. Okay, so I know it's a totally dated 80's film, but it was in the VHS box that I bought at the Burbank yard sale. And it seemed just right for my movie trip across America.

I woke up super energized. I had watched another of my dyslexic TV hero, Stephen J. Cannell's reruns, an episode of

*Baretta* and I dashed Shadow through a brief walk and back into the red BMW. Off we went. It was a speedy drive into Chicago. Okay, I went way over the speed limit, but didn't get caught.

Hello, Chicago! It's a great, big city, and in a lot of ways it reminded me of New York City: the architecture, the feel of it, and the population. Okay, so a ton of movies have been filmed in Chicago, *The Hunter* (a favorite of my father's) *The Untouchables, Risky Business, Home Alone, Sixteen Candles, When Harry Met Sally, My Best Friend's Wedding, Soul Food, The Blues Brothers, The Color of Money*, and *High Fidelity*—just to name a few, and ('un-dork' myself). So I left Shadow at the dog-friendly Marriott Hotel and started out on my Ferris Bueller movie tour, something I had put together by myself.

The character Ferris Bueller says, *"Life moves pretty fast. If you don't stop and look around once in a while you could miss it."* I guess that's what I'm most afraid of. Okay, so I've officially entered dork-ville, but I had a total blast checking out the garage that Ferris drives the Ferrari out of. I strolled past the Tribune Tower, the Sears Tower, and I took a taxi around Wrigley Field. Wow! It was the special movie-sight-seeing day, followed by really good Italian pizza from Giordano's, which the taxi guy recommended, when I asked where the best was made. It's so fun to be a tourist.

Cleveland, Ohio, was my next destination. Some of the movies that were shot there are *The Deer Hunter* (my father's favorite), *Light of Day, Major League, Antwone Fisher* and *American Splendor*.

When my mother left my unemotional father for the Panamanian coffee grower, my father said, "We'll have to fend for ourselves," and then he tossed out my mother's coffee mug. It was a plain ceramic and lightweight; she didn't like holding anything heavy in her hands. He never yelled, he never threw the things she left behind on the floor, and if he cried at all, he must have done it in the shower, because I never heard a thing. Nothing!

There's a line in the film *The Deer Hunter* when the character Julien says, *"When a man says no to champagne he says no to life."* I can't remember ever seeing my father drink champagne after my mother left him. I forgot about being excited to be in Cleveland, when I checked into the Comfort Inn. Not because I didn't like it, but because I was suddenly so worried about seeing my over-educated, workaholic 'forever single' father, again. SINGLE? Please don't let me end up like him.

# 12

## DREAMS

Wow, I was having sex with Ashton Kutcher in my dream. I mean, I actually woke up in my Comfort Inn bed—feeling flushed, exhausted, and well, to be truthful, wet between my legs. Wow, he was good. He was tender, focused, and he had speed. I'm not a star f***er in real life, but in my dream life, I have been a fantastic whore.

Okay, so who have I been to bed with in my dreams? My list is as follows; dead actors first, James Dean, because I believed him in *East of Eden* and *Rebel without a Cause* (and also he seemed moody and a bit intimidated by females and that just turned me on). Next, River Phoenix (from the film *Running on Empty*), but to be totally honest—we were only skinny dipping in my dream. It was still enjoyable, because we were both naked, jumping in and out of a secluded lake, with crystal clear water. Yup, I could see his naked body. I woke up grinning.

Foreign actors: Hugh Grant (UK), because he's handsome and wildly fun in all the movies he's acted in that I've seen, like *Four Weddings and a Funeral* and *Love Actually*, and okay, the Hollywood Boulevard or Sunset Boulevard "alleged" scandal, that garnered him a mug shot—just made him more desirable. I like the idea of him being lonely and seeking out comfort on the street—I think I've felt that same loneliness and horny desperation myself. And then French actor Tcheky Karyo (from the *La Femme Nakita* film), because I replayed the scene over and over where he bangs his hand against the door and kicks it, and he wants so much to go back in and kiss Nakita. And he's rough, older—and I found him really hot to watch.

FYI, this wasn't a sexual dream, but I did dream that Alec Baldwin's brother Stephen Baldwin was trying to give me a religious cleansing (maybe to cure me of my male lust and penis envy). The dream was very short—Stephen Baldwin said, "You're cleansed. The spirits are free," and poured water over my head and the dream ended.

I've had a threesome in my first and only musician sex dream—I was in bed with Jack Johnson and Ben Harper. Okay, so it wasn't the typical threesome. I mean, Jack Johnson played his guitar and sang while Ben Harper and I were having sex, and then, when I had sex with Jack Johnson, Ben Harper played guitar and sang. It was really 'mellow' sex, and I woke up really, really mellow!

Speaking of sex dreams—one time I dreamt that I was having sex with my former friend Heather's ex-boyfriend Ryan. Life is stranger than a movie sometimes and you can quote me on that. For the record I had never, ever, ever thought of Ryan as a possibility because he was her midwestern guy and he wasn't my type at all. So, when their relationship ended and he was just the ex-boyfriend (as in whatever)—I basically forgot about him. But then one morning, I woke up in my Los Feliz bed, having dreamt of him stripping off his carpenter pants and leaping into my bed. Yeah, I did just say leaping. The wacky thing is that the sex seemed real—so I called him. Yup, I just called him and said, "Ryan, this Vivien, I know I haven't talked to you in a few years, but we were having sex in my dream and it was fantastic." I was going through a phase of saying whatever I thought without censoring it—that phase didn't last long.

"Uh, yeah? I like the sound of that dream," he said.

I was stunned. I mean, I knew he hadn't thought about me and that he would never have called me up. I was off his radar. He was living in Oakland, California and Heather had moved onto another guy. "Come visit me!" he suggested, and two days later I had booked a South by Southwest flight out of Burbank, all because I had had a fantastic sex dream. Okay, so the question is—can a sex dream actually turn into a reality worth having? It did this time.

To be totally truthful, there was no 'great romance' at all. Ryan picked me up at the airport and we both laughed. We didn't kiss, didn't even grope each other. Then I spent an hour rearranging his bed, because his lower back had been aching and he hadn't flipped his mattress over. After that, he cooked us a healthy meal (as in no meat). Yeah, I guess I like guys who can cook. I'm kind of a healthy menu girl (as in I can choose nutritious items off a menu). After we ate, we took off our clothes super-slowly and got into bed and we did 'it'. He was excellent, and so was I. The other thing I should confess about Ryan is that he's well-endowed, and he was rather shy about it. How sweet is that? Come on, how adorable is that? Of course I was thrilled. Let's just say I gave him lots of praise.

I don't know whether Heather cared about the size of his cock, because we never talked about intimate stuff like that and she never said anything about him as a lover. The surprise was worth it. I'm not the same in bed as any of my friends—no one is the same in bed as their friends. Okay, so in my opinion; most guys who are well-endowed have matching egos. And it can get boring when they wave it in your face and tell you how terrifically fortunate you are. That happened once, not twice, and luckily not with Ryan.

Anyway, it was a weekend-stand, vs. a one-night stand. I called him once trying to get us to do 'it' again, not because I was horny (okay, probably I was) but more because I just didn't want it to be a weekend stand. But it never happened again. Go figure.

Months later Heather dropped me as friend, not because "I did it" with her ex-boyfriend (they had been broken up for three years), but because I didn't tell her. The idea of me calling her up and telling her that it 'only' happened because of a sex dream I had, not because I had ever, ever wanted Ryan—seemed impossible. Friendships end when one person chooses to dump it lock-stock-and-barrel. It ends like a death, non-retrievable, that much I learned from that.

Paloma, on the other hand, is the opposite. She's so proud of being a Puerto Rican and bred in NYC that if I had slept with one of her ex-boyfriends, she wouldn't care, nor would she ever take it personally. I know that for sure, because she caught one of her ex-boyfriends eyeing my acting headshot that was nailed to her wall. He asked her to set him up with me, because he was going to be visiting LA and she called me up, saying, "Vivien, if you do him, you better be good, because otherwise, I'll have to make up for it." I pretended I was going to be away filming on location. The real reason I don't like remakes are because the first movie should stand as it is, unless it was terrible. As in life, I act the same. The Ryan sexual weekend 'mini movie' was enough!

"Goodbye, Cleveland," I shouted out of the car window as Shadow and I headed for Pennsylvania. Some of the movies filmed in that state are *Rocky, Boys on the Side, Blue Valentine, I Am Number Four* (I saw it, because the lead actor looked cute) and *The Sixth Sense*. There's a line in *The Sixth Sense*, where the character Cole Sear says, *"Some magic's real."* I guess I like to believe that about my own life.

The road sign read ENTERING HARRISBURG. Hello Pennsylvania!

I had booked us in a room at the Comfort Inn in Harrisburg for three reasons: it was close to Hershey Park, the Hershey chocolate stores, and the Harrisburg State

Hospital. After checking into our wonderful room, I took Shadow around the dog-friendly grounds, and then headed off for chocolate. Okay, so probably the Swiss make the best chocolate in the world, but for old fashion, yummy American milk chocolate—hands down it's Hershey.

The movies that have had 'chocolate themes' that I've seen so far are, *Willy Wonka and the Chocolate Factory, (Como Aqua Para Chocolate) Like Water for Chocolate, Forest Gump, Matilda* and *Blood & Chocolate.* Going to an amusement park is usually more of a 'couple' thing to do, but I didn't care. Milton S. Hershey created the Hershey Park, and the chocolate factory. I mean, he just had to have been a very enjoyable, 'yummy,' man.

I bought myself tickets for the amusement rides. I went on my first roller coaster at Coney Island when I was six and now I can never get enough. So I went on the Fahrenheit three times; the Comet once and didn't throw up. It's really satisfying to scream at the top of my lungs in mid-air. I think doctors and shrinks should make amusement parks mandatory, once a month, for all people trying to juggle their humanness. And I did it while eating an almond-covered Hershey bar. Chocolate can replace sex, sometimes. Wow, how much fun I had and the sight from above is a bird's eye view.

Back at the Comfort Inn, I fed Shadow and ate a tofu walnut salad I had bought at a health food store along the way. I rested, and then put on my black jeans with the sewn-on patch 'LOVE IS', my black long sleeve shirt, and my Nike sneakers. I was headed to the Harrisburg State

Hospital, the location central to the movie *Girl Interrupted*. Okay, so not to get morbid, depressed or suicidal—I've only seen the movie five times, and the actress part of me thinks I was supposed to be in it. Go figure! I decided to take Shadow with me; he could sit in the car while I walked around the grounds.

The hospital had opened in 1851 because of the efforts of a female humanitarian named Dorothea Dix, but had since closed. Crazy is crazy, and, well, this was on my movie-location-across America-trip list, and I was about to cross it off. It was a quick drive and I parked near the entrance. Bizarre, it looks just like it did in the movie. I stood there, watching the movie scenes fly past me. I have an auto replay in my mind for films, but not for TV.

In the film *Girl Interrupted*, the character Lisa says, *"If I could have any job in the world I'd be a professional Cinderella."* I stood there, not caring if one person heard me as I said, "I wish that, too!" Actually no one was around: it was deserted. I think one of the buildings was being used as a government office, but I'm not a hundred percent sure. In a way, I felt as if the mentally ill, the mentally challenged, and the others who had inhabited this complex had left their 'ghosts' behind. I stood motionless and silent; I think just maybe I could have heard their pleas. But who knows. I think too much!

So I took a Facebook shot of myself in front of the engraved sign HARRISBURG STATE HOSPITAL. The best way to show my trip across America was by uploading photos to Facebook wherever I stopped, I'll admit that

Shadow was in the majority of them, but he's a very photogenic dog. Before going to bed, I put on my all white Hollywood bikini and went swimming in the totally outstanding Comfort Inn pool—feeling a little like a half-sane Cinderella.

# 13

# *SEX*

Shadow and I drove fast towards New York State, listening to Frank Sinatra's greatest hits; it was time to get into the city and be off my movie-location-road-trip. Forget about the movies filmed in NYC; there are too many to list, and besides, home doesn't count. Hello New York! I'm back!

Paloma's place on the Upper East Side was my first stop. My dear, big apple—my beautiful, overcrowded, noisy city. With Paloma's friendship, I have never had to worry about being 'perfect' or failing her, because, as she once told me, "Friendship is about connecting. When it's thick, it's thick, when it's thin, it's thin, but it don't ever have to be broken." I felt like crying when she said that, but I stopped myself. Sometimes I just stop myself from feeling things that are too multi-layered, mysterious and profound.

Paloma is 5'3", curvy beyond curvy—and she has the 'best' Latin skin. I mean, it's the best. If she ever had a pimple, I never saw it. She's got thick, firm thighs, 32 B boobs, a shapely butt, and she likes clothes that stick to her figure; she hides nothing. Her hair is long and black, and the one time she cut it short, she sobbed for two whole weeks because she didn't recognize herself. Paloma is pretty, with a capital P. Her father and mother have told her that, and, of course, guys and strangers on the street have, too. She's just that pretty.

Paloma was the first one to set out to learn about sex and I tried to follow her. By thirteen, we were into bras; she needed one and I was just hoping. She was into makeup before me. I'll admit it—I covered myself up in black turtlenecks and baggy jeans. Anyway, we liked boys and we had crushes 24/7. It was around this time that fate stepped into our lives (we'd just turned fourteen), and we were introduced to a 'sex lady', an educated older woman, who oozed sex appeal. It happened like this: we were in Macy's, looking at beautiful, fancy lace bras and underwear in bright colors. Okay, so I wore black on the outside, but I loved color. Bras that aren't white or black, but are dark purple, butter yellow, or lime green are what I like to buy. Only I wasn't buying them at the time, because I was flat-chested with nipples only. Paloma found a pair of sheer underwear on a Macy's hanger. It was so unusual, so different to us, that we couldn't help but giggle.

"Why do women buy these, when they can just be naked?" Paloma asked. Remember she was fourteen.

"It's the chase, the tantalizing lure of the smell of your vagina that intrigues males," said the Sex Lady, who looked older than our mothers, but not as old as a Grandmother.

We both stared at her. She had un-brushed shoulder length brunette hair, tight jeans stuffed into brown knee-high leather boots, a sheer top showing her black bra. There were lines around her eyes, and her lips were glossy. She could have passed for a Broadway star. She was hauntingly beautiful and wild—we didn't dare move.

"You know, don't you?" Paloma asked. God, how I wished I had been the one to ask.

"Come on, we'll have a drink and I'll tell you girls some things. This is what I do. I help women understand their sexual joy," she said.

"Sexual joy?" Paloma asked.

"Hmmm, yes," she answered. She had been running a women's sex group out of her cozy, West Village apartment for years. She taught women how to orgasm, how to free-up or maneuver their sexual power, even how to ask for pleasure. Oops—I'm jumping ahead.

We followed her, our arms linked as we headed over to Elaine's, on the Upper East Side at 57th street. That was the restaurant Woody Allen used in his film *Manhattan* (my father's other favorite, one of the few he still owns as video, rather than DVD). FYI, the restaurant is no longer around. She bought us tall iced teas, not cocktails. And we ate something, only I can't remember what, because she was telling us about orgasms and how we had to have our own; that if we didn't, we'd be forever caught up in pleasing men and not ourselves—she said, that was the true difference between a sex life lived and a sex life served. Oh God!

Most of what she said floated over my fourteen-year-old head. I had only fooled around with a boy (Eugene) when I was eight, playing hide the skin stick in the hole (a silly game), but it wasn't bona fide sex. We had even tried dry humping like his mother and her bearded boyfriend had done, but we didn't know how to do 'it'. I was just into kissing and wanting to be kissed, and, well, hoping a teenage boy wouldn't be pissed off that I was flat chested. I was even doing 'titty enlarging exercises' that Paloma's fifteen-year-old neighbor Cleo taught me. I'm not alone, millions of other teenage girls have done exercises to make their boobs grow—I think.

Paloma sat, elbows on the table, leaning towards the Sex Lady, trying to memorize all of 'it'. I mean, she was the pupil with her teacher, while I played the part of the invisible teenage friend. So, it was natural that Paloma had an orgasm first, and fell for a guy in Washington Square Park and made him her first sex partner. Usually girls get their periods around twelve—not us. At sixteen she got her period, but I had to wait until I turned seventeen-and-a-half. By then my father had moved us to Cambridge, Massachusetts. I finished high school as an outsider, a New Yorker craving for her city and her best friend. So finally, I screwed a teenage boy (a nobody) in a closet at party, just to do it. I didn't orgasm; that came later with another guy—and on a bed.

Paloma was in a ruby red dress, midnight black high heels, swinging a crimson leather bag and waiting in front of her Upper East Side building when I pulled up in the red BMW.

"What a shock, wow, look at you, best friend!" she shouted. Paloma can make anyone feel welcomed; especially me, that's the way she is. We hugged and she gave Shadow a dog bone. Paloma has two tiny teacup dogs, Spoon and Plate, but she had left them in her mother's apartment so that Shadow could be the only dog.

Paloma's mother lives in the downstairs apartment. Her father left for five years, moved to Spanish Harlem and lived with two women, but one day he came back and no one said a thing. He still disappears, but only for three to four days a month. Paloma once said, "He's probably got other kids," but then she changed the subject, and I knew it was a closed topic. Before she passed away Paloma's grandmother used to live in the apartment Paloma has now. When you get a rent controlled apartment in NYC, you keep it.

I remembered how the Sex Lady had invited us to drop by her West Village brownstone, if we ever wanted to learn more, but we'd have to pay a small 'fee'; those workshops were how she supported herself. She told us that sex wasn't 'free,' that it came with a price. That price was pleasure or pain.

"Like crying?" Paloma had asked.

"No, pleasure is about erotic joy, erotic stimulation. If you cry after sex, it has to be because you felt pleasure deeply. Negative emotions brought into sex will ruin the pleasure," the Sex Lady had told us.

"I'm not going to be negative," Paloma told her.

I don't know why, but I couldn't say anything. I guess I was too worried that I'd end up a failure in bed.

"Don't become bitter or angry, no matter how bad a man treats you, just move on," she said and those words hung over us, like a glass about to fall from a shelf.

"What about oral sex?" Paloma had asked.

"Make sure to have oral done to you, since men like their penis in your mouth, and they expect admiration."

We both cracked up—I don't remember what else, or if anything else was discussed because I was still laughing. At the time I had no penis envy. In fact, I thought the penis hanging with the scrotum sacs looked weird.

"Girls, you must know the lips of your vagina," she had told us.

"How?" Paloma had asked.

"Masturbate every day," she had answered with deep-seated conviction.

Masturbation? Was I ever naïve. See, I had thought only boys jerked off—that only boys had wet dreams, because they got to have 'boners' and we didn't. "M.a.s.t.u.r.b.a.t.e," Paloma had repeated like she was learning a new foreign word and didn't want to forget it. Paloma lived by that rule.

While I lumbered along tearfully, full of uncertainty and confusion, my body wanted so much sex. Penises flew through my dreams like obnoxious clouds and yet my mind told me that I couldn't have a penis without love. When I gave in at that party in the closet, it wasn't for pleasure, it was out of desperation—I wanted the sex to be hard and fast, and it was. Like I said, he was a nobody and I was, too.

Paloma had it better. I guess I have always envied her. She and the Washington Square Park guy—actually an NYU Freshman did 'it' the right way. He licked and kissed her everywhere for two weeks and then they had sex. She called me up and said, "I like sex. It's as good as the West Village lady told us it would be." Ugh, I wish had been more like her.

Anyway, New York City looked the same, filled with a mix of old and modern buildings, all fighting to be respected. The city's color is light grey.

"You can't destroy our spirit," Paloma had said a few days after 9/11.

It's always been that way; 9/11 just reinforced that belief for the whole country, or so I like to think.

In Los Angeles, the colors are white and neutral for fashion, with accessories in bright colors, but in New York City, even in the summertime, you wear black. Paloma prefers everything she wears to be bright, bold and clingy. We stood grinning at each other—we had been cell phone friends for too many years, and now that was over and I felt so relieved.

"You didn't get killed by gunshot, I'm so damn happy. You know, I would have been destroyed if you had," she said and we hugged. We had never really talked about my being held up at gunpoint in the Hancock Park section of LA.

"I gotta 'heart' plan for us," Paloma announced after we dropped my suitcase and bags in her apartment and took Shadow to Central Park. It is one of the best parks in the world—even though I haven't seen all of the parks. We plunked down in the middle of Strawberry Fields. We weren't the only ones there, as usual. Paloma took out two Tiffany boxes from her crimson leather bag. In each was a thin, silver-chain with a delicate silver heart hanging from it. She gave one to me.

"This is for attracting 'true' love," she said.

She put hers on and I held mine in my hands, and then we made a pact out loud to find 'true' love and to claim it forever. "We hereby say no more casual dating, no more yo-yo relationships. YES to true love that leads to getting engaged, getting married and having a family to love and cherish deeply forever and ever."

Paloma had just dumped her on-again-off-again boyfriend for good. It might sound selfish and immature, but I was so glad we were both single at the same time, and that she had a love plan for us. She was the one who thought up my move out West, so I could have a thousand experiences, and I did. Of course, I had thought I was moving to Hollywood to be discovered, to become a big-name actress. Oh well, not every dream comes true.

# 14

## RITUALS

Okay, so now it was time for me to prepare, I had three seriously important events coming up: 1.) Going to my father's place. 2.) Seeing my Aunt Helen die. 3.) The 'true' love pact. That meant doing rituals. Thank God, I had gone to the Hollywood Y's counseling center for those $25.00 an hour sessions, because that's where I had learned about the power of rituals. Like I said before, that amazing counseling-girl-in-training had totally helped me. Well, she introduced me to mini-rituals, as well as putting an end to my bar hopping.

"Vivien, don't give your mind that much time to worry or be sad. Limit it." She had said, during one of my sessions.

"Limit it? Like, how?" I had asked—I know, I sounded like a 'Valley Girl' minus the 'Like totally'.

She suggested that I buy glass jars with cork stoppers from the 99-Cent Store and fill them with my 'worried' or 'sad' thoughts. For twenty minutes every morning I scribbled as many worries as I had—and then stuffed them into the jars. Wow, I ended up filling five jars in two months. Good news, it worked!

She had said, "Whatever ritual you do, just believe it will work and never dis-believe."

Now that I was in NYC I was going to stay at Paloma's for a few days. So I had the chance to get my mind, body, spirit, and heart ready.

For my first ritual—I went and got my teeth cleaned at my old dentist, Dr. Underly's office. I met him during my college years, and he had acted like my shrink, my priest, my go-to older platonic male confidant. Of course he kept my teeth healthy, while he listened to me with genuine interest and concern. Back then, I was overfilled with many worries, anxiety over guys and fear about whether I was going to make it 'big' as an actress.

Here I was, all these year later, coming to see him after not having made it 'big' in Hollywood. And I was 'single' again. Dr. Underly is a handsome, athletic man, who loves his wife and being a dentist. He once said, "Vivien, it must be hard to be you!" and I didn't say a thing. I just nodded, and now I was ready to tell him—he was right—a hundred percent right. Go figure.

His office used to be in Bronxville, but he had relocated to another town, so I headed to Grand Central, my favorite train station in the whole wide world, and took a train out to see him. His face looked older, but he was still athletic and still handsome. I told him all about 'failing' in

Hollywood, how I had nothing to show for my years there and all the time I spent when I could have been hanging out with my Aunt Helen. And I cried; I couldn't help it. He just listened, and when I stopped crying, he said, "You didn't fail. You just have to wait and see what happens now. Don't be surprised if it's better than what you imagined." A few minutes later his hygienist came in and cleaned my teeth and my dental confession was done.

I left his office feeling semi-better. Back in the city, I took Shadow to Central Park, telling myself to write it out. I knew I needed to scribble out 100 fears, and that's just what I did. I scribbled out 100 fears on Post-its. Okay, so not exactly 100 different fears—I repeated some of the same ones over and over.

After that I went to dinner with Diego, Paloma's brother, who is super good-looking, as in 'hot'. First we headed down to SoHo to walk around. As I said, Diego is hot looking. That means not only do women check him out, but men do, too. He's 5'8", 180, toned, with stunning Latin skin and razor-cut hair. And he's a construction worker. If they ever do a construction worker calendar, he would be the hottest one.

So I asked him, "What's it like being hot...hot-looking?"

He smirked, and then said, "It's all right."

"What's going on, dating-wise?" I asked, carefully.

I asked carefully because Diego had gotten herpes when he was twenty-three and Paloma and I were nineteen. He credited getting herpes to saving his Latin ass from getting

SIDA (AIDS). He had to stop racking up the numbers and opt for a 'real' relationship. I think what happened to him protected us, because neither Paloma nor I do 'it' without a raincoat on the—you know what.

We sat on a stoop on Mott Street and a woman flirted with Diego, her gestures begging him to flirt back. He said nothing. Diego doesn't talk much. He had only dated a non-Latina once, a Chinese girl when he was in high school, until her parents and friends found out. He actually got badly beaten up by a Chinese gang that her brother ran with. After that, he just started dating like a mad dog with rabies. And then he got herpes, and only had long-term girlfriends. But he was suddenly single again. After a long while of silence, I asked my next nosy question.

"Do you believe in true love?"

He stood up and glanced down at me, but I wasn't going to budge until I got an actual answer out of him.

"Yeah, I do believe in it. I'm searching for it. Besides, I have to give my mom some grandkids." I nodded, and we headed into a Chinese restaurant, where he quizzed me on what qualities a guy had to have to be 'my' true love man. It was fun. I had only a basic list: nice guy, no baggage, wants an LTR that turns into marriage, great sexual ability, and family oriented.

"All right, shut up," he said, and I did.

Third ritual: guy list. So that night, with a glass of white wine, (Paloma's choice) I wrote out what my future 'true' love needed to have and be. It took me two hours. I mean, I really wanted to think about it, and I did.

Meanwhile, Paloma was choosing clothes for her 'online' picture; she had decided that she wanted to try a dating site. Paloma is fearless. I fell asleep before she chose between a deep blue dress and a purple jumpsuit.

When I woke up, Paloma was gone. I glanced at my Smartphone. The Tennis Actor had emailed me some nude shots, which was very sexy to see at eight in the morning. I deleted them and told him in an email not to ever post any online 'nude' photos to anybody now that he's on a TV show. In LA, gossip sells—it sells better than water or food or humanity. No public bathroom is safe in Hollywood, not with the camera phones in everyone's pocket.

Well, he always looked yummy naked, but it was over and the 'love' had only been casual. Casual, as in my heart never raced. On top of that I had never felt that he was the one 'true' one. I had spent time with him and all the other guys always knowing that it was all 'causal,' as in casual affection—as in temporary and fleeting.

Why had I done that? Why? Okay, so I knew I was starting to think too much, and I looked over my true-love-guy list and reminded myself that I have three years before thirty—that equals possibility, but only if I stay open and un-jaded—that meant a 50-50 chance at finding 'true' love. Who is he? Who is this future guy?

Paloma said we couldn't 'fork-it up'. She felt she had been going down the same street because she stayed close to her family because she kept the rent-controlled apartment, and because she didn't really move out of her 'comfort' zone. And now she wanted us both to get 'it' together and walk down the street of TL (true love) towards the 'true' guy, not the 'temporary' guy. Paloma has read every biography and autobiography of every major actress, established singer, or successful business woman—and she wants to be remembered as they will be.

She had decided that online-dating was the only way guys who would never see her otherwise, could see her. So when Paloma called, wanting her purple pumps, I had to race over to the West Side and meet her at the photo shoot. Okay, so most people just take a regular photo and uploaded it on Facebook or on a dating site and that's that, but not Paloma. She does photo shoots. She gets character shots, glamour shots, and now 'online' dating shots. When Paloma vows to do something, anything, to improve her life—she does it to the fullest.

The photographer Neal was a serious techno-geek with vibrant tattoos, ear piercing, and wearing Paris chic and Saks Fifth Avenue. He had turned his Upper West Side condo into a photo studio, and had his fashion photos framed on all the walls. It was furnished with a black sofa, white modern chairs, and a Plexiglas coffee table covered with a stack of expensive photo books by five world-renowned fashion photographers. Paloma's makeup artist friend Andre was already set up when I arrived. Paloma was wearing her sapphire satin bathrobe, looking like a true princess. Or an over-the-top-crazy woman. Paloma gave me a hug, grabbed her pumps and ordered me to watch her photo shoot all in one breath. I plunked down on the white shaggy rug and watched Paloma transform. Okay, so no feathers or leopard print layouts; just classic photos of her from the waist up—real and pretty. She only had wanted her purple pumps because they made her feel 'extra' confident. Go figure! The photo shoot was digital of course, so Neal, Andre and I got to review every single photo.

"Remember, this is for 'true' love, no hookups or friends with benefits bullshit," Paloma warned us.

I selected the seventh and fifteenth shots, because she looked so relaxed and genuine. We voted, and in the end she chose number fifteen. Sometimes it feels good to be right. Then she had Andre, who not only does hair and makeup, but computer stuff as well, set her up on the 'online' dating site. All of a sudden, Paloma's private password was selected, her personal profile was written, and her TL (true love) photo uploaded.

After that, Paloma treated us (her and me only) to a manicure/pedicure back on the Upper East Side. We laughed out loud. FYI, waxing the pubic hair is trendy in NYC, too. However Paloma's boycotting it and keeping her bush. She told me, "I don't want not to be untrue down there. And no guys ever complained neither!"

Anyway, I felt such an urge, such a desire, to stay in NYC and not to go to Cambridge, not to face my 'single' father and his broken heart or my dying Aunt Helen—but I see life like one big movie with a million scenes in it. I want my life to not be an XXX rated one, but a better rated one (like a decent R). So that meant I had to face my family.

I had only the next morning to do my final ritual; walking across the Williamsburg Bridge and hollering whatever came to my mind towards the East River, and the air. I got up super early, walked Shadow and then marched down to the bridge. There's nothing like walking in NYC.

The odd thing that happened to me was that the only word that came out of my mouth while I raced across the Williamsburg Bridge was—'RESCUE'. A peculiar word. I wasn't sure if it meant I needed to be 'rescued' or if I was going to be a 'rescuer'. Then I remembered what my dentist Dr. Underly told me, "You didn't fail. Now you just have to wait and see what happens. Don't be surprised if it's better than what you imagined." And I mumbled, "Let him be right, please let him be right," over and over on my way back to Palmoma's.

# 15

## ARRIVIAL

Films shot in Massachusetts are *The Friends of Eddie Coyle* and *The Verdict*, some of which was filmed in NYC. And wow, Paul Newman delivers a 'soulful acting' performance, top-rate. And *The Brink Job*, (my father made me watch it four times). *Jaws, The Paper Chase, Good Will Hunting, Monument Ave, Next Stop Wonderland, The Crucible, Mystic River,* and *The Departed,* just to name the VCR's in my yard sale box—like I said, it was a large box. Oh, and the make-you-cry film that I watch when I really want to sob is *Love Story,* filmed in Cambridge. In that movie, the character Jennifer Cavallier really knows how to love unconditionally and the character Oliver Barrett IV has to learn how to love on a more profound level and that was the problem that I thought about on my four-hour drive from New York City to Boston.

I went right away to the elder care facility on Mass Ave to see my Aunt Helen. She had moved in there, having decided to give up her own home. I waited at the front desk, while they announced that she had a 'guest'. There were fake flowers in vases and an oil painting of a summer-scenic-beach-scene, none of which helped get rid of the feeling that the place—was and is—the final stop before death. If I could play God's role, I'd put an age limit on aging. I'd top everyone off at a hundred. Ugh! Next life—I'll be back to coordinate the future.

"Ms. Helen will see you, in suite 21, located on the 2nd floor."

I wrote my name into the 'guest' book, which had only eleven signatures in the last two weeks.

"It's a real shame, but what can we do?" the fifty-something woman said, having read my disappointed expression. She had the picture-perfect face for being cast in a doctor drama TV series—for the scene where a patient is going into 'code blue'. She'd say something like, "Now hold on. You can make it. You've just got to pull through," and the camera would go in for a close-up on the dying person, as 'hope' slips away. Okay, back to reality.

"My dad said he thinks she's near the end, uh-hum, that's how he phrased it. Is that true?" I asked her.

She gave me one of those looks which makes you think you've accidentally said, "Motherf***er."

She cleared her throat and said in a lower voice, "She's doing fine. No one knows when they'll get the call; that's the Lord's business."

I nodded, because I couldn't top a line like that. I mean, life really can seem like a movie, or at least like a TV show—that never ends until the final blackout. So I turned and headed for the stairwell. The way I figured it, I would see less misery or loneliness on the stairs than on the elevator.

As I rounded the corner, a geeky, college-age guy, with blackheads and whiteheads across his face, stared at me like he hadn't seen a female in a really long time, if ever.

"Who are you here to see?" he asked, in a deep voice that just didn't fit his soaring, lanky frame. It was hard not to want to imitate him.

"My Aunt Helen, room number 21" I said, grabbing the railing.

"She's my friend. She sews a lot," he replied.

"Yup," I said as I climbed a step. Eek! He was following closely behind me.

"Oh, I just remembered she said you were coming. Your name's Valerie."

"No, it's Vivien," I said, wanting him to buzz off.

"Common enough name," he said, like I was supposed to agree.

"No, it's not, I was named after Vivien Leigh from the film *Gone with the Wind*," I corrected him.

"That's new information," he said.

"And yours?" I asked, hoping it was awful or boring.

"Gabriel," he said.

Cool name, so I couldn't say anything mean.

"Names say a lot about a person, before they're even a person. We shouldn't get named until we're at least five," he said.

"Yeah, I guess," I said, wanting him to go away. I felt like I was in a really bad made-for-TV movie and he was the annoying sidekick—the pimply, annoying kind.

"How come you have two last names?" he asked like he cared.

Ugh, he knew more about me than I wanted him to know.

"Some women don't believe in losing their identity by using only a man's last name for their child," I answered.

"Are you one of those feminist types, too?" he asked, as if we were at a speed dating meet-n-greet. I didn't bother to tell him about my penis envy and how I thought that canceled me out for the feminist label.

"I don't know yet," I lied. He knocked lightly at my aunt's door. She didn't answer.

"You've got a guest, all the way from the West," he said, as if he was a radio announcer.

Aunt Helen was in bed with a quilt over her. Her hair was all white and fell past her shoulders. She looked a million years older.

"Vivien, come here," she said as she stretched out thin, very veiny hands toward me. I hugged her bony body— what there was left to hug.

"You've got a choice; get sad or be okay with me," she whispered in my ear so that the pimple-faced geeky college kid couldn't hear. "Sit down, I have lots to tell you and I want to hear everything," she added.

I didn't look over at Gabriel as he slid a second chair over toward the bed, because I was trying to hide the fact that I was crying, which was really stupid and really impossible. I tried the 'something's in my eye' routine. FYI, when you have to stop yourself from crying, there are only three things I know to do: pinch yourself really hard, force yourself to cough until you really cough, or picture something totally gross. So, I pinched my thigh while trying to cough, and pictured Gabriel pulling his pants down and mooning the nursing staff. Triple gross. Aunt Helen normally would have caught onto this, but she was too weak to notice. Ugh, reality!

There used to be a nursing home smack dab in the middle of Melrose Avenue in the heart of Hollywood (it would be like having one across from Macy's in Manhattan or across from H&M on Newbury Street in Boston), and it used to make my skin crawl. I just don't like the idea of aging while everyone else walks back and forth, shopping, eating and enjoying their lives. Awful, but what do I know? Maybe when I'm eighty, I won't care.

"Gabriel, please hand me my bags," Aunt Helen said. She had turned me on to using canvas shopping bags, instead of those plastic white bags—supermarket bags, way before that was in fashion. Because of her, I bought biodegradable poop bags.

"On the dresser," she said, and Gabriel went over to it. There were two Trader Joe's canvas bags, and Gabriel carried them over. Both were full. "Thank you so much, my friend," she said, as her bird-like hands dumped the first bag on her quilt. There stood a stack of cloth patches that she had cut into at least two dozen odd letters, not yet formed into slogans.

Aunt Helen had grown up in Des Moines, Iowa, the eldest daughter of Slavic parents. She and my dad were the only ones left; like I said before, they had once been a family of five. They had grown up wearing handmade clothes (she had sewn most of them). The story goes that my dad had gotten a job on a farm a few miles from their home and had come home wearing Levi's and a button-down shirt, and from then on, never wore handmade clothes again. My Aunt Helen, being the eldest, had continued their mother's tradition of making quilts (everyone got a new quilt for the holidays). Cloth letters were applied across the quilts that said sweet things across them, but after college I had asked her if I could wear them as words on my jeans. I picked up a brownish-blue letter U. U for uterus, U for umbrella, and U for universe. Gabriel rushed over and plopped a pair of blue jeans, Levi's, of course, in front of me, because she had pointed to the folded up pair on the dresser.

"Hope you're still a size 6," she said.

"Of course, because there's no sugary, chemically processed crap in this body," I answered.

She winked. I spread the jeans face down across the bed, grabbed the single letters, and formed the words 'U MAKE U HAPPEN'. Gabriel, who was still hovering in the room, brought over a tiny pine box. Aunt Helen had gotten it from her mother as a child, it contained thread and needles.

"Your dad brings my food supply once a week," she said, "Gabriel, will you see if they could serve us some organic apple juice and protein bars?"

Excellent, a reason to get him to leave her room.

"Sure, don't worry, I know where your supply shelf is," he said as he left.

Aunt Helen was still running her own ship, healthy foods and beverages (she had shown me the way).

"So, is dad dating somebody? I mean, he doesn't want me to stay with him for longer than a few weeks," I asked.

"He's used to being alone. I don't think he knows how to change his situation," she said sadly.

My dad had collapsed (not physically) when my mother left him for the Panamanian would-be coffee bean grower. And then our dog died unexpectedly a week later. A heart attack. My mother had bought the half-Beagle mix in Prospect Park from some junkie for twenty bucks. He was only a year old. She and I named him, "Bridge", after the Brooklyn Bridge. After both losses my Dad just continued to work. I was, at the time, in the world of high school; I entered it as a 'misfit' and graduated as one as well. I couldn't think past my own needs, so I wasn't able to help my father. And now I was back from Hollywood, and already I could feel that he hadn't changed a thing—that he had stayed in that state of utter, sad abandonment.

"Vivien, I think your father needs a secret admirer. Even if it's a 'pretend' one," she said, as if she was scanning my worried mind.

"We'll have to 'trick' him. Like Rachel, the girl in grade school with the ketchup period. Only we won't let him find out that it's fake," I answered.

Rachel had actually wanted her period at eleven and had shown her mother a pair of bloody under pants. Her sister Lily fumed over all the special treatment Rachel got. I was invited to go with Rachel and her mother to witness the buying of her first box of maxi pads (extra thick). Pads? I never went that route because Paloma had said that when we got our periods, we had to use Tampax—that way we would be able to swim and wear white pants. I'll admit I was jealous of Rachel; I tried to get my period by hitting my crotch every night with my hair brush. Month number three of Rachel's period, her sister found a ketchup bottle behind the toilet. Rachel was grounded for lying (it was like a really bad after-school TV special).

"Yes, you must fool him. Please try," Aunt Helen said.

"I will," I replied, as I finished sewing the words cross the back thigh of my new Levis.

An elegant, short bobbed grey haired woman blurted out, "Have you seen Clarence?" Wow, she must have been near ninety and she had pale pink-colored lipstick on. She was perfect for a movie.

"He went to the store; he'll be back soon," Aunt Helen said, without glancing up. She was holding the Levi's as I sewed.

"This is my niece, Vivien."

The old broad slithered over and touched my face, with her long wrinkled fingers.

"Hello, sweetie, have you seen Clarence?" she asked me.

"My aunt said he went to the store," I said.

"Shall I sing for you?" she asked. I peeked at Aunt Helen, who nodded.

"Yes," I said, expecting show tunes, but she broke out in a very scratchy operatic voice. She was one of those people who didn't make it big in the field of her dreams. She sang the beginning of the 'Violetta Aria' which I only recognized because my Los Feliz neighbor L.J. used to blast it through his open windows every weekend. Of course, it was sung by the great Maria Callas.

"Where's Clarence?" she asked, again.

"He'll be back soon," Aunt Helen replied. And then I got it, Clarence wasn't coming back—he was dead. Why live in the 'truth' when the end was so near. She waltzed out of the open door. Clarence must have been a Mr. Darcy type man.

# 16

## TRICK

*Casablanca* will always be one of the top ten favorite movies of my overworked, academic forever 'single' father—my beautiful father, who was so wrongly dumped and abandoned by my mother in a matter of days when I was fifteen. Okay, so I like the movie, but I hate the ending. Why the hell does Rick, the lead character (played by Humphrey Bogart), have to end up without Ilsa, the lead woman played by actress Ingrid Bergman? Is my father destined to the same fate as Rick? Will he always just have the fifteen years of marriage with my mother, plus the two years they dated? Is that all my father gets? I can't accept that.

When I had swung by my father's two-bedroom Cambridge apartment to drop off Shadow, my suitcase and bags, before heading over to see my Aunt Helen, he was in the living room that had been converted into a library/office. He got up to pat me on my head, pet

Shadow, and ask, "How long are you staying?" And I answered, "Not long, don't worry. I won't move one of your beloved books!"

"How long is not long?" he asked.

Rude? Maybe, if it wasn't coming from my father. He's just like that.

"A few weeks, don't get scared. I'm not moving in with you; my tits are still perky, and if I have to post myself on eBay, I'm sure some desperate guy will buy me," I said, and marched out. I don't usually talk crudely to him, but I was outraged.

After spending time with my aunt, I went reluctantly back to his place. It was time to end his 'single' lifestyle once and for all. Trick or treat? It was time for the trick. He was out, and I stared at the piles of new books that he bought over the last several years. It had been eight months, since I had last seen him. When he came to Los Angeles to see me, it was at least amusing, because he theorized and pontificated (AKA) babbled about Hollywood and 'Hollywood'- type people, which made me laugh.

Shadow was stretched out on the two-tone grey sofa and my father had left a post-it on his laptop screen ('Gone to Trader Joe's'). What would we do without Trader Joe's, the West Coast food store that came East (smart move).

I immediately took Shadow to the Charles River, one of the best spots to walk and think. Tricking my dad about a 'love interest' and dealing with Aunt Helen dying meant I needed to make a fast plan for myself.

An hour later, when I returned, my father had prepared a gourmet veggie meal for us, even removed his books from the square birch kitchen table. Big step for him; my father likes to leave his books everywhere, and never move them. Weird! He's a cross between Sam Shepard and Clint Eastwood. So what woman wouldn't want him? It's just that he's completely bookish; he thinks books and talks about books.

He sat down after feeding Shadow and proceeded to tell me about writing two essays, one on Napoleon and the other on Caesar. I listened, because that's all I can do. Once he was done eating and talking, I asked, "How long has she got?"

He studied my question as if it was typed across my forehead.

"Not long," he replied. That's when I began to set a trap for him.

"A woman stopped me on my way into the building. She asked about you," I said.

He looked at me without any interest. God help him if he rejects a nice woman he encounters outside of his apartment. I mean, she'd feel like a piece of shit.

"Did you come onto some lady last week at one of your Harvard lectures?" I asked, like I was serious. He looked mildly confused.

"Did you?" I asked, as if the imaginary woman had actually stopped me.

"I don't think I did," he said, now slightly concerned, and he stood up.

"Well, you must have led her on," I said.

"I didn't," he said, defensively.

Ha, ha I got him. I watched him stride out of the kitchen and I smiled.

"Not going to be easy! But I will win," I told myself.

I had heard all the rumors about the late, great author J.D. Salinger, writer of my all-time favorite book, *Catcher in the Rye*. He had lived life as a recluse after the success of his book, even his marriage was short lived and I guess I felt that my father was in the scary process of following in his footsteps—minus the best selling book.

My father walks a mile-and-a-half every morning, and then sits slumped over his desk, reading; he ignores the phone whenever it rings. He lets his mail pile up and only sifts through it at the end of each month. He never has friends dropping by, never wants to go to a movie (he prefers rentals) and he abhors eating out. He has his routine and goes ballistic if it's broken. He wears the flannel button-down shirt or navy blue turtleneck, loose-fitting trousers, and suede walking shoes—every day. He showers every few days and manages to comb his hair, brush and floss his teeth daily, but other than that, he does nothing to 'switch up' his routine. Aside from saving for retirement, he donates to educating those in need. And the Harvard students adore him; they follow him around campus and bring him meals and wait for him to pontificate more academic stuff.

When my mother loved him, he was a 'giant' in my eyes. The odd part is that my father is tall in a professor-type way, and women ogle him constantly, but he looks through them; he even ignores them when he talks to them. I don't know why I should care, why it bothers me. If I was at all brave, I would sit his long, tall body down on the couch and say, "Dad, you need to get laid. You need to fall in love! Dad, I'm sick of you being lonely; it scares me for my own future," but I'm not brave. Besides, he's an adult— and he's got a brilliant mind. My father and I don't argue. We've had maybe six fights, in twenty-seven years, most of which took place during my 'semi-turbulent' high school years, go figure. We just exist with each other.

As days passed, my father didn't even ask about my Hollywood life or what I'm planning to do with my future. Instead, I could feel him counting down the eleven-day stay in his apartment. I didn't tell Aunt Helen how sad I was beginning to feel, not wanting to worry her. She was dying, after all, and she needed me to save her brother and to be the niece she had always invested in.

Paloma called in the middle of all this and told me to put my dad on an online dating site without telling him, and to screen the women and then set him up on blind dates. Now, that was a trick worth considering. But I wasn't ready yet. Not while living under his roof, and not while spending visiting hours with my aunt. "Paloma you're wicked," I told her and she just cackled and then told me how she was going on second dates with a white-collar Manhattan lawyer, a Williamsburg-based artist, and a Connecticut contractor, and that all three were really good guys. We made another 'true love' pledge over the phone;

"True love, nothing less than the best, no settling for less. Amen," and then we hung up.

The next day Aunt Helen told me that my mother had called her to say goodbye—I almost vomited. I mean, shit, okay, she's dying, but my mother calling to say "GB" just made it so extremely real and filled me with anger.

"Why did she leave my father? What did he do? Did he stop having sex with her? Did he ignore her? Did he become too overeducated for her?" I asked.

She looked at the ceiling and then at me; she spoke slowly as if she was cautiously selecting each letter, each syllable, and each sound.

"Your father did his best, and your mother did her best. Blame holds no importance," she said.

"But..." I tried to go on.

"You must promise me that you will stop blaming your father, and that you will see him for the heartbroken man that he has been and help free him, even if you have to pretend," she said.

"I don't want to blame him anymore," I replied.

"Don't waste your life with blame. Just do your best," she added and then she closed her eyes. Not to die (TG), but to sleep, or to pretend to sleep or to give me space to leave, because I was crying. Not out loud, not so anyone could tell, but I was crying inside myself. I had blamed my father. I had been blaming him since I was fifteen. Because frankly I couldn't deal with how easily she left me. Bam, she disappeared. She had Facebooked me and I had 'friend-ed' her, but I never responded to her private Facebook messages.

Outside of my aunt's care center, I burst into visible tears, and cried all the way down Mass Ave on my way back to my father's apartment. TG for sunglasses (I have nine pairs—it's an LA thing). When you cry with sunglasses on, no one really notices.

Okay, I'm a daydreamer, I'm an actress, I live in movie scenes, and suddenly the best director in my life, my Aunt Helen, was fading out. It killed me. It felt like an actual murder was happening. No one in the world ever called me on my 'stuff' like she did and soon she would be gone and all I'd have left would be my two best friends and my father. Suddenly that just seemed like nothing, nothing much at all.

# 17

## OPPORTUNITY

I needed a new place to stay. It was day eleven and my days crashing with my lonely, overeducated father were numbered, so I called Laurel. She was the first rich friend I met during high school, and her parents had just moved to Martha's Vineyard, leaving her their four-bedroom Cambridge house (a few blocks from Harvard Square). Her parents also own a condo in Palm Springs, and, of course, a treasured summer home on Martha's Vineyard. Money is freedom—when there's millions of it. Laurel looks like the 'all-American' girl, with blonde hair and blue eyes. She majored in business in college, but her minor has always been in men. Fact of the matter is that these days, she does less business and more men.

"I'm off to make love to a divorced, Italian banker, I met him on Facebook," she screamed into the cell phone, skipping hello and how are you.

"Laurel where are you? I need a place to stay while I'm in Boston," I hollered into my cell phone.

"I'm at Logan Airport, en route to Italy," she boasted, as if this was normal.

"Right now? Oh, bummer," I said, at a loss.

"Perfect timing, you can house sit for me for a few weeks." she said.

"Like totally yes," I said, acting like a California valley girl to cover up my depressed feelings.

It was pure relief. Laurel is one of those girls who doesn't wait for opportunities to happen to her; she makes them happen. Laurel quickly went onto tell me where she had hidden her spare house key. Incidentally Laurel won't talk about sex, but she'll talk non-stop about being 'in love'. Whereas Paloma and I have always gabbed loudly and obnoxiously about sex—even going so far as creating a list of sexual categories. #1, a GUNNER (100% sexual, but with an evil twist of violence—avoid and run fast. #2, an ACCESSORY (a guy who agrees to 'do you' on your terms and likes it). #3, a ZIPPO (as in I should have gone shopping, that was really 'dumb' sex). #4, NAPLOEY (short for Napoleon, as in not well-enough-endowed) or as in "Shit, I couldn't feel a thing." #5, a ONE-ER (as in one time only, don't ask for details). #6, a NEWEY (as in inexperienced, couldn't find my G-spot if it spit at him). #7, a ROMEO (an equal partner/a guy you could spend your whole life with, a Mr. Darcy-type through-and-through).

Okay, so maybe Paloma and I have had too much time on our hands. Okay, also maybe we're foolish actresses who believe 'Romeo' exists, one for each of us. Maybe?

It was Laurel who once asked, "What is life, if you're not in love? What is it?" At twenty-two I thought this was a totally 'dramatic' question, but now at twenty-seven, it suddenly seems so profound. I mean, what is life without it?

"Shadow, we have a new home," I shouted as I clicked off my cell phone. Dogs can temporally replace the feeling of being alone, as in 'single'. TG for that. The fact that Shadow was my dog was a precious thing in itself. Of course, you've got to not mind having your face licked by a warm tongue. And you've 'gotta' speak dog (the language), which thanks to LA, I can do. I had found half a dozen stray dogs in LA that my friends Mitch and Gary would foster 'til homes were found. They were a couple I met because Shadow liked to rumble with their boxer, Lips. They were both infected with the AIDS virus. At the time I first met them, they were trying all sorts of remedies including drinking their own urine. FYI, people who don't want to die will do anything to live longer. Luckily, they had already cheated death by nine and ten years, put together, nineteen. It was Gary who said, "Dogs make you go outside, and they make you meet people you wouldn't have ever met."

Fortunately thinking about him saying that—was what made me come up with a way to trick my dad. Not wasting a second, I put Shadow in Laurel's house and sped off in the red BMW (it was due for a drop off in Connecticut in a few days) over to an animal shelter. It was less than half an hour before closing, when I rushed in.

"I want to adopt a medium-sized dog with short hair, if possible. Shaggy if that's all you have," I said. The guy pointed to the back room, "Go pick one out," he said. He was a muscular type, the kind that looks as if he works out 24/7 and drinks protein shakes four times a day.

"What? I don't want to see all the dogs waiting to be adopted, knowing that not all of them will get adopted and some will die. I won't be able to sleep or eat, and this will cause a major depression that might last months, even years. I can't. I won't. You have to help me. That's what you're being paid for in the first place, to help people like me," I said in my most hysterical voice. Being an actress has its perks and I still had an actress living and kicking inside of me.

"We don't do that," he replied.

"Do you want to save a dog's life or not? I have cash," I said, not backing down.

He gave me the glare that guys give when they think you're a royal 'b-i-t-c-h' which didn't bug me.

"Wait here," he said, and got up and went into the back.

"Medium-sized, please," I yelled, which was stupid, but I couldn't take it back.

I waited and I waited. There were a row of chairs, all metal. The walls were tan, and the place looked as if was hosed down weekly. All the dogs were suddenly barking; he had left the door open, on purpose I think. So I stood there, plugging my ears as I thought about the late 80's movie *The*

*Accidental Tourist*. In the film, actress Geena Davis plays a really wacky dog walker/trainer and God, I swear I felt like I was suddenly playing her part. She ends up saving actor William Hurt's character. So my father was next. I mean, sometimes life can be like a movie—if you cast it right.

The animal guy came back in with a low-to-the-ground-type mix (looking like something the director Tim Burton would have cast in a weird film).

"It's a male," he said, like he was fixing me up on a date.

I put my right hand out and the mixed mutt licked it. I patted his back and he responded with a sit. So someone had once spent some time training him.

"Is he neutered? Can I take him now?" I asked.

In LA, all dogs have to be neutered first before they are adopted, and that means picking them up at the vet in a day or two.

"He's fixed. Fill out the papers and pay the fee," the animal guy said, like he was impatient to get to the gym already. Maybe I was being too harsh. I mean, the guy has to hear the dogs yelp for adoption during his whole shift. Suddenly I felt for him, and I didn't want him to think I was a real bitch. So after I had paid for the mixed dog mutt, I hugged the animal guy. I mean, I wrapped my arms around him, pulled him into me and hugged. He was shocked. Either it was unusual for a dog rescuer to do this, or he hadn't been hugged in a really long time. I didn't say a thing, I just walked out with the dog-mutt on a 99-cent leash I had in my Chanel bag. FYI, always carry a spare leash, in case you find a runaway dog.

The dog-mutt didn't tug on the leash. In fact, he strolled, and that just proves he still had his spirit. I had to set the scene like any first-rate movie director would; my father can sniff plagiarism. But my mother always said that he didn't change my diapers or blow my nose and ran away at the sight of vomit, so I knew he wouldn't get near enough to smell the fake ketchup blood.

I dashed over to CVS, leaving the happily adopted dog-mutt tied to a pole. I bought gauze, medical tape—and Heinz Ketchup. After all, I needed the blood to look as real as Rachel's period had. Then I got back into the red BMW and drove us quickly to my father's place. I got out, picked up the sixty-pound dog-mutt and with one hand, squirted his belly and brushed him so that some of the fake blood was on the left side of his face. No one on the street watched us; if they did, I was too busy to care.

I wasn't going to let my father near the dog-mutt until I had cleaned it off. Panic is what this 'drama' scene required, and I was game for it. I felt a rush that actors feel when they are about to step into the land of 'pretend' and make it real. I headed to his building, carrying the 'bloody' dog-mutt in my arms, and started breathing really fast as I banged on my father's door.

"Dad, open the door, hurry up," I yelled with fully 'pretend' panic rushing through my voice. My father swung his apartment door open.

"Some drunk just tried to shoot this dog and it was running down Mass Ave. It's hurt bad. Oh my GOD," I screamed.

He looked anxious and troubled. I was thrilled!

"You should take it to the vet right away," he said, with great concern. Ugh, he's so predictable. Wait a second, that's what every good scene needs.

"All right, I will. You wait here. I'll be back. I hope it doesn't DIE," I said, letting a super, emotional tremor go through my voice.

The dog-mutt whimpered, as if on cue. I mean, it was exactly what would have happened had this been a scene in a Disney movie.

"Damn it, I'll come with you," he said, and started to reach for his keys.

"No, no, no, wait here, I'll do it, I'll go. Just wait here," I said, as I backed away and bolted with the dog-mutt in my arms before my father could tag along. I got out of the building and raced around the corner. The ketchup blood covered the sixty-pound dog- mutt's paws and he was now licking it. I laughed, because we were technically off-camera. I love acting—it really works if you work it. Hey, I didn't steal that line from my AA actor friends; it's just true.

Two blocks away I set him down, and we ambled back over to Laurel's place. After all, I couldn't get back into the BMW with a ketchup covered dog. In Laurel's backyard there were party lanterns hung around the fence. I found the switch that turned them on and then heard Shadow barking, but I had work to do. He, my beloved dog, would have to wait. I cleaned off dog-mutt and put him onto the porch, where I bandaged his right hind leg. Shadow watched from the window, no longer barking, because he knew I was just helping another dog. I stalled around until just before nine then I walked dog-mutt back to my father's place. He opened the door after the first knock.

"He's going to live," I said breathlessly.

My father took dog-mutt from me and carried him into the living room.

"I can't keep him, I have Shadow already," I said in a very stern, but kind tone.

My father examined dog-mutt who whimpered a bit, this time, I think, from fatigue. What a smart dog. I mean, really, he whimpered.

"He needs water," I said.

My father rushed into the kitchen. I pinched my face to keep from screaming, "Holy shit, you're gullible." He returned with a salad bowl filled with water.

"He's skinny, the drunk was wicked to him…and blah, blah, blah, blah" I said, not really knowing when to stop myself. Once I get started acting, I never want to just say one 'line'; I want to monologue it all the way.

"He needs to rest," I informed my father. He hoisted the dog onto the sofa, and dog-mutt licked my father's long fingers. That sealed the deal.

Best dog names from the movies that I really like are as follows: Toto from the *Wizard of Oz*, Asta from my father's favorite (the *Thin Man* films), Benji, because that film was called *Benji*, and, of course, Bruiser from *Legally Blonde*, Nannok and Thorn from *The Lost Boys*, and, of course, Shithead from Steve Martin's film *The Jerk*.

# 18

# REST

Aunt Helen was up early and I plopped down in a chair beside her bed. I was on my way to Connecticut to drop off the LA girl's BMW. Her cheeks were flushed and her eyes seemed extra alert.

"So it worked. Dad has a dog. I still have to pretend to take it back to the vet in a day or two," I said, and I told her how the whole thing went down.

She clapped. We laughed at how gullible her brother really is, a fact that only she understood because she used to trick him all the time when he was a kid. Aunt Helen had raised her brothers and sisters when their mother became bedridden. No one ever said what my grandmother came down with, they just said she got sick, got in bed and stayed there, and one day she died. Everyone said she had been a very kind mother. Sometimes my aunt couldn't stop talking about her childhood, and how important it had been for her to make sure all her brothers and sisters were married and settled into good lives, because she had promised her mother.

Gabriel came in, carrying a tray of natural food from her stash. He stared at me and I stared at him. Gabriel's a typical college-looking guy, but he doesn't seem to do anything about his acne. If it was only blackheads, okay, but his whiteheads were oozing. That was double gross—and I had to stop myself from wanting to squeeze them. He's actually attractive in a geeky sort of way, but totally unaware. He sat down when no one asked him to, and acted like he was watching something interesting happening outside the window. I rolled my eyes at my Aunt Helen, hinting to her to get rid of him, but she just put her finger up to her lips to silence me.

So I pulled out my father's map of Connecticut—he has a huge collection of maps and he figured I could skip using the GPS for once. I got my driver's license in LA, so I wasn't a seasoned East Coast driver. While I was running my finger across the map and drawing neon arrows along the route, she said, "My mother came to visit last night." I looked over at her, a bit annoyed by the idea of my mother coming to see her and no one telling me ahead of time. So I started in on a long, mean monologue about my forgotten mother and her famous departure for 'true love,' and how I didn't even think about her (blah, blah).

"Your grandmother!"

I stopped. Suddenly her room felt strangely cold. Even Gabriel had turned his head to watch both of us, which I'll admit I didn't like.

"She sat down where you are. My mother asked how I was feeling, and I said, 'I'm tired, Mama' and she told me it was time to rest, and—" I interrupted her on purpose.

"Rest, as in take your time to feel better, because your niece just drove a million miles to be with you," I countered.

"I can't walk anymore, I have to be bathed," she explained, softly.

So I said. "A loofah scrub brush and Trader Joe's French lavender soap is all you need, and I can help."

"I'm ready to die and you'll need to take care of my affairs." The lump in my throat was turning into a gnarly knot.

"You mean sleep with men your age?" I asked. Okay, I'm lame at telling jokes, but I try anyway. I mean, one day I just might tell a funny one. Maybe!

"I think a nice man around your age, give or take a year or two, is best for you," she said, and meant it.

Aunt Helen had loved only one man, who sadly died of cancer when they were in their mid-twenties, and never found anyone to feel serious about after that during her eighty-plus years. No one even bothered to fix her up—not one of her siblings. Didn't they care about her? Didn't they think she'd want to marry?

Which reminded me of the time Laurel had arranged for me, her, and a girl named Kathy to screw the same guy, a few minutes after each other. The stud was Nick, a 5'9", 198-lb football jock who was rumored to be a 'G-spot' wrangler in bed, which meant he made you cum at the same time. I was nineteen then, and believed that love mattered. But Laurel persuaded me by saying, "If our friendship matters, you'll do it!"

"But you don't even like American boys." I said.

"This one I chose. Be my friend."

"But I don't even like jocks."

"Vivien, you don't know him. He's really nice, he's not dumb. Are you this judgmental?"

"I'm not judgmental. He's probably okay," I said. I was nineteen, remember.

"I'll go first; if he's awful, you and Kathy don't have to do it."

So Kathy and I waited in the living room. Laurel's parents were in Harvard Square at the time, dancing at a church that hosted a 'Dance Free' event every Wednesday night. They were rich hippies, which is the only way to be a hippie; at least, that's what Laurel told me. Kathy and I waited while Laurel was upstairs doing 'it' with Nick. All of sudden Kathy started to hyperventilate, which was so odd because she had been badgering me when I had tried to back out.

"Why are you always so scared, Vivien?" Kathy had asked and I didn't bother responding. Now she was bright red and her forehead was sweating.

"I think I'm having an asthma attack; I need to go home and get my inhaler," she said.

I was about to stop her, when we heard Laurel shouting from upstairs

"Vivien, YOUR TURN!"

I looked at Kathy who was putting on her windbreaker, when we both saw Laurel, dressed in her mother's bathrobe, staring down at us. We were by now both inches from the front door.

"Come on up!" she shouted like she was the announcer on a 'porn' game show.

Eek. So I had to climb up the stairs and head into her bedroom. I heard the front door slam shut and I knew Kathy had left, and probably wasn't coming back. I walked in and Laurel closed the door behind me.

I had to stand in Laurel's light blue bedroom and wait until Nick was done showering. Yup! I just stood there, listening to him talking out loud while he showered; he was talking about something stupid like how good he was at long distance running. Then he walked out with just a blue towel around his waist. He was super fit in that jock way— and I was too tense to say a word.

"You're not my type. You're one of those arty-farty girls," he said, as he combed his hair.

Phew, I felt relief, I didn't have to go to bed with him; I mean, I wasn't his type, right?

"That's me and I'm planning on becoming an actress," I said.

"I saw you in a play last year. You're right for it," he said. "Laurel's a crazy girl," he added.

"Yeah, ah, well, she's afraid of dying," I said, trying to sound profound.

"Is she ill?" he asked.

"No," I said.

He walked over to Laurel's bed, and tossed off the light blue top sheet he had used with her, and then threw her cloud-print comforter on the bed and hopped on it. I stood there, frozen. Then he patted the spot next to him, and for some stupid reason, I walked over to him.

"Take your shoes off," he said, and I did.

"Come over here," he said. And I got on Laurel's cloud-print comforter.

"Lay back," he said and I did, and he did, and we just lay like that.

"You're not a virgin, are you?" he asked, ever hopeful.

"No. I've slept with two guys already, one in a closet, don't ask, and the other on a bed," I said.

He brushed my hair off my face and sort of played with it for a bit.

"I'll make you feel good," he said, and then he started sucking on my neck. He was a hicky-type guy and it relaxed me, because I had always wanted a 'hicky'. I think they're so cool. Hickies, in my opinion, say, "I've had pleasure! What about you?" Okay, so I have an ego, a 'competitive' edge; I'm not enlightened. Oh well!

He took my clothes off, felt me up and down, spread my legs, and wrangled for my G spot, which he found (I mean there really is a spot that, when touched properly, releases everything; it's so fantastic).

"I'm DYING," Aunt Helen said loudly, snapping me back into the reality of the current situation.

"I don't want you to," I said, and she reached out and we held hands.

"Twenty-seven, three years before you turn thirty; this is a very important time in your life," she cautioned.

"Yeah, if I don't mess it up," I said, suddenly feeling extra sorry for myself.

"You'll hold out for love, and you'll go from being an 'I' to being a 'we'. And you'll like it very much," she proclaimed, like a fortune teller.

"You didn't become a 'we'," I said, not trying to hurt her feelings.

"My biggest mistake," she said, and that sentence hung in the room over us, like the start of a rainstorm that doesn't happen, but you can feel it wanting to pour down.

"Not true," I said, wanting her to agree.

"Very true," she replied.

And that's when Gabriel got up and stood in front of her door with his 6'1" back to us. He was like a human door.

"We'll talk it about it another time; you have to hit the road for Connecticut before it gets too late," she said. I got up and folded the road map. I asked with fear, "You'll be here?"

"I'll be here, but be back by tomorrow morning," she said. I agreed.

All at once I understand the expression 'to walk with lead in your feet'. It was so hard for me to walk out of her room. Gabriel followed me.

"Can I go with you?" he asked. I looked at him. "I'm fond of long drives," he added. Twenty and wearing grudge clothes that looked as if he slept in them, but he didn't; it was just his style.

"Sure," I said, because I didn't know how to say no, and maybe I would get to pop his zits for fun.

"Let me get my knapsack," he said.

"Look, we're not staying overnight. We'll hop on a train back to South Station," I said, not wanting to spend too much time with him.

"Yeah, I know," he said, as he entered a room four doors down. I waited in front of it. The truth was, I had glanced in during one of the days I was visiting and I had seen the woman in it. She was dying, like everyone else in the care center, otherwise known as a hospice. My father had said care center, because even he couldn't say hospice. Hospice!

The art of movie making is about creating illusions, and then selling them to the audience. I'll buy illusions over reality any day. *Terms of Endearment* is way up there on my 'dying' movie list. Not that I would have ever told Gabriel to watch it, but I knew when he walked into the room why he was hanging out in the place. There's a line that Shirley MacLaine's character, Aurora Greenway, says in the movie when her daughter's dying, *"Come close...come close...come closer."* And suddenly I understood it, and I wanted to share it with Gabriel so badly.

# 19

## GAMBLE

I drove as Gabriel took over the road map. I had left Shadow at Laurel's with a promise from my father to walk him twice and feed him, so I was free to just enjoy the mini trip. Unfortunately Gabriel made wise cracks about the fashion designer's red BMW—for its over-the-top wealthy look; he hated everything that was flashy or trendy.

"What would you buy if you had to get a car?" I asked, not really caring.

"A Volvo," he said, and went onto explain the reasons why he thought it was a well made automobile.

If any driver tailgated us or nearly cut us off, he'd yell, "You jerk!" I tried to explain that the word jerk was dated, and that it was best left to comedian Steve Martin to re-use, but he didn't listen. He had theories about everything, and he went on and on about eating organic food, the cost of shipping tomatoes, and the antibiotics fed to chickens and cattle.

When we stopped at our second gas station, I said, "Gabriel, I get it, you're a college kid, but just shut up for some of the ride." His face got red, his whiteheads looked terrible, and his eyes watered; I swear he was about to cry.

"I have to wash my face," he said, and off he went with his knapsack.

I stood there at the Rhode Island rest stop and felt like screaming, "So this is what failing feels like? This is what not being a working film actress feels like? This is what having almost no family feels like? This is what single feels like?" I would have continued, but the car behind me, honked. So I got back in and parked, and went through the convenience store to the bathrooms and then waited for Gabriel. He came out with a pinkish complexion. He had attacked his acne and shoved the Proactiv bottle back into his knapsack.

"You look better," I said, trying to sound supportive.

"I'm not used to being with girls," he said. "Girls that I don't know," he corrected himself.

"No worries," I said. It was a gamble, but I wanted to try and connect if we could; I mean we were both about to lose people we loved. I bought us bottled water, oranges, and trail mix.

"Can we go to Foxwoods?" he asked, as we crossed the Connecticut state line. He took out a Wikipedia computer printout about the largest gambling casino on the East Coast. He talked with accelerated speed about why he wanted to go there and try out the *Wheel of Fortune* slot machine. We were only a few miles away, so I said, "Okay, why not!"

I mean, I wasn't exactly in a hurry to drop the BMW off at the fashion designer's parent's house in New Haven; I also wasn't in a hurry for anything, because the clock was ticking for my aunt and I wanted to delay it. I know you'd think I'd be in a mad rush to return, but in the movies you get to re-watch the ending. In real life you don't. It just ends.

So off we went to Foxwoods, and that's when Gabriel informed me that he had dropped out of Harvard, like Bill Gates and Mark Zuckerberg. Only he wasn't dropping out to invent something, he was just saying a long goodbye to his mother.

"Academia isn't going to be my life," he said, like he had figured it all out. Meanwhile I tried to explain to him how great college is, not only for the education, but for the experience of learning with peers and professors. He started laughing. Yup, I sounded like my father. Gee, how did that happen? I mean, you plan on not being like your parent or parents, and then suddenly you say or do something they would do. Go figure.

"Do whatever you want," I said, as we pulled into the level one parking area of the Great Cedar at Foxwoods. A very shiny, gigantic MGM Grand building that stood out like the Empire State Building. The elevator by the outdoor parking lot was surrounded by handicap parking spaces, the most I've ever seen any where. Either the architect had handicapped family members, or just knew that if you add enough spaces, they will come.

I pulled out my camera and took a shot of us for my Facebook page that I had been neglecting. Gabriel didn't have a Facebook page, or a blog, and wasn't on social networks—just an email account.

"Do you have any friends?" I asked, after his long-winded rant about the invasion of privacy via the internet and how information is tracked and gathered and can be used for defacement scams or worse. He didn't elaborate on what 'worse' meant and I didn't ask.

Oh well. Foxwoods. Wow, what a mammoth place. When we got into the Great Cedar Casino, we were like kids at a candy store. FYI, there are two other casinos in the same building and the place looks like a massive indoor mall, with a movie theater and shopping and exotic food. It's amazing!

Gabriel wanted to be in the smoking section, because he had brought along a Cuban cigar and wanted to smoke it.

"You're a bit young to smoke a cigar," I said. Shit, a second comment that sounded like my father. Help me!

"I'm twenty-one as of this morning," he said. He then went on to tell me how marvelous it felt to be in the casino. I was going to sing him happy birthday, but I didn't want to sound like my father once again, so I just said, "H.B." And he said, "Thanks," and then pulled out four hundred dollars in twenties. His mother had sold her house and given him his inheritance, which he was keeping in a safety deposit box at a local bank; he didn't believe in checking accounts or ATMs. Go figure!

"Where are the *Wheel of Fortune* machines?" he asked a guy, who looked like he had just lost his shirt gambling, but seemed eager to show us the slot machines. He was in his seventies, with hair and eyebrows dyed brownish red, and wearing a suit jacket with slacks. He limped a bit, just enough to give him character. I would have cast him as a co-star in a gambling movie. Maybe an indie 'gambling-shake-down' film set at Foxwoods. Maybe filmmaking will be my next career.

The old guy told us which machines he had won on and lost on. Gabriel was grinning, and I realized it was the first time I had seen this college-dropout smile.

Still, the poker tables seemed more exciting, and I wished Gabriel knew how to play or at least wanted to try them. But he had read about a man winning on the *Wheel of Fortune* machines two months ago, and he had a theory it was time for another big win. We stood in front of the *Wheel of Fortune* machines and Gabriel said he needed time to study them. So I wandered off.

In the movie *Casino*, Sharon Stone's character is dressed sexy and I looked at myself, blue jeans with the word 'HOPEFUL' on them didn't cut it, nor did my black wrinkled blouse. Fortunately, I had my Chanel purse and so I went to the bathroom to re-vamp my makeup and hair. Not that I thought I would meet Mr. Darcy/AKA Romeo, but I would at least appear not so loser-ish. I applied cover-up, cheek powder, and eyebrow pencil, made my eyelashes extra thick, and put on brown lipstick, which made my lips look dramatic. Paloma had given me a travel pack of mini hair products, because she knows how to keep it styled even on weird or sad days. So I poured gel goop into my messy hair and made it seem like I was a rocker wanna-be, a better role than an actress-going-nowhere.

After I'd made myself presentable, I walked back to find a huge shock—Gabriel had won $10,000. It was surreal. They were checking his ID and giving him his money voucher and offering him a birthday drink on the house. He ordered a draft beer. I rushed over and took a dozen cell phone pictures as proof. I mean, who'd believe this? Birthday- dropout-wins-big; only in the movies, right?

"Buffet meal on me," he said, as if he'd suddenly become seven feet tall.

"Now you're talking," I said, still totally amazed about his win.

The buffet was out of this world. FYI, you can have grilled vegetables, exotic fruit, seafood, meat, gourmet pizza, Sushi, Chinese food, even Mexican food and beautiful desserts. Everything! We filled our plates and the waiter took our drink orders. We had just started to eat when Gabriel launched into a hefty explanation about artificial insemination. Yup!

He walked me through the process as if I had a penis. He told me about sperm banks, and how they offer pornographic material so that the donor can ejaculate after stimulating his mind. He kidded me about becoming a manager of a sperm bank. I would be in charge of buying the sex magazines.

"How would you buy them? In person, or just order them online?" he asked.

It's true I'm not shy with a guy, but I'm actually totally a private woman. I'd never be able to buy a Playgirl, let alone a vibrator in front of a cashier—I'd be too afraid my photo would be taken and uploaded onto Facebook, Twitter, Ning, Taxed, Orkut, or friendster. Okay, so I'm paranoid.

Gabriel laughed; he had bought a stack of vintage Playboy issues.

"That's because you're a guy, guys are supposed to buy that stuff. In fact it makes you look healthy."

"It's called third party reproduction, when a woman gets impregnated by a sperm donator," he said; he was on a roll. I nodded as I continued on my second plate; he was treating, so the least I could do was act like a good listener. He told me sperm banks were modern day baby supermarkets where a woman could select anything she wanted—from blue eyes to olive skin to even an 'Ivy'-educated sperm donor. He told me how the upscale sperm banks collect a voice sample of the guy and print out a fact sheet about his education, race, and religious background, even his choice of fashion, favorite color and zodiac sign. "Virgo," he said. And I just looked at him.

What could I say, I wasn't a Virgo. Okay, so I had dated a Virgo once, but without McKenna (the LA astro-queen/art model) around, I knew nothing about Virgos.

"It's the sixth astrological sign in the Zodiac. Symbol is the Virgin Maiden. It's an earth sign…blah, blah," he said. I zoned out. Gabriel noticed.

"You're a jerk; I'm telling you something important," he said.

"No, you're rattling off Wikipedia info as if I can't Google it," I countered.

That's when he explained that the reason he was talking about artificial insemination was because he was a 'sperm' donor baby. His so-called biological dad was just a printout and a voice-recorded message lasting only minutes.

"So, you've got nobody when your mother dies?" I asked and he nodded. Now I know why the character Charlie Brown, says "Good Grief." My favorite animated films are *Pinocchio, Bambi, Fantasia* and *Toy Story*.

We walked back through the casino so he could smoke his first cigar and collect his money. Let's just say, after coughing nonstop during his first several puffs and exhales, he put out the cigar, but kept it as a symbol.

Then I watched him collect his $10,000 in cash—it was first-rate. The funny part was when he stuffed it into his knapsack. For a second I thought I was on a reality TV show, because it was just so bizarre.

We stood staring down at the parking lot, now dark, and debated about driving to New Haven or staying in the casino's hotel room, but Gabriel said, "Let's drive, I'm a great driver, and you can always take a nap in back." Since it was his birthday I said, "Sounds good," and off we went.

We waved goodbye to Foxwoods and hopped back on the freeway.

We got to New Haven by eight-thirty and dropped of the fashion designer's red BMW at a modest home a mile-and-a-half away from Yale. Her father offered us the guest room, but we both wanted to head back to Boston, so he dropped us off at Union Station, where we bought one-way train tickets.

No sooner had we sat down on the train when Gabriel started talking about Herman Hesse's novel *Siddhartha*.

"Siddhartha realizes that time is an illusion. Do you believe time is an illusion?" He asked with complete earnestness.

I laughed; he really was odd in the coolest way, but I would never tell him that.

"Gabriel, I read that book a long time ago, try Freshman year in college and, all I can remember is the river, it seemed so vivid that I could actually picture it."

"Me, too," he said smiling.

"You're not alone," I said. It just flew out of me as if I was sensing some search, some unspoken worry emanating from his pimply face.

"I think people try to distance themselves too much," he said.

"I'm going to adopt you as the kid brother I never had. I'll draft up the papers and you can sign them," I said, half-joking. That's when he pulled out a super small Swiss Army knife, "Forget the paper work. Let's seal it—"

"Wait a second! I guess there's one thing you don't know about. Like, we can't mix our blood, not with HIV around. I've been tested already and maybe you have or you don't need to yet, still that old custom is over for good. So let's do a hand shake with a double hug," I said. And we did just that.

Wow, I was eager to have family, and anyone who thought as deeply as he did belonged in my family, or I belonged in his.

## 20

## *TASKS*

The next morning, I showed Aunt Helen my Facebook page on the Apple iPad with my new-brother pictures all over it, and she clapped. I had made her so happy, as if she had wanted this relationship to develop all along, but was afraid to imagine it. I wasn't sure if Gabriel would really act like my kid brother, or if he had just been caught up in 'winning' at Foxwoods, but it didn't matter. I mean, a brother for a day is better than not having one at all.

I helped her sit upright. Her two Trader Joe's canvas bags were on her bed, and she was anxious to show me things while she still had enough stamina. When a foreign film ends, the screen usually has 'fini' and sometimes I think that looks better.

"I haven't got long, that much I know," she said in a hoarse voice.

"I don't want you to leave, I've just gotten back and things are starting to click," I said.

"You can always keep me with you by thinking of me."

"Like Jill?" I asked.

"Yes, just like Jill and Finch," she said.

Jill had gone to the same high school I did, and I had gotten a two-week crush on a guy named Finch (his real name was typical and boring, so he took the nickname Finch from the purple bird well-known in Massachusetts). Okay, so I even tried walking behind him to high school, you know, trying to casually 'bump' into him. And my then-new high school friend Cheryl had cut out a picture of the Purple Finch for my locker, but all of a sudden Jill and he became high school sweethearts—they just fit together. So I was done with my crush. Then she and I ended up at Sarah Lawrence College, and she taught me body sculpting and the best way to stay physically fit. She even designed an exercise floor routine that I still do eight times a month.

SLC was made up of many anorexic/bulimic women and Jill hated that, so she taught a lot of them how eat well and work out (five days a week). She was pixie in size: small boned and slim. Jill had promised when I 'made it big in the movies' that she'd fly out and be my personal trainer from time-to-time. We used to laugh about that dream.

Jill once lent me her room for the weekend. And, well, I used her bed for the coolest sex I ever had! The super-amazing kind where my eyes rolled back into my head from sheer bliss. Wow! It all happened because Jill was by then not dating Finch, and had gone away to try to forget him. And I went to the local dance held in our college cafeteria with my redheaded friend Gemma, who wrote poetry.

Incidentally I was on crutches because of an aerobics accident; last time I ever did aerobics. Gemma made me go with her, so she didn't have to walk in alone. Well, anyway, one really chiseled-faced guy from Purchase College came over to me. "Want to dance?" he asked. "I'm on crutches," I answered. "So what," he said. And onto the dance floor he led me. Standing in the middle of the dance floor, me holding my crutches as he danced spastically all around. He had that Abercrombie & Fitch photo-shoot look—so he could get away with bad dancing. His name was Erickson, and his older brother was on a soap opera that filmed in Manhattan. He was planning on becoming a businessman like his father.

He helped me hobble back up to my college house, a non-dorm style living space that SLC offered. I led him into Jill's room. It was after midnight, and I felt excited to be in her room and with him. I sat on Jill's bed, which was covered in white sheets (ala Shabby Chic style) and seven white fluffy pillows.

"Let's take our clothes off," he said.

"Okay," I said.

I was wearing a black skirt and a jade colored blouse. He took off his jeans and shirt and his pinstriped CK boxers. He stood in front of me naked. Having never yet bought PLAYGIRL, he became my November, December, January, February, March, April, and all the rest of the months.

When he slid inside me—both our eyes popped. I mean, he really just 'fit in' and it felt so incredibly fantastic and profoundly amazing. I daydreamed for weeks that he was going to become my college boyfriend, but unfortunately, he ended up as only a ONER.

Life's not like the movies most of the time. Jill and Finch hooked backup after college ended, and they eloped, which everyone joyfully wanted—but what no one ever expected was that on their honeymoon they would be hit by a car and die instantly on the side of a quiet, serene Georgia country road. Gone a future doctor; gone a future veterinarian; gone their love. Gone her fun, kind and grudge-less friendship.

My Aunt Helen had closed her eyes and I was waiting for her to open them. A heavy set nurse came in with a bedpan; now, in Beverly Hills, she would have entered with a decorated hatbox with a bright ribbon (stylishly hiding the bedpan). I nudged her awake as the nurse took a position by the other side of the bed.

"I'll wait in the hallway, and then we can look over the stuff in the bags," I said, as I scooted out of her room.

The hall was off-white, (with a strip of frosted cream-tone paint, in the middle of the wall as if this was the finish to HEAVEN or HELL). Gabriel raced up the linoleum corridor to me.

"The doctor said I can take my mother for a day trip! We're heading down to the Cape," he said. I hugged him and then, as he turned towards his mother's room, he said, "So long, Sis," and I sighed. Family, I want it all.

The nurse bustled out in just the same way as she had bustled in. My aunt was still propped up, her white hair combed away from her face. I think white hair is cool.

"Would you put that coco butter cream on my hands and read to me?" she asked.

"At twenty-seven, I can multitask," I kidded her. After I had lathered her veiny hands. I stood in front of her small collection of beloved poets.

"In the mood for poetry?" I asked.

"Yes," she said.

I grabbed the heaviest book and plunked myself down in the chair that had once belonged in her living room, when she had a place of her own.

"At least you get to decorate your room as you like," I said.

"When you're tired and not feeling well, it really is a comfort," she said softly.

"If you need a good yell, I can wheel you outside," I said, realizing that I hadn't seen her stand up once.

During my first year of high school, she had taught me the 'Yelling Method'. Simply find a place outside, where there is a lot of traffic noise, and yell about anything you can't stand. When I was in high school, the 'yelling method' meant I yelled every single school day. Yelling works!

She also taught me how to be able to recognize people who release their anger, frustration and sorrow and people who don't. She named them Bottle-Neckers, people who hold every little frustrating moment in their body.

I once had sex with a Bottle-Necker. Most guys get pissed off and blow off steam, but I found one who didn't. He worked at a café on Beverly Boulevard in the heart of Hollywood. He was an actor, of course and whose girlfriend of two years had dumped him. For some stupid reason, I was single and lonely. He took me to a traditional, petite Italian restaurant down on La Brea, just before Olympic Boulevard, where he tried to talk positively during our meal, but he was really pissed off about the GF dumping him. A warning sign! I should have listened to it! But I was new to LA and really, extra lonely. Go figure! Why would anyone talk about any ex during a date? Why? Anyway, he took me back to his Hollywood apartment and straight into his bedroom. He had a great looking cock, which he covered in a purple condom (a bad color for condoms, but that's just my personal opinion). I think he was screwing his 'girlfriend' using my body. The screwing was 'bang, bang, bang,' style like a GUNNER, but without the violence.

Back to reality, I looked at my Aunt Helen.

"I have no more screams left. Please, read me a Daniel Kilt poem," she said.

So I ran my finger over the index of poets until I found his page, then I read, '*Dirt on Mouth*' "*Through the harsh blast of stoned wind*

*I fell across your path;Dirt on mouth, your gentle touch*

*Cupped hand to chinI lifted dirt on mouth to yours.*" Later, I watched her shift a stack of letters around in one of the TJ canvas bags. Love letters—wow, I thought, a huge stack of them—the hair stood up on both my arms, my lips quivered, and I felt an urge to giggle with excitement.

"You must return these when I'm gone, along with a letter I've written; it's important to me," she said.

"I will," I said, excitedly.

The thought of returning her love letters to some kindhearted, elderly gentleman humbled me.

# 21

## *ROOMATE*

I was carrying the two stuffed TJ canvas bags towards Laurel's house when I realized that I hadn't checked back with my dad about the dog-mutt. My father doesn't text, doesn't email, and avoids the phone at all cost; he prefers snail-mail, but I'm used to that. Good news is always welcome, and there it was: my father in his favorite wrinkle-resistant button-down shirt (his style is L.L. Bean meets L.L. Bean), brown chinos, and Rockport shoes, walking dog-mutt outside his building.

"Hi there," I said, hoping my father would realize that I needed a hug, but he didn't.

"I've named him Twist, because Twist reminds people of the continuation of man's need to own man. That slavery hasn't perished. That there are countries that still practice it; Oliver was an owned boy, he was a slave, he represents man's worst trait—"

"Twist is a cool name, Dad," I said interrupting him on purpose.

He had found a local pet store to buy healthy dog food.

"So, you're keeping the dog?" I asked, because it was funny to see my father so attached to anything that wasn't a book.

"Are those the letters?" he asked, ignoring the obvious. I told him how Aunt Helen had asked me to return her love letters.

"Love letters? Good luck finding him," my father said, as he and Twist trotted off in the opposite direction.

Suddenly I felt furious. He really didn't care about talking with me, and clearly was relieved that I had to return the love letters instead of him. At least some man had been writing her love letters. But why hadn't she told me about him? Why not?

I hurried back to Laurel's to drop off the bags, grab Shadow and to go for a long walk to get rid of my confusion and the sadness that was mounting inside of me. There he was in her driveway, cutting slabs of wood, with my dog Shadow sitting happily a few feet away.

"What's going on?" I asked, annoyed.

"Hello, I'm Tristan," he said, British accent full-on. He babbled about what a cool dog I had, and how Laurel had requested an addition to the porch to be added for her wedding.

"Wedding?" I asked, dumbfounded. I mean, she had just flown off; no way could she be getting married yet, not before me.

"Oh, luv, didn't you hear? She's getting married to a divorced Italian banker, his third marriage, her first. Should be a jolly one, this time round," he said. As far as I was concerned, there was nothing 'jolly' about it.

"How come you know before me?" I asked, like any third grader would.

"Check her Facebook page, silly," he said, as if he was a schoolmaster.

Damn it! I stormed into the open house, followed by Shadow and Tristan. What a dumb name, but I didn't bother telling him. He threw his blue jean shirt in the room opposite mine (I was staying in Laurel's bedroom).

"What are you doing?" I asked.

"I'm your new roommate, staying until the job's done, she returns and gets married in the back yard," he said.

"Great," I said and I didn't mean it.

A roommate? I felt like kicking him out—instead, I slammed Laurel's bedroom door and flopped on her bed, ignoring Shadow scratching at the door. I grabbed my Apple ipad and looked at my Facebook messages. Three dozen postings with color photos were from Laurel about her 'Italian-style' American wedding, to be held at her Cambridge house in two weeks. Two weeks?

That's when it really hit me. "What happened to my Hollywood dreams? What happened to my life? What the hell happened?" I glanced at the canvas bags of love letters I had dropped on the floor and cried. I couldn't help it. Everything seemed so messed up.

Sometimes I re-watch the movie *Bonnie and Clyde*; there's a scene at the end of the film where they're setup to be gunned down by the cops—and they look at each other. They know it's over, but they look into each other's eyes, and I think they're saying, "I love you, you love me." And then I imagine Jill and Finch on that open, wide, beautiful southern American road—but just before the car careened into them, I picture Jill and Finch looking at each other. They're not holding hands, but their eyes are locked, as if to say, "I love you, you love me." That's how I picture their final moment.

When I think too hard, I usually fall asleep, and that's just what happened, deep sleep. Okay, so I woke up not feeling really rested, and in an extra grumpy-mood. Everyone was on my shit list including Shadow who had seemed so happy with Tristan. I marched out of Laurel's bedroom into the smell of home cooking. Yup, Sir Englishman was standing at the stove in the gourmet kitchen that Laurel's parents had designed, with Shadow watching his every move.

"Still sour?" he asked. A comment which only made me extra mad.

I ignored him and walked to the fridge, removed a fancy bottle of water and marched out. Drat, I wanted to stop myself, but really, I was on autopilot 'bitch' mode. I went into Laurel's bathroom with the sunken, double-wide tub and poured lavender bath salts in it. I locked the door and called my father's machine. I knew he wouldn't pick it up, so I could leave a nasty message. It went as follows: "Dad, you and your brothers and sisters did nothing to help aunt get love, she never got to get married and you and everyone else GOT EVERYTHING. I hate you for failing her. I hate you," I said, and I hung up.

Then I called Paloma, because when I spin out of control, I always call my first best friend, and she always helps ground me.

"Oh, girl, I'm going on date number eight with the Argentinean filmmaker. He might be Romeo," she shouted into my cell phone. Wow, suddenly that made two best friends with new men and me with none. Double drat!

"Where's Argentina anyway?" I asked, feeling sorry for myself and totally dim.

Paloma laughed, "You loca today or what?" she asked, in that tone only she can use with me.

"I would hump the doorknob at Bellevue, if they'd let me in," I said, which meant I was extra, extra crazy. I told her about everything and she said, "Oh, me, oh my, oh no," over and over, which made me feel really listened to. Paloma can do no wrong.

"Shut your mouth for twenty-four hours. Say nothing mean or nasty, and put your love necklace back on, stupid," she said.

How did she know I had taken the 'love' necklace off? Then she told me that being unhappy helps nobody, and that my Aunt Helen needed sunshine, not a tropical emotional storm.

"Okay, message received," I said, and then I asked about the filmmaker. She told me that he made independent films, and that he was 5'8", with beautiful skin, a mohawk, and a beard (a full beard). That was a surprise, the full beard. Paloma laughed when she said what a good kisser he was and that she hadn't slept with him, because she had decided to hold off til 'true' love was in place. Wow, did my first best friend just grow up without me? Can I catch up to her? I hung up and slid into the hot bubble bath to purify my angry, black-and-blue mind. Also, to get rid of my pity; pity parties only last so long—and mine needed to end.

I found my new roommate on the living room couch, listening to David Gray singing *Lately*, Shadow beside him. I scurried into the kitchen, made some tea, and then sat down across from him. He looked over, winked, and then went back to reading the *New York Times*. Tristan is 5'9", lanky, with stubble on his chin, short dark brown hair, (think that English actors Jude Law and Alex Pettyfer had a son, I know that's not possible but just image their looks mixed into one). His style is happy-camper/carpenter. He's highbrow with a bit of lowbrow tossed in and seems to have that 'I'm content' attitude.

I felt like a wet mop next to him, but I had on my 'love' necklace, a black lace blouse, my black jeans with 'GOOD VIBES' sewn down the back leg, and my Steve Madden black leather pumps. My hair was wet, styled with a little Paul Mitchell. I was following Paloma's rule of saying nothing negative—which meant I couldn't say a thing. He got up and returned with a tray of hot food.

"Oh, God, do I deserve this?" I asked in my mind, but I said, "Thanks, I'm really hungry," and he nodded and went back to reading. Shadow watched me, but he was stuck on Tristan, and didn't move from his spot. Okay, so I'm not the best at following directions, because after complimenting him on his cooking, I asked, "Are you one of Laurel's ex's?" He laughed. Laurel's always had international men, whereas I've had American plus American times whatever. So it seemed natural, because Laurel always ends things nicely—she knows the art of romance and the art of ending romance. Go figure.

"She dated my cousin," he said, and then added, "I've never even kissed her." As if that mattered to me.

"Night," he said, and sauntered out with Shadow following behind him. Okay, I was not trying to come onto him, but suddenly I freaked out that he might have thought I was. I wasn't, I swear! So much for trying to straighten out my really 'bad' day for a better night and so much for having a loyal dog—thank God, there's always tomorrow.

# 22

## CRY

I woke up at 6:00 in the morning, feeling terribly lonely because of my strange set of dreams, so I crept out of Laurel's room and opened the guest bedroom door. Tristan was asleep, and Shadow was on the rug below him. "Shadow, come on, come with me," I begged, and my dear dog got up and ambled over. I hugged my half-Shepherd mix. His warm tongue licked my face, and I sighed.

"Anything wrong?" Tristan asked, with his eyes half closed.

"I had strange dreams, I don't feel so good," I said. That's when he moved his pillow back and patted his bed, and I walked over. Second guy to pat a bed in Laurel's house, but this time it wasn't sexual—it was just comfort, and I welcomed it. I told him my dreams.

"My first dream was in 3D, it played out just like a movie. There was a very handsome man swimming across a clear, sea-blue ocean. He had been visiting his woman, who had long wavy, light brown hair and (she looked like a younger version of my Aunt Helen). As he was swimming away, I thought sharks were after him, and I became scared. Then, just like in a movie I could see under the water. There were white horses with grey wings swimming behind him. When the horses' wings flapped, they looked like shark fins above the water. Two men hollered to him; they were floating in the same clear, sea-blue water, and they called out in British accents, "M' Lord, M' Lord," and then my dream ended."

"And your second dream?" he asked, now sitting up and leaning against the sham pillows.

"It was extra strange, but too weird to tell to a stranger," I said, trying to wiggle out of telling him.

"You woke me up, the least you can do is tell me about it," he said.

"Okay, I was in the Malibu home of a guy who looked liked like Shawn White, the Olympic athlete. He and I were about to go to bed together, but I told him we had to be in love, really 'in love'. I went into his bedroom and his friends wanted to watch us, they wanted to be with us. The dream ended."

And then I laughed, because Tristan stared at me like I was crazy and I felt ridiculous.

"I'm a big dreamer, that's my problem," I said. He messed up my hair, like you would do to a silly little brat.

"Good on you," he said, pretending to be Australian.

I walked out of the guest bedroom and away from my new roommate. Thanks Laurel, I felt like texting, but I didn't. I dressed, did my makeup and headed to see my Aunt Helen; she would solve my strange dreams. Well, not the second one, but the first. I was wearing my favorite pair of old blue jeans that she had sewn the words 'TRUE TO SELF' across the front of.

My father stood at the end of Laurel's block with Twist at his side. I had left Shadow with Tristan. Oh, no. I felt shaky; I had blasted my father on his answering machine, and now he was ready to confront me. I slowly walked toward him, because maybe an argument wasn't the worst thing in the world to have.

"Let's walk," he said, and we did, to the Charles River. That's when he told me how he had listened to my message, and it had prompted him to go have a talk with his sister.

"You did?" I asked, because my father never wants to talk about anything that isn't written in a book. Then he told me how he had arrived in the nick of time, because Aunt Helen had taken a turn for the worse, and he was with her when she breathed her last breath.

"But you never got to talk." I said, because it was easier than thinking about her death.

"She was fine with her life, she told me so. She wants you to take the letters back to the girl," he said.

"The girl? What girl?" I asked, totally confused.

"Your Aunt Helen had a teenage pen pal, and she wants the letters returned along with her goodbye letter. Leave it to her to try to help one more soul during her lifetime," he said, and gave a heartfelt chuckle. Not as in ha-ha, but one of those laughs as if you're smiling from the inside out.

"Pen pal?" I asked, "But, what about the love letters?"

"If she had those, which I'm sure my sister did, she destroyed them. She was very private," he said.

We continued to walk.

"A troubled teenager, not love letters, that's a bummer," I said, feeling really ticked off, sort of 'goosed' by my aunt.

"Now, watch it," he said.

And after that, we both went silent. My father doesn't yell and he never uses crude words, he loves the English language too much to muck it up with toilet vocabulary, as he calls it. I remember learning the F-word for the first time—along with the word 'shit'. Wow, it felt like being an adult, just to say them out loud when I was a kid.

"She wrote you a note," he tapped his breast pocket. "There's a letter for the girl in a brown envelope in the bag," he added.

I held out my hand and waited for him to give it to me. I wasn't mad at him, I wasn't mad at her, I just felt so confused by my family, what little there was of it. No one really communicated fully. Not that I knew how to change that. He handed me her handwritten note and I shoved it into my Chanel bag to read later.

"My sister Helen is with my mother in the old kitchen, cooking. My mother's got a quilt wrapped around herself; my father used to put her in a chair before going off to work in the coal mines. My other sisters and brothers are asleep, but I was watching from the stairs. Our mother was a kind, sickly woman," he said, as if he was back in Des Moines, Iowa.

"You've never really told me about Grandma," I said.

"My sister Helen could take leftovers and turn them into a new meal, I've never met anybody else who could do that," he said proudly.

I felt as if he wanted to break down, but he wouldn't let himself—he was the last of the five children born to Slavic immigrants in America, pride is pride, I guess.

He abruptly picked up speed with Twist and that was my signal, as if he was a director who wanted a scene change. So I dropped back and let him continue without me. He was going to walk the whole length of the Charles River—that much I knew. I headed back into Harvard Square because I wanted to be in a crowd, I wanted to be surrounded by people, even strangers.

Smack in the middle of it, I imagined being in Ridley Scott's movie *Aliens*, playing Sigourney Weaver's part of Ripley. Me with a machine gun in my hand—ready to blast death—the thing, the real thing, that no one can ever run away from. The movie scene faded from the front of my mind, as I walked through Harvard University, pretending I was attending it to get my PhD; pretending I was a brilliant, learned woman.

I kept blocking out the thought of my Aunt Helen's lifeless body, of my father being in the room to hear her last breath. It should have been me who was with her, I think. There were things I wanted to say, mostly just 'thank you." Ugh.

I walked up the steps to the library, and opened the heavy door, and slipped passed the guard, continuing to act like a real Harvard University woman, wandering through a long row of bookshelves. I love such movie scenes; there must be over a hundred movies with scenes filmed in libraries. It's homey, and it feels safe, like a church or temple, the world of books. I don't know when the tears started to fall, but they did. I made no sound. Just my eyes cried.

I found a desk facing a courtyard window and stared at a New England tree, lush with green leaves. I cried more, only this time over violence, war, diseases, crime, even white-collar crime, over bad TV shows, rotten movies and stupid money-grubbing remakes, over rich vs. the poor— over making it in Hollywood vs. not making it, over everything I could think of. Finally I decided that I should form a crying corporation that produces jars of tears to sell for $29.99 with free shipping. I imagined going on the QVC channel in a bright dress, perky hair and loads of glossy make-up, selling to everyone in the world, because so many people don't cry, or won't cry. I figured that after that, I might as well open up crying schools or academies where people could learn to cry. Night classes, day classes and, of course, online crying classes.

Then I thought about my early years of attending acting classes and how we had had to do scenes from all the classic plays of Shakespeare and Beckett, Chekhov, Miller, O'Neal, Ibsen, Pinter, Foote, Hellman, Wilson, Rabe, Wasserstein, McNally, Kushner, Shepard, Mamet, and a dozen other greats. The one that suddenly stood out in my mind was Thornton Wilder's *Our Town,* the classic play about death.

In it the whole town is dead and one-by-one they come back to tell their stories. And it hit me in my stomach, that my aunt was no longer a living, vibrant human being—now only a memory, a ghost in my mind. That in the future I would point to a photo of her and say, "That's my Aunt Helen, I wish you had met her," and that hurt, it hurt so bad I felt like screaming in the prestigious library—like a crazy lady.

One of the greatest 'crazy' films (in my opinion) is *Frances* starring Jessica Lange. It's based on the real actress Frances Farmer who made it in Hollywood. Jessica Lange not only got to be the lead actress in it, but she got to act alongside her real-life love Sam Shepard (back when they were still a couple). Now that's called making it big in both ways. Shepard's character, Harry York, says, *"Frances, you're crazy,"* and Lange's character, Frances Farmer, says, *"Don't tell anybody."* That just about killed me. I guess I'm a sucker for drama films—I like long monologues, and the way everyone lashes out at each other. And I like the cinematography. Frances Farmer was the subject of at least three books and films, but the one quote I always remember that the real Frances Farmer actually said, (not what a Hollywood screenwriter decided she should say), *"I have learned that to have a good friend is the purest of all God's gifts, for it is love that has no exchange of payment."* And, well, aside from my Aunt Helen being my aunt, she was my good friend, and I'll always feel that way.

I was done crying; my eyes were red-rimmed and I was ready to walk out of the library smarter—a lot smarter.

The morning was over, and I wished I had had a camera crew following me. Okay, so technically, I hate reality TV, but this was the one time I wished I had been filmed crying, because I don't think I'll ever cry that much again.

# 23

## *JEALOUSY*

Jealousy is healthy. It has to be, because I sometimes have it. Tristan was in Laurel's backyard, having just constructed half of an outdoor wedding canopy, a raised stage with four wooden poles. The door bell rang nonstop with deliveries of all the wedding stuff Laurel had ordered from various online sites. I was in charge of signing for everything and texting her what had arrived. Shadow was watching Tristan work when I stomped outside, annoyed that all the fuss was about her and not me.

"You'd think she could have waited until she returned," I said, wanting Tristan to agree.

"She wants it all set up when they arrive, and for the guests, too," he said, as if it was a smart decision on her part.

"Are we her minions?" I asked. He took the nail from between his lips and held it like a cigarette.

"I'm getting paid, luv. And, well, you're one of her best friends," he said.

"Tristan, feel free to not respond to everything I say," I said in a snotty way, and he nodded and went back to hammering.

And then the nightmare arrived—in strawberry colored six-inch heels and a tight white dress: Deeda, the 'decorator' from Long Island.

"I'm in charge of pulling off the most unforgettable American-Italian picnic-wedding ever," she said, as she walked around the backyard, not impressed, and deciding what needed fixing ASAP. Tristan sat down, awaiting instructions.

"Flat ass," I said to him in passing, and he chuckled.

Deeda turned around and winked at him, which is one way of handling being laughed at. She took a seat at the makeshift table Tristan created with plywood and spread her 'decorating' book out for us, showing us the look Laurel wanted. My mouth watered. Soft white silk draping side panels around the canopy, off-white chairs surrounding it, and imported ivy hanging everywhere, red roses intertwined. Even the picnic menu had been chosen with elegant food in mind.

The last time I wanted a party celebration hosted for me in my Los Feliz studio apartment happened a few days after I was held at gunpoint. I had attended a commitment ceremony between a B-rated actor and a very established producer, a cool event held in Hancock Park (an upscale neighborhood) at the producer's house. It was black velvet and red roses, with a heavy metal twist (the band). When I say black velvet, I mean the chairs were covered in it, as were all the tables, and even the napkins and the canopy that they stood under as they exchanged vows. It was gothic-meets-rock-meets-the smell of crushed roses. The place was swirling in roses and I loved it. The over-the-top style and design made it so fantastic. I was single at time, and went with three guys who happened to be gay and very close to the producer. I had seen the actor/groom on TV, but I didn't know him personally. I ate the best hors d'oeuvres and drank sangria like it was lemonade.

I am not like Paloma and Laurel at parties. They seem to meet everyone, whereas I usually select a few people and have discussions about films, pets or travel, my three party topics.

Okay, so this time, I flirted with one of the cater-waiters. He was an actor, of course (think a young Richard Burton). It was easy, because we hit it off. He served me the most mouth-watering appetizers and kept my sangria glass full. I wasn't driving because I had come in one of the other guy's cars.

"Want to make out?" he asked, several hours into the party.

It wasn't like we were going to start dating, it was more that, with all the love going on at the party, we were both desperate to have some 'pretend' stuff. I mean, I hadn't been kissed in months, so I was really open to the idea.

"Sure," I said.

We ended up in a jade-tile bathroom with a huge sunken tub (that easily could fit three people or four super slim people), and a black toilet and sink. Want to know real wealth? Go into the bathrooms of those who have made it in Hollywood and you'll want to strip and use it. Okay, so I have that urge.

This time, I just leaned against the cold, jade-tile and let the super-cute cater-waiter- actor kiss me. It was so first-rate, I felt like informing all the guests. Some guys kiss to get in your pants, and some kiss because it feels so good, and they just might want to build a connection. I couldn't judge his reason, because my mouth and lips were sangria intoxicated. When I told the three guys I had come with that I had been happily making out with a cater-waiter-actor, two were happy for me and ran off to copy.

"I'm jealous of you," Ron said. Incidentally he's 5'7", thin, with black hair cut short in front, longer in back (not a mullet), and a freckled face. I tried to pick out a few guys for him, but he didn't respond.

Meanwhile the cater-waiter-actor was back working the party and his boss was watching him, so we didn't speak again until he slipped me his card as I was leaving.

Okay, so I might have called him if I hadn't gotten held at gunpoint. The celebration ended and the other two other guys had 'hooked' up, so Ron and I walked to his dark blue Acura, which was parked a few houses up from the producer's place. It was midnight and a Sunday. As we got to the car, Ron, who I really didn't know that well, stopped me and said, "My life has no meaning. I don't have a purpose. I feel useless." He wasn't drunk, which was a bummer. If he had been, I would have tossed his bony ass into his Acura and driven him home.

"I feel like I have no purpose, like I'm just taking up space," he continued. He held his car keys in his hand, as we stood by the trunk, into which he had just put a bouquet of red roses that the host had given him.

Okay, so my mind started to freak out, as in, what if Ron commits suicide? What if I'm the last person he talks to before he kills himself? Those thoughts are what made me not rush to get into his car. I was trying to not appear drunk, superficial, or uncaring. So there I was, attempting to come up with some 'preventive' monologue, when a dark Honda (can't remember the color) carrying four young guys came our way. I saw them, but I didn't have time to study them. At a quick glance, they looked like 'possible' Hancock Park residents.

They were eighteen or nineteen max. Two got out in front of a house just down from us and the Honda drove off. Suddenly they came toward us, and I knew I had to run. I had no time to yell, I just ran, but one ran faster and tackled me onto the manicured lawn of a Tudor-house and put a gun to my temple. I stared at the grass, not wanting to see his face because I didn't want to give him a reason to shoot me. What if I recognized him later in a lineup? FYI, I had seen almost all of Dick Wolf's *Law & Order* episodes and I knew about lineups. He asked me which house we lived in. I wanted to laugh, because I wished I lived in one of the Hancock Park houses—a mini Beverly Hills. I wished

I had had that lifestyle, but all I had was my Screen Actors Guild membership card, a rescue dog, and a lease to a studio apartment in Los Feliz, with money enough to coast on.

"We don't live here, we were at a celebration. We're not rich," I said, keeping my eyes focused on the grass. I heard Ron moaning in the background.

Then my heart sank. My Hollywood dreams were about to be blown away; I was going to die as a 'nobody,' having gone nowhere. And then I swear I heard the voice. It came into my head—it was God, and he said, "You won't die, it's going be all right," and then it felt like my whole body sank into the grass, into the earth, and I wasn't scared anymore.

"Come on!!!!" the other young guy shouted. The Honda had come back around and the young guy jumped off me and dashed for it—and drove away. Ron was on the street a few feet from his car. He was sobbing—uncontrollably.

It had been so surreal, so out of a made-for TV movie that I actually looked around for the director, any director, as if expecting him/her to holler "CUT". I mean, sometimes life is like a movie scene. It is!

Then I shouted to all the neighbors on the block in my loudest New York voice, "Come out and show support, come out and show support," I said it over and over and over. In all the action films, there is always a crowd scene. And damn it, I wanted mine.

Five minutes later, the LA cops came and they wanted to know why Ron was crying, he hadn't been shot, and he hadn't been robbed.

"Good news, I don't think he'll kill himself," I told the seasoned cop after I tried to describe the guys and the car. Then I jumped into a cab that had cruised by and went home alone. I never saw Ron or his friends ever again. All I know is that I spent a few days wanting gifts, presents, bouquets of flowers from all over the world to arrive—I wanted to slip into a gorgeous designer dress, with matching high heels and Harry Winston jewelry (why not!), and attend a black-tie party in my honor. I wanted that!

One of my favorite French films is *The Red Balloon*. Okay, so I saw it as a child and technically it's a kid's film. The filmmaker made it with his son as the lead in it. The ending is the best, but I won't spoil it—maybe that's why I wanted presents to arrive for me.

"The last and final gesture of the ceremony will be the releasing of a dozen White Doves, followed by a candlelit dance," Deeda said, snapping me back to the plywood table and Laurel's future.

"White Doves," I said, having the sudden urge to suggest geese instead. FYI, Boston has a Canadian Geese population that wanders around. They have the right-of-way when crossing the street and it's fun to watch the worried, angry drivers sit in their cars, watching the line of geese slowly, very slowly, crossing the street.

# 24

# *LETTERS*

My father bit into a chocolate-glazed donut in Dunkin'
Donuts. "Maybe we'll see Aunt Helen from time to time in
our dreams," I said. He was looking at the tabletop as he
slurped his regular coffee and continued to munch on his
donut. Later, he looked up at me and nodded.

I needed to get out of Laurel's house, which was turning
into her lovely, enchanted garden, but I still had my own
stuff to do and things to work out. My father avoids all fast
food chains, but he was feeling lonesome because of his
sister's death, and jumped at the chance at sit with me in
Dunkin' Donuts. Shadow and Twist waited outside, their
leashes wrapped around a meter.

"The letters?" my father asked, like it was his duty to
follow up.

"Yeah, okay, I'll bring them to the teenage girl," I said,
reluctantly.

"We've got to meet with Helen's lawyer soon. She drafted a Will, and it's going to be read to us," my father informed me.

Wow, I was shocked. My aunt wasn't poor, but she wasn't rich, so what kind of inheritance did she leave us? As if reading my mind, he said, "Knowing her, she'll have tasks that we'll have to carry out," he said, and I laughed. Aunt Helen was always trying to orchestrate things—good things, of course, but in a way she was like a forceful movie director, using life as a film. Then I told him about Laurel's upcoming wedding, just so he wouldn't schedule the lawyer for the same day.

"When are you going to get married?" he asked.

"Married?" I said, annoyed as I shook my head like a mad dog. Didn't he notice that I was single, without an acting job or my own home?

"You're single, how do you think I got this way?" I added, in fully-mean spirited tone, I couldn't stop myself. Go figure.

He didn't hide the fact that my words stung. He slid three unopened letters across the Dunkin' Donuts table.

"These came from the pen pal, but as you know, I only open the mailbox once a month. They were forwarded from Helen's former address to mine," he said.

"It's a wonder you have a roof over your head, what with paying your bills late each month," I snapped. He stood up and glared at me.

"I always overpay the amount due, if you must know, daughter," he said as he left.

I watched him unleash Twist from the pole— and I know I should have raced out and apologized, but it would have been a forced gesture and I needed time to cool off.

After that I took Shadow on a walk through the Mount Auburn Cemetery. It's such a wonderful place to stroll through. Sure, there are graves with old headstones and fancy monuments, but it's peaceful. I knew my aunt hadn't bought a plot, because she didn't believe in being buried. I figured she'd want her ashes scattered in the Charles River or shipped back to Iowa; she still had a friend her age who lived in her hometown.

I looked around, hoping for some sign—something to make me feel not so angry and not so scared. Having only three years until I turn thirty made me feel anxious and apprehensive. Would I ever get married? Where would I live? Would I still be an actress? Then I saw it, the Purple Finch. They look like sparrows, only with a light purplish color. This one was eyeing a female Finch. I swear they were flirting. And suddenly I felt as if Jill and Finch's spirits were hovering over me. So I stood there holding Shadow's leash, watching them.

LOVE was the message that I got from the birds. I had been turning love away and acting like a bruised apple-doll instead of a woman. Okay, so I made a vow right there and then to just act with love, to think love, to be love.

When I got back to Laurel's house, Tristan had finished the canopy and was painting it white. He had bought the wood to build an outdoor bar that Laurel had not only wanted for the wedding, but to keep as well. I stared at the wood like it was something important because Tristan was so proud of it, and I kept my vow to act 'loving' at all cost.

"Does your family do woodworking?" I asked, softly. Tristan laughed.

I couldn't have asked a more stupid question. His father was a prominent financial investor, along with his other two brothers, and he was from a very well-to-do London family. He had traded money for wood, and it made him happy.

"Does your father approve?" I asked, deciding that I had to keep trying.

"If my brothers weren't both finance investors, he'd have an issue, but two out of three sons, not a bad return on his paternal investment. It all comes down to ROI'S," he said, with louder laugh.

I watched him: he seemed filled with happiness, much more than I'd experienced.

'Change yourself,' I said inside my head, a chant I repeated ten times. He glanced at me and then went back to the white paint. I was about to head inside when he said, "Hey, your new brother's here, he's taking a nap on the couch. Looks as if he hasn't slept in days, so I told him to get some shuteye. Don't wake him up."

"Is that an order?" I asked. He turned and double winked at me.

"I'm sorry to hear about your Aunt Helen, if you want to talk about it, give a shout," Tristan said.

Wow, he meant it. Cool, a brother and a British roommate, I wasn't really all alone after all. And there was my father, who I knew I owed a gigantic apology to. Still, I decided to put that off for a day, because my father has a thing about timing—he trusts things that aren't rushed. Also, I wasn't sure how to apologize. Should I just say sorry in person? Or write a note and slip it under his door?

Shadow was camped out near Tristan and I went around front to take packages inside because there were packages that needed to be taken inside. My cell phone rang. It was Paloma, so I sat on the front steps and listened to her talk.

"I'm going to Argentina to shoot a film with him. I'm playing a gun-toting-rebel- whore," she blurted out, laughing.

"I'm not jealous, I'm excited for you!" I said, because I was. Paloma's my first best friend and my NYC friend. Laurel's my second best friend and my New England friend.

"Do you think he's the one? Is he Romeo?" I asked.

"I hope so, I'm ready to be a sexy wife," she said.

Then she told me about the white lace underwear she had bought, because she was going to do 'it' with him for the first time in Argentina. It was the longest she'd ever dated a guy without having sex, and she told me that so far, it was the best challenge she'd given herself.

"But what if he's not good?" I asked.

"Then I'll teach him. Still I'll be glad I held out because we've had so much passion, kissing, hugging, and cuddling. I'm hooked," she said.

Paloma really is one of the coolest women I know.

"Diego has a serious girlfriend," she told me. He had skipped dating and just jumped into it.

"Wow, everything is happening so fast," I said, in amazement.

"She's got the same thing, too," Paloma said. She won't say the words herpes or cancer—anything 'medically' serious; she always calls it the 'thing'.

I clicked off my cell feeling happier. I mean, she was really carrying out the vow to fall in 'true' love, and hopefully forever.

Then I unlocked Laurel's front door and carried in the four large boxes. They were from Pier 1, and Tristan had signed for them. I texted Laurel about the boxes and left them in the hallway before going into the living room to peek at Gabriel who was fast asleep on the couch. He looked extra-skinny, but his acne was almost gone. His black knapsack was on the floor, a jacket next to it.

So I sat in the kitchen, waiting for the tea kettle to boil. I was going to drink tea and just be quiet. I still couldn't believe that I had spotted the Purple Finch. There aren't many birds I recognize, aside from pigeons. Okay, Bluebirds, Red Robins and Red Cardinals, but nothing past that. It was a sign—a sign I so needed. I had lived my life looking for signs mostly in movies—I pinched myself on my cheeks, something I do every now and again just to remind myself that I am alive, really alive. The kettle whistled and I sprang up to get it.

Then Gabriel walked in. He had circles under his eyes, his hair was messy, and he seemed sad. "Hi, bro," I said, as I poured myself a cup of tea. He slid a mug near mine and I filled his. We sat at Laurel's square red table. Neither of us spoke, as we sipped our tea. The silence made us notice the sounds in the kitchen, like the grandfather clock her father had put in the far corner, the drip of the sixty year old sink, and the hum of the fridge. It was an old, comfy room, wallpapered in an English horse and buggy design, one of Laurel's mother's ideas. I liked it.

"She's slipping away," Gabriel said, not daring to look at me. I could hear it in his voice; he wanted to cry, but he wouldn't, or he couldn't.

"Can you let her go in peace?" I asked. It just came out of my mouth.

He looked at the grooves in the table and then I did, too.

"Yeah, yeah, I can," he said a few minutes later. I finished my tea because I was trying not to talk.

"Do you like puzzles? Want to complete one with me?" he asked.

"You bet, bro," I said.

Then I followed him back into the living room. He pulled a puzzle box out of his knapsack. I looked at the picture on the cover, a vintage Ford Model-T. I couldn't believe it, because my grandfather (on my mother's side) had learned to drive in one, and later he had saved up and bought one. It was a classic. I had always bought vintage cars in LA; they never lasted more than a year, but who could turn down a 1960 Chevy Bel Air (pale baby blue), or a 1975 Mercedes 450 SLC (chocolate brown), or the last one, 1974 240 DL Volvo Station Wagon (hunter green).

"I love classic cars. They are the beauty of Los Angeles. In that climate you can drive them everywhere," I told Gabriel as he opened the puzzle box and dumped it out on the rug—a 1000 puzzle pieces.

As we started in on it, I thought of that great scene in the classic movie *Citizen Kane*, where the wife is working on a puzzle in the huge, stark, mansion living room, and she's bored to death.

"You've seen the movie *Citizen Kane*, right?" I asked, expecting a yes, followed by the classic 'rosebud' mention.

"No," Gabriel said. Oh, no, my new brother had uttered his first movie 'sin'.

Not seeing *Citizen Kane* is like not knowing about Elvis, or that Key Largo is in Florida, or that Warner Brothers is in Burbank. It's like not knowing that Marilyn Monroe was sexy; like not knowing how to add one plus one, or how to use a YoYo or build a tower out of playing cards, etcetera, and etcetera.

"You're seeing it tonight," I told him, like any sister would.

"I'm game," he said, and then went back to working on the puzzle.

I keep five DVDs with me at all times. They currently live in my suitcase. The famed 'gossip' about *Citizen Kane* is that it was based on William Randolph Hearst, the newspaper tycoon, and that 'someone' found out that 'Rosebud' was his pet name for his girlfriend's clitoris. Who knows if it is really true, but I like to think that is. FYI, if you haven't seen it yet, the word 'rosebud' is not used the same way in the movie.

"You do know who Orson Welles is, right?" I asked, hoping I wasn't going to have to fully educate my new brother.

"He's the actor/director/writer guy that got fat like Marlon Brando before he died, right?" he asked.

Okay, not really the way I like the great Orson Welles to be remembered.

"Shut up," I said.

Gabriel snickered, like any punk brother would. "Yeah, well you should see *Searching for Sugar Man*; it's about a humble musician named Rodriguez, best ever. But it's a documentary, if you're open to those."

"I'm open, maybe I will," I said. Suddenly having a sibling you can joke with, even argue with—well, it's beyond amazing. Go figure!

Finally, Tristan came in with Shadow trailing behind him and plunked down next to Gabriel. Six eyes on a 1000 puzzle pieces are totally necessary. An hour later I had to stop myself from shouting, "Wow, can my life please stay like this," because I felt happy just being there with the three of us, plus Shadow. As if I had a new family—one that I wanted.

# 25

## *WORDS*

Gabriel stayed up watching *Citizen Kane* in the living room, while I sat on Laurel's bed, still wide awake from having finished the 1000 piece puzzle with the guys, a task which lasted well into the early hours. I dumped Aunt Helen's heaviest Trader Joe's bag out on Laurel's canopy bed. Her bedroom had been re-done in the style of an African safari, which her parents had taken her on when she turned twenty. They had exposed Laurel to a terrific life of travel and adventure; no wonder she wanted to marry an international man.

Okay, so I haven't been to Europe yet, and I know, at twenty-seven, it's a total embarrassment. Paloma had been to Puerto Rico three times as a teenager and now she was going to Argentina. How do I find 'true' love, get engaged, get married, and travel the world by the time I'm thirty? How?

I looked at the pile of pen pal letters. I counted them. There were nine. Then I looked at a clump of words sewn as patches that my aunt had made for me. I couldn't believe it. Now I knew why the bag was so heavy. I read them out loud to myself: 'DREAMS UNLIMITED' and 'BALANCED' and 'ACT AS IF'. The fabric letters were all cut from various colorful clothes, and she had pinned them across heavy denim strips. The letters really stood out. All I had to do now was to sew them across my pants and a few jackets.

Okay, so Laurel's got really expensive good taste. She buys everything from fashion shows and sample sales and everything is current. Paloma is a mix of 14th Street-meets-Macy's. She buys knockoffs and no one would ever guess it. Paloma and Laurel met once, but I've kept them as separate friends and they both like it that way.

I dumped out the second TJ bag, and out came a stack of brightly colored envelopes that had my initials on them. They were filled with magazine cuttings about furniture, gardening, and other 'homey' stuff. Leave it to my aunt to save magazine clippings for me. At the bottom of the bag was a brand new jean jacket with the words 'I AM MYSELF' sewn across the back of it, and inside it was *To Cassidy from your pen pal Helen.*

I rummaged through my Chanel bag and found the letter she had written that my father had given me. My hands were shaking. She wrote the following: *Dearest Vivien, Please go see Cassidy; she's only sixteen and she's a bright girl, and I want you to give her my goodbye letter and the blue jean jacket. I hope it fits her. Please give her her letters back, I wouldn't want her to think that they were tossed out in the trash, as I very much enjoyed reading every single letter. What a pleasure it was for me to open my mailbox and find a pen pal letter waiting for me. I hope letter writing will last forever, even with the next generation and the next. Oh, dear me, I do hope so. Please give her my best and make sure she's good and safe. Love your Aunt Helen.* I folded it back up. My aunt had been so selfless. I suppose it was disrespectful, but I decided to read all the letters Cassidy had written. I only did it because something in my mind kept nudging me to read them, all of them. Okay, maybe being delirious from a lack of sleep made me decided that or maybe it was just my curiosity to hear the voice of a sixteen-year-old.

I picked up the stack of letters, written with red ink, in all capitals, all in order. The first letter was about being sixteen, living in Chelsea and going to high school there, wanting to become a dental hygienist and really wanting to have a cat, but her stepfather said no. She had two stepsisters, both were in middle school. Her mother didn't work. This was more of an introduction letter, and she had drawn a picture of herself on the back, which showed a teenage girl, kind of chunky, in pants, a sweatshirt, with shoulder length hair hanging over her face. It didn't seem as if she was trying to draw herself as all that happy.

I was almost ready to read number two, but I fell asleep.

Oh, what a dream I had—the late TV creator, Aaron Spelling, (*90210*, *Melrose Place*, and *Dallas*, just to name-drop a few of his mega television hit shows) was still alive and was in a Hollywood hotel room, and I was meeting with him about creative ideas. All of a sudden, he pulled opened a bottom drawer of a dresser.

I asked him, "What if a world opened up that you could enter, whenever you pulled the drawer open?"

And Aaron Spelling said, "Where love lived in full motion."

Then the dream ended and I woke up to see Tristan walking into Laurel's bedroom and looking down at me.

"Hey, can you help me out?"

I sat up and blurted out my dream.

"Yeah, well, I'm not building drawers, but I am building an outdoor bar and I need a steady hand to hold some wood while I cut it," he said.

So I got up, raced into the shower, and then headed down stairs and out into the yard to hold the wood very still while he cut it correctly. The bar was to be curved and seat at least six. Nothing was going to be left to chance for Laurel, with the help of Deeda, who had thought of everything.

"This is going to be amazing!" I said.

"No worries, I won't tell her you're jealous"

"Listen, smart ass. Okay, so I was jealous, but I'm not now. I'm really excited for Laurel," I said, as he went back to trimming the wood without my help.

Gabriel was up and heading back to see his mother. He had been staying at the Harvard Inn in a small single room that had been rented for him in the hopes I guess, that he wouldn't drop out, and in support of his inevitable loss.

"Stop back anytime, any hour," I said.

And Tristan echoed, "That's an order, mate," and Gabriel sauntered off with his black knapsack over his shoulder.

I headed into the house, racing upstairs to the stack of pen pal letters because I wanted to get through most of them in one sitting. Shadow stared up at me and I said, "You don't need a walk, you're incredibly spoiled by the British roommate and me, but you can have a dog treat." I gave him a rawhide to chew on and he wandered off happily. Wow, what an easy dog.

Letter number two was Cassidy thanking my aunt for writing to her and saying how much it meant, and that if she told her any secrets, would my aunt promise never to tell. It was such typically teenage stuff that it amused me. Pen pal letters number three and four were all about having to baby-sit her stepsisters, because her mother was going places with her new husband, how she was staying up late to finish her homework, and how she wanted to visit my aunt, how she'd never been to Cambridge (only to Somerville once to that Target because her mother wanted something that the Everett one had run out of). How she couldn't wait for my aunt to write again; that even though she had Facebook, Tumblr and email, she liked letter writing better.

Letters five and six talked about her future and moving away, and how she was trying to get good grades so she could get into a good dental school. She thanked my Aunt Helen for advice on homework and goals and asked when she could visit her in Cambridge, and how she had one good friend, but she had gossiped about her and now they weren't friends.

I was about to open pen pal letter number seven when Tristan walked in and sat down next to the pile.

"These love letters?" he asked.

I laughed, and explained to him how I had thought they were, but that my aunt had befriended a teenage girl in Chelsea as a pen pal. And I opened letter number one again and held up the red ink drawing for him.

"This is her self-portrait," I said. Tristan took it from me and looked it over.

"I had a pen pal, once," he said proudly.

"You did, when and why?" I asked.

"It's rather nice. I was in my first year of high school, and she lived in San Francisco and was nice-looking."

"That's called trying to get an American girlfriend," I informed him.

"She was nice," he said, with a smirk.

"You slept with her, right?" I asked, already knowing the answer.

"I got to come over to the U.S. for the first time at fifteen-and-a-half, and I stayed with her family for a month," he said, and then he winked, which meant that he had done it with his American pen pal.

*SOS* the text read; it was from Paloma. I hit redial. "My best friend's in trouble," I said, as I sprang away from the canopy bed.

"Meirda, el esta casado, el me mintio. Shit, he's married, he lied to me," Paloma started screaming into my cell phone.

When she's really upset and really angry she always talks really fast, while translating Spanish to English or English to Spanish.

"Va a tener un divorcio, he's getting a divorce, but she's in no hurry, she's an actress in the film. Meirda, shit, meirda, shit, shit." Paloma was hysterical.

So I told her that international men are different, because that was what Laurel had told me (only I left out how I knew that) and that if he had said he hadn't gotten divorced yet, she would never have agreed to date him, let alone be an actress in his independent film. And I told her that at the end of the day, it was about being actresses—that was the key to our identities. Paloma and I had both wanted to be known on the silver screen or the TV screen, to leave our mark, like Rita Moreno, her hero, and like Faye Dunaway, my hero. And that we could never forget that.

"Think of Rita Moreno, you're going to be a success like her," I said.

Then she reminded me how once when Rita Moreno was young she dated Marlon Brando, the once public rumor was that she had had a breakdown over the ending of it, but she did overcome it—and she did go on to find another man—a healthier one.

"Did you sleep with him?" I asked, suddenly worried.

"Mine is mine, he never got any," Paloma cackled, because the day she was planning on letting him in between her legs, his wife came over and introduced herself. And we both laughed; it was like the timing couldn't have been any better.

"Tell her thanks," I kidded. I mean, the worst is to give your body willingly to a guy you think is single, only to find out he's not. Then you have to feel not only cheap, but also dumb.

I couldn't tell her about what happened to Laurel when she was twenty-five, because it was Laurel's story and I kept the friendships separate, like I said before. Laurel had gone to France to take a summer cooking class, okay, really to meet French men, and to fall in love while learning to cook French cuisine. She had dated an Israeli journalist who was working for a French Newspaper for the summer and anyway, they dated, they spent 24/7 together, and she went to bed with him.

"Israeli men make love like they might die tomorrow or in an hour; their soldier training makes them extremely passionate." That's what Laurel had said, quote un-quote. Anyway, a short-haired, well-toned Israeli woman came to the apartment one day and he introduced Laurel to his wife, and she never heard from him again. I can't even begin to go on about how many pounds Laurel lost. It took her six months of therapy, until she was ready to meet a new international man.

Thirty-five minutes later Paloma said, "Soy un actriz. I'm an actress, Thank God, gracias!"

"You bet. FYI, you could end up meeting Romeo at the Sundance Film Festival if the film gets in, so the best is yet to come," I said. And that got her daydreaming again, and we hung up. I walked to Laurel's bed to find Tristan's face twisted as if he was in pain.

"She's in trouble," he said, with concern.

"No, she's okay. She's going to focus on the film and being an actress," I answered.

"I'm talking about the pen pal," he said with uneasiness.

I looked over his shoulder at the letters. He had turned them all over, revealing the ink drawings Cassidy had done on the back of each letter, her self-portrait in the middle. There was a drawing of two girls with halos floating above their head (stepsisters), with their feet above the ground, followed by one of a woman who looked out of shape, wearing a super-huge dress (her mother). The next three were of a man who looked like Freddy Krueger's twin (*Nightmare on Elm Street*) with a hook (the kind the animation character Captain Hook has). The others were of flowers with knives as stems. I looked at the nine ink drawings and then at Tristan; he was, after all, from the homeland of Sherlock Holmes.

"Well, Sherlock, what's she telling us?" I asked.

"She's being abused," he said.

"Wait a second, she's sixteen, she was writing to my eighty-plus aunt. It was just a high school teacher's project, not a social worker's," I tried to explain.

He picked up one of the images of the 'Freddy Krueger twin,' the stepfather.

"This guy has to be stopped. See, the buckle keeps getting bigger," he said, and that's when I saw that the hook wasn't a hook—it was a belt buckle.

"My dad gave me some more letters," I said, and quickly pulled them out of my Chanel bag.

Tristan tore them open. The last two drawings were of an old lady with the initials GM written under it and a map of Florida.

"GM stands for Grandmother, we have to get her there," he said.

"Get her where?" I asked.

"Florida," he pointed to the map.

Wow, this girl talked in codes; how she imagined my Aunt Helen would have figured it out was too sad to think about.

"We can't pass up the chance to save her, she's crying out for help," he said.

"See something, say something...do something," I said as it hit me in the pit of my stomach, "Okay, let's rescue her," I added.

I had saved stray dogs and cats—why not a teenage girl? Why not?

# 26

# *RESCUE*

Okay, so every actress waits to land her biggest, leading role—the role whereby playing that character she will forever be changed. Incidentally it's the same for male actors. I hadn't booked it in Hollywood, and now I was about to play 'it' and play it for 'real'. Of course, not in front of a film crew, or TV cameras, or on the radio—but person-to-person. I felt a rush; just the thought of performing to fool a troubled mother and a dangerous, treacherous stepfather gave me the drive. So when you accept your role, you have to review the script—and really know how the scene has to be played out. That's just what Tristan and I sat up doing for several nights in a row.

We decided not to do the 911 thing (chances were the girl would hide the abuse out of fear), or the call to a social worker (who may or may not be able to get her out of the house or even have enough time to meet her due to backed up case loads). And also Tristan had had a friend who was never saved because of red tape, and now sits in jail because the abuse ate way at his non-violent soul and he fought back with a gun.

In movies, the victim is usually safely rescued, okay, so sometimes it doesn't turn out well on HBO. But our made-for-not-TV-movie was going to have a happy ending. I knew he needed to be the cop and me the social worker in order to get Cassidy safely to her grandmother's. We figured that when she turned eighteen, she could decide whatever she wanted.

"Just tell me what to say, and I'll fake a Boston accent," Tristan said, like an actor entering his first acting class.

Suddenly, I was not only setting up our 'rescue' scene, but training Tristan, and we were about to form a seamless rescue ensemble. I only wished that my Aunt Helen could have seen us, she would have been proud.

I had left my father a 'SORRY' note hung across his reading chair. It was painted on a scrap of canvas that Tristan had in the back his Land Rover. Incidentally, he has the Defender model—how perfect an auto name is that? It was his idea for me to use the canvas, because he said paper notes get tossed away too easily.

The 'sexy' cop uniform was still in my suitcase from sexing the grip/actor—only now it looked serious and authentic on Tristan. I had to stop myself from becoming aroused. "No, no, he's your roommate, and you're on a mission," I thought. I don't think he saw my mouth almost pucker up. I hope not. I had three wigs, a reddish with bangs, a blonde and a brunette one that was perfect for a bookish person. I had belly and breast padding and very cheap makeup. My acting motto-have costumes will travel. All I needed was the outfits.

"Check Laurel's mum's closet," Tristan suggested, as if he had worked on the stages of Paramount.

"You're good," I said, as I leapt up and he followed.

"I think so," he added.

Laurel's mother had left a lot of clothes hanging in a bedroom closet, like any smart woman who likes to travel lightly. I needed two outfits, one for the social worker role and one to wear when I met Cassidy for the first time.

Okay, so before you act in any role in any film or TV show, it has to get the green light, meaning the official 'yes', the project is happening. And for us with our real life rescue, we needed to be sure that Cassidy wanted to be rescued, and that she was indeed being abused. So I decided that a blonde girl, a friend of Aunt Helen's would show up and talk person-to-person with her. Then, if it was 'yes,' I'd wear the brunette-bookish wig for the social worker with belly and breast padding to age me a bit and give me a more professional appearance. When Tristan pulled out a bright jacket and skirt, we both laughed.

"I can't wear cherry red," I said. Then he selected a dark, conservative blue suit with pants and a semi-matching jacket.

"Social worker?" he asked.

I put it on and walked around the room, imagining the padding.

"That's her," he said.

"I'll need a fake ID," I said, anxiously.

"No worries, I know a guy who makes ID's, real ones, but he'll make us fake ones."

I couldn't believe how focused Tristan was on getting our rescue job accomplished.

"Try this sweat suit on, with the blonde wig," Tristan said, like he'd been in show business for years.

"I can't believe Laurel's mother wears that. So, have you ever wanted to be an actor?" I asked.

"God no, that's a tough biz," he said.

I tried on the brown velvet sweat suit. It had no logo on it, and was tight and clingy, not the kind I'd ever wear as my real self. For the blonde character, though, it was perfect.

The pen pal letters had been sent care of the high school, but on the second-to-last letter Cassidy had scribbled out her home address, another example of her cry for help. We practiced the way my conversation with her should play out; I would ask if she was being physically abused, and I would tell her what could happen, as in a cop and social worker arriving to take her away and having her mother sign a form that left her in the 'legal' care of her grandmother (who we were 99% sure lived in Florida). And that, if her grandmother agreed to care for her, we would buy her a one-way ticket, and the rest of her life would be up to her, and that my Aunt Helen had wanted to help her as her last dying wish. It was Tristan's idea to mention her for sentimental value.

We ended the night watching the first *Hangover* movie, because Tristan had the DVD and thought we should watch something funny. I'll admit it, I love to laugh, but the whole time I just kept thinking about Cassidy's mother. Why was she allowing her daughter to be abused? Why didn't she send her to her mother's? Then I couldn't sleep, but I didn't want to wake Tristan, who had fallen asleep before the movie ended, so I got up and started ironing the red and white frilly cotton table cloths that Deeda was going to be using in less than a week for Laurel's wedding.

Early in the morning, Tristan took off; he wanted to get a few things covered in case our rescue plan was a go. I walked Shadow and continued to prep things for Laurel; just to stop myself from thinking about my first meeting with Cassidy.

By one o'clock I took the Red Line to Park Street, and from there I caught the Green Line to Haymarket, all in less than thirty minutes. I'll admit that I was nervous during the train ride, until some white-collar-type guy gave me a flirting look. Oh yeah, I was a blonde. They have to have more fun, because at least four other men smiled at me in that 'hint-hint' way. Everyone who's a non-blonde woman should wear a blonde wig for a day, just to see what it's like.

I jumped on the 111 bus and headed to Chelsea via the Tobin Bridge. I felt keyed up and energized. We decided that it was better if I tried to meet Cassidy on her way home from school. After arriving in Chelsea, I walked by her home, which I found through a map on my Smartphone. Actually I stared at it from across the street—it was a regular single-family house that looked unkempt, but not out of place on the block. No one was around, not that I would have looked suspicious. From there I headed over to Chelsea High School. I got there early, so I walked around for a few minutes. I knew what she looked like, thanks to Facebook, so I didn't have to carry the ink self-portrait drawing. I figured she would walk out alone, because in her pen pal letters she had mentioned having difficulty maintaining friendships, and I knew the stepsisters went to a local middle school.

The high school doors flew open and a pack of students rushed out. I spotted her, in baggy pants and a large pink sweatshirt. Her hair was in her face, but I saw that she was wearing some makeup. Her left arm was in a cast and that spooked me. Still I followed her until we were two blocks away.

"Cassidy?" I asked. My heart pounding.

She just gave a blank stare.

"Your pen pal Helen sent me," I said, with full conviction.

Cassidy's eyes went wide.

"She says you're being abused, that I have to rescue you, and send you to your grandmother's home, ASAP," I said, all in one breath.

That's when her tears started—there wasn't anything she had to say; her pain was all over her face. I pinched myself to stop myself from crying, we couldn't both be seen crying, not with other teens ambling by.

"Walk near me, I'm going to go over everything that is about to happen."

She nodded, and then I told her. She repeatedly asked about Aunt Helen, but I didn't tell her that she had passed away. I couldn't. We were about a block from her house.

"Are your stepsisters being abused?"

"No, because they're his kids. He doesn't like me."

"Does he beat you with a belt?" I asked. I felt guilty asking, but I had promised Tristan that I would, and that promise I had to keep.

"Yeah, all the time. He blames me for everything," she said.

"And your arm?" I asked, deciding that I needed to know.

"Yeah, he broke it, but I didn't tell anyone. I said I fell."

Then I asked the hardest question of all, "Does your mother know?" and she nodded.

"Say it out loud, when you say it out loud you own the truth," I said. Those words basically flew out of my mouth unrehearsed.

"Yeah, she does know he hits me," she finally said.

"Okay, I need your grandmother's phone number. Then you'll need to keep your head up, because tomorrow morning it will happen," I said. She gave me her grandmother's info and I walked away.

After that I jumped back on the 111 bus. And the whole ride back into Boston, I found myself thinking about the movie *Mommie Dearest*, and how much courage it must have taken Christina Crawford, (the adopted daughter) of famed actress Joan Crawford to go public by writing a tell-all book about the abuse she experienced. Who would want to believe that 'The' Joan Crawford abused her kid? Wow, would I have told if I had been her daughter? I don't know, I really don't know.

Forty minutes later I reported everything to Tristan. I was shaking when I told him, I felt frightened and so out of my comfort zone. We talked about calling child protective services, but in the end we decided to stick with our rescue plan. I quickly rattled off her grandmother's number that I had memorized, since I didn't want to be seen writing something down. He had scored his friend's dark blue; four door Ford that would be our 'unmarked' cop car, since so many Massachusetts cops drive them. I glanced at the outdoor wedding bar—it was done. Tristan winked; he knew his woodworking was beyond just good, it was the highest-quality.

"Come on, we need to get our ID's made," he said, so I raced upstairs and changed into my social worker outfit, with the padded belly and breasts and brunette wig—in full character to the max. Okay, so I'm going to brag: I really looked like a 'social worker'. Wow, how could I ever give up acting? I dashed downstairs, but when I heard the doorbell ring, I scurried into the living room, while Tristan intervened in perfect timing. More wedding packages for Laurel—we laughed after the UPS guy drove off. Tristan's Land Rover was in the driveway and I hopped into the back seat. Okay, so we were acting like a cast in a spy film.

Tristan drove us to Marblehead to his friend Mark's home, his Boston accent (no R's) was what Tristan was copying for his cop role. FYI, the easiest way to practice the Boston accent is to say, "Pahk the cah in Hahvahd Yahd (translation: "park the car in Harvard Yard"). Try it!

I took my 'social worker' pose in front of an off-white poster board. It was so professional, the set-up. Mark had the real name of a social worker who had passed away that he put on the ID.

Tristan had disappeared into the bathroom, only to reemerge with a shaved head. He was going to play a bald headed cop. I couldn't believe it. It was smart, he wouldn't have looked real in a wig and with the shaved head—he seemed completely authentic. On the cute 'cop' side too, in my opinion, which I didn't share. We all laughed as Tristan practiced his cop walk and flat footed stance.

After that I needed to call the Grandmother pretending to be the social worker to find out if she could take care of Cassidy. It was Tristan who wanted me to double-check. Mark gave me a throwaway phone, and I felt like I was in a James Bond film, minus the sexy outfit and sensuous name. Note to self, audition for action films. Tristan and Mark went into the kitchen to make something to eat, because I was worried about getting nervous and we didn't want Mark to know everything. He just knew a teenager was in trouble and that was enough for him. So I altered my voice because I love changing into different characters. I looked at the ID, and then I dialed Cassidy's grandmother in Saint Augustine, Florida. A sweet old woman named Rena-Jo answered, and when I introduced myself to her, she sounded suddenly shaky.

"If we send your granddaughter to Florida tomorrow, can she live with you?" I asked in my best social worker voice.

"She sure can; I've been praying for her to come down here," she said with a slight southern accent.

"We want her to be removed from the house, because the stepfather's beating her," I said, sounding even more like a social worker.

"Get her here and I promise I'll raise her right," she said, and I felt a lump in my throat. There really was a loving person waiting for Cassidy. I hung up after getting her address and making sure she'd be home to greet her.

I raced into Mark's kitchen. "It's all set," I said. The guys were munching on grilled cheese sandwiches with chips and dip. I felt too excited to eat. I knew right there and then, a hundred percent sure—that this was why Aunt Helen had gotten Cassidy as her pen pal.

We left Mark's place late, because the guys played back-to-back games of Ping Pong, and headed back to Laurel's house to press our clothes and go over the scene. We had to go over "the-what-ifs," as in what if the stepfather got violent (we couldn't arrest him), what if the mom didn't sign the guardian release form.

"What if Cassidy changes her mind and doesn't want to go? I asked.

"How it unfolds is how it unfolds, no regrets," Tristan said.

Go figure. The Brits came up with the slogan, '*Keep Calm And Carry On*'.

"Okay," I said, as I headed into Laurel's room, feeling nervous, but needing to sleep.

"Night," Tristan hollered.

It must have been two in the morning when I heard the sound of a wolf howling. A wolf in Cambridge, Massachusetts? I thought no way—but it sounded real. Okay, was I on the set of *True Blood* or *The Vampire Diaries*? Or was this a horror film, and I was playing a woman about to be eaten by a lone wolf? Then I heard Shadow barking nonstop from downstairs, so I got up and grabbed Laurel's fuchsia Victoria Secret robe and walked into the hallway. That's when I saw Tristan heading down the stairs.

"I'm coming with you," I whispered, "I heard when in danger, go in pairs," I added.

I hoped that was true. Tristan grabbed a broom from the kitchen and we headed to the porch door. By then I was hiding behind Tristan, when all of sudden he started chuckling.

"Look at our wolf," he pointed.

There was Gabriel under the wedding canopy, crouched, drinking from a bottle of Jack Daniels, and howling like a wolf. Tristan went out to fetch him so that the neighbors didn't call the cops. That's all we needed. His hair was wet, his mouth and clothes smelled of JD, he was wearing what he'd worn days prior, and he was laughing and crying at the same time.

"The trouble with this life is that you die at the end, you die," Gabriel said, as Tristan sat his skinny butt in one of the kitchen chairs and poured a cold cup of coffee. I knew then that his mother had died. Shadow licked his hands as if trying to calm him down, but Gabriel was too drunk to notice.

"Drink the coffee, then it's time to sleep it off," I heard Tristan say as I headed back to bed; finally too tired to be scared about the rescue mission.

# 27

## ACTION

I couldn't sleep, so I read all of Cassidy's pen pal letters again; it was like reading a script before call time (AKA when you arrive on set). Lights, camera, ACTION. Only this was real action. At six in the morning, I found Gabriel holding Tristan's cop outfit.

"What are you guys up to?" he asked, now sober and super-wide awake.

"Nothing," I said.

Tristan tried to tell him that we weren't robbing a bank, he knew that, but he was full of questions, and I just blew up.

"BUTT OUT! You're going to ruin everything," I screamed, like I was five-years-old. Before he could react, I left the room and headed into the bathroom to put on my social worker costume again with belly, breast padding and my brunette wig. I didn't mean to be rude—he had just lost his mother and I hadn't even gotten to talk with him about it, but I was afraid we wouldn't get Cassidy out of the house and on a plane to Florida.

I took a few deep breaths and then, like a trained actress, in front of the ornate bathroom mirror, I got into character. When I emerged from the bathroom, Gabriel was waiting.

"Tristan told me. I'm doing the airport part," he said.

"Cool, bro," I said, letting out the biggest sigh of relief. I would have hugged him, but I was in character and needed to stay in character. Gabriel and Shadow watched as the cop and social worker entered the unmarked car. We wanted to get there early so as not to draw attention from the neighbors, and it was Saturday. We didn't talk during the drive over from Cambridge to Chelsea; we were well rehearsed, and knew what to do.

It unfolded like this: we arrived at the house, the cop knocked on the door, the mother answered, and I, as the social worker, spoke first.

"I'm from Boston's Children Social Services."

She opened the door, we stepped in without hesitation.

"We're removing your daughter Cassidy due to physical abuse by (his name). She will be placed with another family member," I said, word-for-word.

The mother was smoking a Marlborough and we followed her into the living room, right off the hallway entrance.

"Who says?" she asked. Her eyes were glazed, she appeared out of it, but I wasn't sure what from. The room was gloomy. Only a ceiling light and the TV, with low volume were on. It was a messy, sad, crummy living room, with cheap used furniture.

"She's to be removed now," I said, not backing down.

"Yeah?" the mother asked, without any emotion. Thank God, Cassidy came in the room.

"Get your things, we're taking you out of here today," I said.

"Tell them they're wrong," her mother said, glaring at her.

Cassidy lifted up her Miley Cyrus T-shirt, showing welt marks from the belt her stepfather used (it was horrifying) and I had to hold my breath.

"GET YA CLOTHES," the cop yelled, in a perfect Boston accent. The mother stared at the floor like she was trying to find something—suddenly he rushed in, his face was round, his nose was thick and his gut protruded over black boxers. He wore black socks and his hands were fists.

"Get the F*** out," he said, about to punch Tristan, (cop). But he stepped back, and the stepfather fell against the wall. Then Tristan grabbed him, locking his hands behind his back.

"You stupid? You wanna go to jail?" Tristan the cop asked in a mean voice.

"This is my house, I call the shots," he barked.

"Not anymore," Tristan the cop countered.

"F*** you!" he shouted.

"Leave him alone," her mother said.

"Shut the F*** up, bitch," he yelled.

Cassidy was carrying a small duffle bag (I think she must have packed it the night before).

"I'm ready," she said.

"Sign this, or he'll go to jail for assaulting an officer," I said.

The mother turned and looked at me. I thought she'd put up a fight, but she grabbed my pen. I had the guardian release form on a clipboard.

"Your daughter will live with another family member. When she's eighteen, she's free to do as she wants. She may contact you at any time, but it will be up to her. She will no longer be under your care; you're signing away your rights to her," I said.

She signed. Tristan waited for my signal, I checked the signature and nodded. He let go of the stepfather, but not before giving him a sharp warning.

"F*** yourself," the stepfather said as he slumped onto the dingy couch.

"What?" Tristan the cop asked.

"That's to her, not you officer," he answered.

I wanted to hit him myself, but I didn't. I took a deep breath.

"This way," I said.

We headed to the front door, as he continued to shout at her, "You brat, slut, piece of trash (cuss, cuss, cuss)." Cassidy was shaking, tears rolling down her face as she followed me. Tristan (cop) was the last to leave. We entered the unmarked car, Cassidy and I in the back seat. The cop was behind the wheel again, and he drove us to Logan

Airport, which took all of five minutes. While he drove, Cassidy and I talked about the following: "When will I meet Helen?" she asked, her nose running and her eyes glazed.

"You won't. I'm sorry to inform you, but she passed away, but not before contacting us," I said. I couldn't drop out of character, too many years of acting. Also, Tristan and I had agreed that our secret rescue mission was our own secret and no one else's. So don't tell!

Tristan found a few napkins and passed them over. I waited while she blew her nose.

"Not fair, I wanted to meet her, badly. I knew she would understand my secret," Cassidy explained, still tearful.

"Not a secret to keep. Now, your grandmother is waiting for you and you will live with her. This is your airline ticket, and pen pal letters. And in this change purse is travel money. I won't be coming with you, but an undercover agent will be on the plane to make sure you arrive safely. From Jacksonville, you'll take a long taxi ride down to Saint Augustine, right to your grandmother's door. Just act confident," I said. Cassidy nodded.

FYI, we used a pre-paid credit card to buy her ticket with.

"She didn't care," she said, and I knew she was talking about her mother. I wanted to say so many terrible things about her mother, but I knew it wasn't my place.

"Deep down, she wants you happy," I said. I passed Cassidy the ticket, letters and change purse (actually it was a nice chunk of Gabriel's Foxwoods win; to help her get a new start with).

"When you get off the plane, grab a taxi," I reminded her.

"I can't wait to be with my grandmother," Cassidy said.

"Here's something from your pen pal, take it with you," I said.

Cassidy took the jean jacket. She studied the words on the back, I AM MYSELF, and then on the inside where it was embroidered with *To Cassidy from your pen pal Helen* and then she got out and headed towards the Jet Blue sliding doors. That's when I saw Gabriel. He had on new black jeans, and a Red Sox jacket and cap as he went in the door just behind her. He didn't miss a second; if only his mother could have seen him. Wow.

Tristan pulled the unmarked car away and off we went—a mile or so later he pulled into a Dunkin' Donuts parking lot and quickly changed in the front seat into his faded jeans and green T-shirt and work boots.

"I thought I was going to have to pummel that bastard into a pulp," he said with a huff.

"Well, I thought I was going to have to jump on his back like Joe Pesci did in one of those *Lethal Weapon* films," I said, laughing.

"You should take the wig and stuffing off, I'll go get us some food," he said.

"Tristan?" I said. He looked at me through the rear-view mirror. "We did a good thing," I added. He winked and got out.

I took off my wig, the jacket and blouse. I was so ready to lose the top-heavy breasts and stomach padding. Okay, maybe I overdid it, but it looked real. As I yanked off the belly padding, Tristan got in the back seat with the Dunkin' goodies.

"I like the stomach, but the boobs were a bit too much," he said.

"Ha, ha," I said.

"The blonde wig's better," he added.

"Well, I don't think we'll be rescuing teens on a regular basis," I said.

He sipped his coffee as I slipped into pair of leggings, a black V-neck dress and ballet flats.

"There were two girls I remember being abused, and as a kid I never thought I could protect them. I just tried not to think about it," I said.

"Yeah, I know."

"We made up for that today, don't you think?"

"Yeah, maybe. Hope she gets a happier life in Florida," he said.

"She will," I said, because I can't help but believe in 'happy endings'. After all, if I was making a film, the ending scenes would be Cassidy attending a new high school where she fit in, and yes, in the last shot, falls in love with a super-kind high-schooler. Fade out, the end! I can't sing, but when I was looking at Cassidy, I could hear that song, *Sixteen Going on Seventeen* from the film *The Sound of Music*. The innocence was so missing from Cassidy's face, from her body, from her speech and her life and I wanted her to get it back.

I thought about when I was sixteen, and the tall, dirty-blond guy, named John, from Jamestown, Rhode Island, came up to visit his friend Abigail Borowitz, a girl who had just moved to Cambridge. I went to her apartment, not far from M.I.T. Everyone was drinking Southern Comfort, only I didn't. I don't know why drinking and drugs weren't my thing, but I sat in the circle and watched him. There was another John there, so he was John H. and I thought he was so beautiful and I wanted him to want me. I was thinking that, "want me, want me". We left Abigail's mother's apartment (her father still lived in RI) and one of the senior guys drove us to Brookline to an ice cream shop that's no longer there. We went in and I sat down at a booth.

Then Abigail came up and she said, "John H. won't come in because he likes you." I was shocked; it was like getting a gold medal, an Oscar and a Tony award all in one second. My first real 'crush' guy, and he liked ME. I walked outside the ice cream shop and found John H. leaning against a leafless, skinny tree. He didn't look at me, but I looked at him, his beautiful forehead leaning against the tree.

"Want to come in and have ice cream with me?" I asked. It was all I could think of. He turned his face and glanced at me, still keeping his forehead against the tree.

"You want ice cream?" he asked.

"Yeah," I said, as I nodded.

I suddenly felt my heart racing and I didn't know how to talk. Why was I so shy then? Anyway he moved away from the tree and next to me and we went back in together. I felt like I was wearing the largest crown on my head, I felt that GOOD. That amazing!

It was a special night, but then he went back to RI (he was going to high school there and lived with his family, and soon after that my mother met her Panamanian prince charming and ran away from me and my father). And I gave up on 'true' love, heartbeats, and innocence. That's why I screwed the guy in a closet at a party, just to get the virginity thing over with.

"Two dollars to know what you're thinking about?" Tristan asked. I opened my eyes and eyed him, snapping back to the present-moment, the moment I don't often want to live in.

"Innocence. It doesn't last. One way or another, it goes away," I said.

"Right," he said.

We ate our tuna fish sandwiches on toasted bagels. FYI, I eat seafood two or three times a year.

"You're a talented actress, you better not quit," he said.

"You played one hell of a Boston cop, perfect accent," I said.

He leaned in and I felt my heart start to beat, it was scary. I glanced down at my hands. Suddenly I felt really shy.

"I'm twenty-nine and I think that was one of the most important things that I've done in my life. I didn't get to save my friend, but seeing Cassidy get out at Logan Airport was—" he stopped himself.

"Ditto on that," I added figuring he didn't need to spell it out.

"Only you and I will remember it forever," Tristan said as he crumpled up the Dunkin' Donuts bag. I didn't know he was twenty-nine, but I liked knowing it.

"Don't you agree?" he asked.

"I agree 100 percent," I said.

He got out of the back seat of the unmarked car and I sat there, stunned. I had wanted to kiss him. I felt like I had wanted that moment, but I'm old fashioned. If a guy wants to kiss a girl, he makes the move. Paloma had made the first move (with a few guys, years ago), but that's because she can. Not me. I just don't like getting rejected. Acting is filled with rejection. Why get any more from a guy?

Besides, maybe he has a girlfriend, maybe she's in the UK, or traveling abroad, or just busy. Tristan got into the front seat and drove us back to Marblehead to return the unmarked car to Mark. We put my wig and the cop uniform in a trash bag and dumped it into Mark's trash can. I no longer needed the cop uniform, and the wig wasn't one I ever wanted to wear again.

Tristan drove us to Gloucester, where he said he needed to pick something up. He parked near the Fisherman's Wharf.

"What are you getting?" I asked.

"Just time," he said.

And we walked along the water walkway in the quaint historical seaport town.

"How are you feeling?" he asked.

"Shocked, happy, kind of sad, but not really sad," I said, sounding like a nervous airhead.

"Me, too," he said. We sat on a huge rock and watched the boats on the ocean.

"You just wanted to come here to do this?" I asked.

"Yeah," he said.

He really was a super-cool guy, and I was so glad Laurel hadn't slept with him. Not that I was thinking of sleeping with him, because I wasn't. After all, I'm on the hunt for Mr. Darcy/AKA Romeo, and not a fling.

"What are your plans?" he asked.

I told him how confused I was since I had no car, no home of my own, and I wasn't sure if New York was the place I should try again or if returning to Los Angeles was the better choice.

"It will reveal itself," he said.

"Ha ha, you sound like an old sage," I said with a laugh.

We walked away from the rocks, and as we headed back to his Land Rover, he put his hand on my shoulder and squeezed it.

Later that evening Tristan cooked dinner while I finished ironing Laurel's wedding drapes. She had sent twenty-two text messages letting us both know that she was arriving the following day. It was about to begin—her wedding celebration.

Gabriel arrived after midnight and we all sat in the kitchen, while he filled us in on the flight, the snack food, the taxi ride from Jacksonville to Saint Augustine and watching Cassidy hug her grandmother, who wasn't an 'old' woman. In fact, she was one of those suntanned, super-fit-senior-types.

"She walked through the condo complex door and it shut. That was it, I turned around and high tailed it back here," Gabriel said and we clapped. I mean, it was the best ending. Could it be that easy? It was for her. As soon as Gabriel pulled out a new puzzle, Tristan made his goodnight exit.

"Laurel's back tomorrow for her wedding. After that, I have to find a new direction in life," I said.

"Yeah, so do I," Gabriel said, as I walked him into the living room.

"Just spend some hours at Harvard one more time, and think about finishing it," I said, like a good older sister would.

"Okay," he said as he leaned back on the couch, pulling the Mexican blanket over him.

"Goodnight, bro," I said.

It had been the most amazing, purposeful day in my life and I had played my best acting role ever. I knew I'd never forget it, as I sauntered up to Laurel's bed. Okay, so no one will know about it. But that's okay. Please, don't tell.

# 28

## CEREMONY

Deeda-the-decorator woke us up. She was dressed in a short, tight black and white dress, with black ankle length boots. Obviously, she'd just been to the hair dresser, and her makeup was ultra-peach-ish. I'm not an expert on makeup, since everything I know, I learned from Paloma who used to get free makeup lessons at Macy's. Every time she tried a makeup product, she would get new information and then pass it onto me. But in my opinion, Deeda didn't have a complexion that could carry the peach color. She seemed super wired-for-sound and had arrived with only two other helpers—and she looked at Tristan and me as her free employees.

"I don't think her boobs are real," I whispered to Tristan, as she hollered for us to carry the Pier 1 Import furniture to the middle of the yard so her staff could 'place it' as she had pictured it in her mind. Oh, and she had lost her designer book somewhere.

"It's like not having the bible for the rest of your life," she said while adjusting her tight dress, probably to show off her figure to Tristan and her two helpers, Paul and Ian.

Laurel phoned her and then immediately called me. "Is it set up?" she asked.

"Almost," I said, because Deeda told me to say that. Laurel was on the Vineyard, showing off her soon-to-be husband. She wanted to arrive at the house with only enough time to change into her wedding dress; that was her style. Gabriel had left when he heard Deeda shouting orders, and took Shadow to my father's for doggy-day care. Luckily, he still had his Harvard Inn room to camp out in. I felt guilty that I still hadn't asked him about his mother's passing, but in a way I think he didn't want to talk about it.

"Tristan, honey, set up the dance floor. It was shipped all the way from Italy," Deeda shouted.

As Tristan headed to the heavy boxes stacked near the canopy, I asked, "Is she on caffeine pills or what?" Tristan smirked at me.

"Vivien, I need you to drape the canopy. Hurry up," Deeda shouted.

I said nothing, because I didn't want ruin anything for Laurel, and I had seen some over-the-top Hollywood party decorators who were loud and bossy, but still set up a party in an absolutely astonishing way. Never mind Martha Stewart, they had their shine on, too. Actually, I like M-Stew a lot better since she did jail time. In my opinion it made her more human and I have one of her interior decorating books to use when I get my own house—hopefully some year soon.

It took me an hour to drape the white silk, and to hang the imported ivy, and to intertwine the red roses. It looked so romantic.

"Come on, the bar needs to be styled," Deeda shouted. She wasn't using her hands to fix or arrange anything. With her peach painted fingernails she pointed out what we should do, refusing to get her hands dirty or chip her nails. Two women caterers had arrived a half an hour earlier and they were busy filling wicker picnic baskets for each of the guests with silverware, white china plates, and wine glasses. Fresh cut red roses laid against the red and white linen tables. It looked beautiful for the split second that I got to check it out, before Deeda hauled me away. The bar was draped with imported ivy, white candles in tall clear vases, and several bowls with floating gardenias. The smell was heavenly. I filled smaller bowls with mixed nuts and organic munchies that the caterers brought.

"Boys, cover the chairs," Deeda shouted.

Paul and Ian began covering the chairs with throws and mini pillows, placing them around the round tables. I helped toss out empty boxes, plastic bubble wrap and other junk in the recycling and trash area. Then I excused myself and headed to the bathroom.

A small clean-up crew inside the house was vacuuming and arranging imported flowers in tall, ceramic, white, Italian vases in all the rooms. It looked incredible, and smelled really fantastic. Laurel and Mr. Italian were going all out.

Later I walked into Laurel's bedroom to change my clothes, but her canopy bed had been covered with white silk sheets, a red silk blanket draped on the edge of it. There was a mega-white vase that must have weighed four hundred pounds filled with long-stem red roses. My Louis Vuitton suitcase was nowhere to be found. In fact, nothing of mine was. I went into the hallway and was about to ask someone where my things were when I saw a decorated sign on the doorknob of the room Tristan had been staying in, saying *Vivien & Tristan.* I looked back at Laurel's bedroom door; it had a huge decorated sign saying *Laurel & Anthony* on it. The door across from hers, toward the other bathroom, had her parent's names on it. I opened the door to Tristan's room. The bed had been made and a vase of sunflowers was sitting on the desk. Below it was my vintage LV suitcase and two matching travel bags.

I had gotten my Louis Vuitton luggage off of Craigslist; I met a very wealthy woman in Beverly Hills at the local Starbucks and bought the set right there, because she was liquidating. I love the LV look. Vintage is so my style. Anyway, I texed Laurel; *Hey, you've put me in Tristan's bedroom?* And she texed me back; *You're welcome.* Oh, no! Laurel likes to play the 'raw' matchmaker, hence the reason I had to sleep with the g-spot jock years ago. Unbelievable. I wasn't sure if I should tell Tristan or just let him find out. I mean, there was only one bed in the room.

I changed my top and stared at the sunflowers (the biggest and brightest); they're one of my favorite flowers because of Vincent Van Gogh's sunflower paintings. I knew Laurel had Deeda's crew put them in my shared room on purpose. That's why it's hard to ever get mad at Laurel.

I raced downstairs. A red runner now covered the hallway from the front door all the way out to the back door, and into the back yard. Bags of white rose petals were stuffed to the side to be tossed on it once Laurel's guests arrived.

I found Tristan, who had completed the dance floor and hung loads of imported ivy all along the back walls of Laurel's very private backyard. It was almost ready for thirty guests and the bride and groom.

"How's it going?" I asked. He looked so cute with a nail in his mouth, a hammer in his right hand, and the ivy in his left.

"Missed you," he said. Wow, I felt my heart start to beat.

"Listen, Laurel put us in the same bedroom because her family's arriving," I said. I had to tell him. Before he could answer, Deeda pulled me away.

"The party gifts have to be arranged," she barked, and off I went, back into the house and in the living room where a white bed sheet had been placed over the rug. On it were thirty white silk bags and on each of them was printed, *Laurel & Anthony, in Love*' in gold letters. Next to them were thirty gold boxes with matching gold ribbons containing Godiva Belgian mini-chocolates. There were also thin, blue, glass bottles. Next to them, printed on off-white handmade paper, were hand-written notes about donations made to the following charities: St. Jude's, AIDS, Susan G. Komen for the Cure, ASPCA, and Greenpeace. I put one in each bottle and then placed them in the silk bags, along with a box of chocolates. It was so elegant and romantic.

Top romance films, in my opinion, are *Eternal Sunshine of the Spotless Mind*, *Say Anything*, *Slumdog Millionaire*, *Wuthering Heights*, *Shakespeare in Love*, and *The Fabulous Baker Boys*. Just my luck, I'm a lot like the character Susie Diamond in *The Fabulous Baker Boys*, as in sleeping with a guy and having to find out if it's ONER or something more. Note to self; don't share the bed with Tristan after Laurel's wedding; that's no way to start something real. I mean, let's face it: I'm twenty-seven, not far from thirty; I have to find Mr. Darcy/AKA, Romeo ASAP.

My father's favorite romance film is *Gone with the Wind*. Go figure! In that film, the man walks away. My father really is a wounded man, but still, he did name me after the lead actress, one of his favorites.

My Aunt Helen liked *Casablanca*, *An Affair to Remember* and *The Bridges of Madison County*.

Okay, so Jill's favorite romance film was *Dirty Dancing*, which she watched 24/7 during her short-lived break-up with Finch. She would sit her pixie body up close to the TV screen and watch the DVD over and over. I caught her a dozen times doing just that in our SLC dorm house living room. She stopped when Finch came back into her life. FYI, she gave me the DVD.

Paloma's favorites are *Jerry Maguire*, *Love Actually*, *The Notebook*, and, of course, her number one is *Breakfast at Tiffany's*. Once a year she dresses up like the lead character, Holly Golightly, and goes shopping at Tiffany & Co.

Laurel's favorites are *Titanic*, *Brokeback Mountain*, *Moulin Rouge*, and *When Harry Met Sally*. She once told me that she fakes her 'orgasms' a lot, and that when the real guy came into her life, she wouldn't have to. So does she cum with Anthony? Note to self, find out. I didn't have to wait long: Laurel arrived an hour and a half before her big event.

Just like a movie star, she pulled up in a limo, accompanied by her older (as in fifteen), slim, divorced Italian banker Anthony—he looked like the Italian actor Fabrizio Bentivoglio (from the comedy film *Scialla*) and he was wearing an expensive tailored suit and hand-made leather shoes. His dark eyes focused only on Laurel. She hugged me and dragged me by my arm up the stairs to her bedroom, followed by two teenage cousins who were carrying her seven garment bags.

"I've missed you incredibly much," Laurel shouted, dramatically.

"Me, too," I said.

"Thanks cousins," she sang out, as they hung her garment bags on the rack set up for the event.

Then she hugged them and they dashed out of her room. Laurel shut the door, leaning against it like a movie star.

"He's the best I've ever had," she said in a super loud voice. It wasn't like she was showing off—Laurel always says what she feels in a super loud voice.

"I think I was waiting my whole life for him. I like that he's older than me and that he was married twice before; he has experience and he makes me happy," she boasted, loudly.

"And how is he in bed?" I asked, not wanting to wait any longer.

She giggled. "I knew you'd want to know," she said, with her hands on her perfect size twelve frame.

"I'm predictable," I replied.

"Stay that way," she shouted.

"Go on, only lower your voice," I said

"Well, I waited seven days," she bragged, in a slightly lower tone.

"Seven?" I asked, wondering if she and Paloma had read some guide to dating book that I hadn't seen.

"Try it sometime, it really works. The kissing becomes crazy sweet, and the hand holding breathtaking, and the heavy petting magnificent." She was glowing as she spoke.

"And then, when you did it?" I asked. Okay, so I like to know the ending of most movies before I see them. Go figure.

"I could never do a 'Sally' (as in *When Harry Met Sally*), because I get turned on when he touches me anywhere on my body," she said, and I believed her.

"Wow, I'm so happy for you," I said.

"Look what I bought you, best friend," she said.

I sat on Laurel's freshly-made silk sheet covered bed as she pulled out my new Ralph Lauren black dress, Victoria Secret black bra and matching panties, sheer thigh-high stockings, and my very first pair of black Prada high heels. Okay, so I saw *The Devil Wears Prada* because Meryl Streep was the lead—and I see all of her films, it's like attending a master acting class. She played the role of Miranda Priestly, and it just killed me whenever she spoke. The true art of being a 'bitch' is shown in that film and she exemplifies it.

"He's got a girl coming, and she's sitting next to him, because he's into her," Laurel said as I glanced up; I had been busy worshiping my first pair of Pradas.

"Who?" I asked.

"Tristan, and don't pretend you don't like him. Don't sulk. You'll be at the same table, number three," she said.

"I wouldn't sulk. I've just met him," I said, defensively.

"You haven't slept with him?" she asked, suspiciously.

"Laurel, I want to get married, too, not just tally up names of guys I've slept with at the end of my life," I said.

"Don't pout," Laurel warned.

"I'm not. Thanks for the pretty things," I said, trying to stop myself from feeling sad.

"Go get dressed, I want you downstairs ASAP," Laurel said. I got up to go.

"Give me a huge best friend hug," Laurel said, and I did.

"You're one of my best, best, best friends and I wouldn't let you down," she whispered in my ear. Maybe—as in she'll pay for my therapy for the rest of my life if I end up single and unmarried. Who knows! I didn't ask her what she meant; I just took my new stuff and ambled out of her bedroom. She was smiling. It was natural: she was in love and about to be married.

It was the longest slow walk back to Tristan's room. I opened the door, taking a deep breath. "Don't cry, don't cry, don't cry," I told myself. He was dressed in an Italian grey suit that Anthony had picked out, per Laurel's request.

"How do I look?" he asked, grinning.

"Handsome," I said.

It was true and I knew that the other girl would think so as well. I hung up the dress and put the bra, panties, thigh-highs and Prada heels on the bed.

"This is going to be a special wedding," he said.

He had the closet door mirror open and I stood there, looking at it sideways, staring at me—single, unmarried, and not in love. God, I wanted to sob right there and then. He came up behind me.

"Hurry up. I want to see you dressed up," he said.

"I will," I answered.

"By the way, I won't be sleeping in here tonight, it's all yours," he said, and that's when the lump in my throat appeared.

"I'm going downstairs. Don't forget, table three," he said, as he walked out and closed the door behind him.

"Don't cry, don't cry, don't cry," I said, as I pinched my arms five times. Thank God for acting classes, I mean, if I hadn't been a trained actress, I would have grabbed my LV suitcase and bags and the Prada heels and marched out. I would have gone to my father's and just hidden myself.

There's this powerful scene in the movie *All That Jazz*, during which director/choreographer Bob Fosse tells about his own life through the character Joe Gideon (played by actor Roy Scheider), it's brilliant. God, I hope when I'm old, I've lived a life I want to make a movie from. Anyway, the character Joe Gideon stands looking at himself in a mirror, and says, *"It show time folks."* And that's what I decided to do.

I stripped off my clothes, spritzed myself with rose water and lathered my body with vanilla lotion and put on the new black Victoria Secret bra. Laurel's first bra was from VS, whereas mine was from Sears. If I have kids and one is a girl, she will get her first bra from Victoria Secret, I swear. I rubbed more vanilla lotion on my thighs. Then I put on the sheer thigh-highs and my first Pradas. You can't be depressed when you're in Prada heels—I understand the hype now. I felt like Cinderella with an attitude. Okay, I can't have Tristan, then who's next? Give me the next good guy, please. I slipped on my RL dress. Pow! Shazzam! Wow, I looked better than great.

"Nothing bothers me, nothing makes me sad, I'm fine, I'm fine," I said five times and then I walked out the door and down to the wedding. Okay, I won't lie, the lump in my throat was still there, but I had picked up my spirits. I was ready to act 'happy'. I saw Laurel's mom and gave her a congratulations hug, and then walked outside into the backyard that looked like an enchanted wedding scene.

The white rose petals smelled fantastic as I walked along the red carpet. I went to the bar. A hunk was serving, but I saw his wedding ring and so I just smiled (surface only) and ordered water with a lime. I wanted to swallow the lump in my throat.

Deeda came up to me. She was in a tight peach colored dress; and her breasts popped out. Her heels were six inches and black.

"Looks beautiful, doesn't it?" she asked.

"You did a superb job, it's romantic and amazing," I said.

"You're at table three!"

Oh, God, if anyone else tells me table three, I'll scream. Composure, act 'as if' nothing bothers me.

"Laurel's always had a large international group of friends, looks like everyone has arrived," I said.

The tables were almost filled. The afternoon ceremony was all going like clockwork.

"Go get your seat," Deeda ordered.

I felt like giving her flat ass a kick, but I didn't.

"Might as well," I said, putting down my empty glass of water and heading away.

I saw Tristan seated next to a freckle faced, pretty blonde woman in a pale cream strapless dress. Okay, so maybe it's true, blondes do have more fun and get whatever they want, too. As I headed there, I could feel Deeda following me. Oh, God, I don't need to be watched. I turned around, but she was talking to a guest behind me. If I could have walked any slower, I would have. As I approached table three, Tristan glanced over at me, and the pretty blonde stared at me and the lump in my throat grew.

"Just a second," Deeda said.

"Do you need my help?" I asked, hoping to be whisked away.

"The name settings are all wrong."

She pulled up the name card of the pretty blonde woman and put it across the table and plunked down my name card next to Tristan.

"Mrs. Millar, have a seat next to your husband," Deeda said.

The pretty blonde sprang up from the seat and went around the table and sat next to her husband.

"Sit down," Deeda ordered me, and I did. I gave Tristan an apology shrug.

"God, you're beautiful," he said.

I couldn't speak; I was too busy looking around for his date.

"Don't you know a Laurel gag when she plays one on you?" he asked.

"What?" I asked, even more confused.

"I told her I liked you, but I wasn't sure if you liked me, and she said she'd prove it, one way or another," he said proudly.

My mouth fell open. Laurel had staged it all.

"Kiss her," Deeda said.

And Tristan did better than that. He pulled me close to him and whispered in my ear, "I'm into you, and you're into me," and then he kissed my ear. Not with his tongue, but a soft kiss. I grabbed his hand and then I leaned in and pressed my lips to his and we kissed—it was fast and fun.

The Italian singer Biagio Antonacci began singing, *Vivimi*. As Laurel and Anthony made their gallant, romantic entrance, everyone stood up and Tristan held me, and I glanced over to see Deeda giving me the thumbs up. It was magical watching them walk down the steps, passing all of us and entering the canopy. They had 'In Love' vows that they wanted to exchange in front of all of us, while an interdominational minister presided over the ceremony. Minutes later Nigerian-German hip-hop-soul singer, Nneka sang *Do You Love Me*. The lump in my throat was gone and I was crying; it was so unbelievable seeing Laurel and Anthony married. All of sudden I remembered back to when she had once asked me (in a very loud voice), "What is life, if you're not in love? What is it?

# 29

# *INHERITANCE*

I woke at 7:00 in the morning from a kissing dream, it was so wonderful and yes, it was Tristan who I was smooching with. He had gone off to bunk with Gabriel at the Harvard Inn. He wanted us to date awhile, which was okay with me, because if Paloma was still waiting to have sex and Laurel had waited seven days—then I was going to copy them. I loved staying in the guest bed, staring at the sunflowers in the large, white, Italian-style vase.

The night had flown by because of the dancing, the picnic meals, and the endless toasts. Everyone had wanted to give a toast, mainly because not everyone was going to fly to Italy for the 'official' traditional wedding. I was with Tristan the whole time—my left hand in his right. He had to learn pretty quickly how to use his left hand to eat and drink with. I had floated into the house and up to the guestroom, and he had followed. We made out for twenty-five minutes. Oh, wow, I could have torn his Italian grey suit off with my teeth, but I didn't.

"Vivien, telephone," Laurel's mother hollered. I jumped up, rubbing the sleep from my eyes and threw on one of Laurel's sexy mini Victoria Secret bathrobes and raced out into the hallway.

"Be here by nine; we've got an appointment to see the lawyer right away," my bookish father said with no enthusiasm in his voice. I didn't bother asking why he hadn't called me on my cell phone.

"Okey dokey artichokey," I said, playfully.

I playfully stomped back into the guest room and pondered over what to wear. God, I just wanted to make out with Tristan again. How could my dear father go on so long without love? No more, I'm not going to allow him to live a passionless life, a single unattached life, with no hugs, and no kissing. No more! I looped my finger around the Tiffany love necklace Paloma had bought for me, because it had worked. So why couldn't I help my father? I sat there and then I decided to say a prayer. It went like this: "Please God, and the powers of the universe, let my father find the right woman, let him have profound love or just simple sweet love," I got goosebumps on my arms after I said it.

After that, I got dressed and dashed to his place. There he was, a handsome man, with a mouthful of bookish, overeducated words and two rescue dogs. Shadow barked when he saw me. I knelt down and let him give me a warm tongue lick on my hands.

"How was last night?" he asked, which was odd, because he never asks those kind of questions.

"She wore a Vera Wang wedding dress, and Anthony wore a dark, dark blue suit with a silk white scarf around his neck and expensive shoes without socks. He looked ultra-European. It was beautifully romantic," I said.

My father chuckled.

"I've met someone who's probably the one, the real one," I said. I couldn't help it; I was in the babble of 'truth' mode.

"Better be the British woodworker," he said.

My mouth dropped open, I couldn't believe it.

"Tristan?" he asked. I nodded as I tried to close my mouth, because it was so strange. My father is never in the loop. Never.

"I can agree to that. Now let's walk the dogs," he said.

"I thought we were in a rush?" I asked, wondering if my father had tricked me into rushing over, just to walk the dogs with him.

"Come on," he said, as he leashed them both and out we went. He wanted to walk along the Charles River because my father never tires of its tranquility.

"Whatever she's left, it won't be much," he warned.

I told him that I didn't care, because I suddenly felt as if I had everything I needed in my life.

"I'm happy you gave me Twist, even if he wasn't injured," he said with a serious grin.

"Me too," I said.

"But I wish you had told me how important having a dog was before, I might have done it sooner," he said.

Ugh. I wasn't about to remind him how I had called from Los Angeles a dozen times telling him to get a dog, but he had just balked at the idea. Besides, he always brought up the loss of Bridge, our family mutt-dog, whom we had all loved.

"Right," I said, and then we didn't talk during the rest of the walk, we just watched Twist and Shadow. How could anything be better?

The lawyer's office was straight out of the film *The Maltese Falcon* (my father's other vintage favorite). The lawyer, Mr. Urbansky, was in his seventies, and had on a 50s style suit with a bow tie; he was old school all the way. I swear it felt like I was on an old MGM movie set. We sat across from him, and he spent the first few minutes consoling us on our recent loss. We both missed her, but we also knew she'd lived a long, good life, and at the end of it, she was content. Then he withdrew her Will from a faded file folder. He sat back down and looked at us in a very grandfatherly manner. It was impossible not to think I wasn't in a 1950s film. He spoke to me first.

"In her last Will and Testament, your Aunt Helen has left you the deed to a six bedroom, three bathroom house located in Rye, New York, just a twenty-five mile commute from New York City. The house is paid off; you'll only ever have to pay property tax on it, and she left you twenty-thousand dollars to fix it up with."

"A house? For me?" I asked, interrupting his very polished reading. It was a total, amazing, thrilling, unbelievable shock.

I stared at my father, who gave me a wink. Mr. Urbansky cleared his throat.

"It needs work. Now, I can only give you the house keys. The deed will be turned over once you have brought her ashes to Panama and spread them in a circle around your mother's house," he said.

"PANAMA? My mother?" I jumped out of my seat. Now I wasn't happy.

"Are you crazy? My Dad and I want to put her ashes in the Charles River," I shouted.

Then I glared at my father, wanting him to protest for once in his life.

"My dear, this is her last Will and Testament, and we must all follow the wishes of your Aunt Helen. After all, she is giving you a house," he said, scolding me.

"Mr. Urbansky, you don't understand, the point I'm trying to make is that I don't know my mother anymore. She has her own life and it's in Panama, which is not in America," I said, hoping he'd finally get it.

"My dear, I'm well aware of where Panama is located, and if you don't know your mother, than perhaps you will, after you have brought your aunt's ashes there," he said.

Then he picked up the Will and continued on. My father's head was down, and he seemed suddenly small, (which for a tall man is not impossible, I saw it happen).

"When I receive proof of your flight there and back, then the deed will be given. As for you, your sister Helen left you a collection of first edition books, twelve in all, and they are very rare. She had plastic coverings designed for them," he said, as he pointed to a stack of cardboard boxes that sat on the floor to the left of his mahogany desk. I looked at my father who nodded, but didn't smile.

"Dad, rare books, how special is that." I said, jumping into sounding positive and cheerful, something I always do.

My father just continued to nod. The phone rang. Mr. Urbansky took the call, and then he got up from his desk.

"Please excuse me for a moment," he said, and he left us alone in his office.

The silence fell. My mother's abandonment had left its mark on my father, and now I was being forced to go visit her, which was clearly my Aunt Helen's last attempt to reunite us.

"I can buy you the ticket, and we can pretend you went," my father said.

"Not with that lawyer. It's all right, I'll just go, but only for a weekend," I answered.

He nodded. I eyed the cardboard boxes, thinking about lifting the first lid and flashing my father one of the rare books, just to cheer him up.

"A weekend's not so long," I said, hoping to make it less painful for him.

"She wanted to take you with her, but I told she couldn't have it both ways, a new man and my daughter," he said staring out of the lawyer's window and away from me.

"I'm glad you kept me," I said. I felt sad, as I always did.

My mother had followed the beat of her heart, but she had left a heart broken in doing so. Love can be like that. Go figure.

Mr. Urbansky returned. He had us look over the Will and Testament, and then he gave us papers we had to sign. After that, a young guy dressed like a bellhop appeared and strapped the card board boxes onto a small rolling dolly. He followed us out and down to my father's parked car. Once the boxes were loaded in, we drove off.

My father told me how he had taken Aunt Helen on a drive through the city of Rye and how she loved how close it was to Manhattan, but he had never guessed that she would have bought a house there—but that was his sister, always doing something good for some member of the family.

I wasn't thrilled with the idea of going to Panama, but having a house of my own was exciting, and I knew Tristan would be pleased. After all, it was an old house and it needed—carpentry work. We could make it ours. My heart started beating and I felt like screaming, "I'm happy! I'm truly happy," but I didn't, because my father had become somber.

"She didn't get everything," I said, "I mean, yeah, she got a new guy, a new location, but she lost me," I added.

"I couldn't lose you," he said in a quiet voice that made me catch my breath.

"A weekend won't change us," I said.

He nodded. There was silence after that as he drove me to Laurel's, where Tristan was waiting on the porch. I got out and waved for him, and he ran over. We hugged, and then he went around the side of my father's car and started talking with him.

I walked over to Laurel's front steps and sat down, and that's when I remembered that Leah Bloom's mother had placed a Craigslist ad asking women to marry her son. And it had worked! So why couldn't I ask a woman to date my father and like his dog? I could! I would!

Tristan raced over, "I'm going with your father to put the books in his place," he said. I grinned, because he was so totally cute I couldn't believe it.

"Goody," I said, and I watched them drive off.

Laurel's mom came out front, "Bet they're having a romantic morning walk along the beach," she said.

"Hand-in-hand," I added. She smiled. Laurel was her one and only and she doted on her too much I used to think, as in 'spoiling', but now I just thought, why not? Why not spoil the ones you love?

"Would you know how I could find my father a girlfriend?" I asked.

Laurel's mother Lynn was ultra-chic and ultra-hip, and she knew a lot of people. She was also very private and could keep a secret. After all, my father is known around Harvard and with the NYU crowd, and if someone saw my ad about my dad, they could tag it on Facebook or worse, it could go viral.

"I know a terrific matchmaker, but would your father be willing to meet with her?" she asked.

"Lynn, my father doesn't know how to get started unless it happens to him, but I'll meet with her. Is it expensive?" I asked.

"She owes me a favor. I'll set it up, so it's free for you," she said.

"Really? I mean, are you sure?" I asked; shy to take a gift.

"Just say thanks, and I'll make the phone call now," she said. That's why Laurel was always able to travel, to fall in love a hundred times, and to finally end up with Anthony, because she was taught to say 'yes and thanks'.

"Thanks! I want my father to be happy," I said. She nodded, and we went into the house together.

That night I met with Madge the matchmaker at her home in Jamaica Plains. She lived in one of those old Victorians that are stunning on the inside, but left unkempt on the outside. She was Laurel's mom's age, and was happily married to a man she'd met through a newspaper ad (pre-internet days). I had to bring two pictures of my father, and I showed her the write-up that Harvard had printed about esteemed faculty—he got top billing. She thought he was very 'dashing'. I told her his faults, and about Twist, his new dog. I also told her it couldn't be a 'date'. It would have to be set up as a chance meeting. She found the "undercover dating' style of it exciting, and knew she could find the right woman to meet him in a 'pretend' way. I got goosebumps just hearing her talk about my father falling in love again.

"How long have you wanted this?" she asked, catching me off guard for a second.

"I think it hit me the hardest during my second year at college, because I wanted him to have love. Of course, I had wanted it after my mother left, but that was too soon and he was too bruised and heartbroken."

"Leave it to me, I'll see that love happens," she said as she took my contact info, and that was that.

"Thanks so much," I said, hugging her.

Then I raced outside to find Tristan still sitting in his Land Rover, waiting for me.

"What was that about?" he asked.

And I told him the truth because I felt that Madge the matchmaker was the real deal.

"I'm glad I'm not female," he said with an extra-smug British tone.

I laughed. I mean, women do think about falling in love more than men, at least in my opinion they do—I could be wrong, but I don't think so.

We went out to eat at an Indian restaurant in Central Square. It was our first official date and I was so aware of that fact—only it felt good that we had already shared so much: Cassidy, Gabriel, Laurel's wedding and now my father's love life.

"Would you want to move with me to Rye, a beautiful section of New York State, because my Aunt Helen left me a fixer-upper house with six bedrooms?" I asked nervously, over a plate of curry.

"Absolutely, but is that before or after Panama?" he asked as he passed me the computer printout of a round-trip ticket that my father had booked for the following weekend.

"Yikes, that was fast," I said.

"He said you don't have to use it."

"Let's go to Rye right away. I'm not crazy about going to Panama, but a promise is a promise and I owe that much to my aunt, even if it's family-style manipulation," I said.

"Let's go tonight," he said, and we clinked our cups of Indian tea as a toast to the fixer-upper, Panama, and us.

Before eleven, we swung by the Harvard Inn and asked Gabriel if he wanted to drive with us; we were leaving right away.

"I was ready yesterday," Gabriel said, as he started packing his stuff.

I called my father to tell him that we were heading to Rye and that we would grab Shadow on our way.

"You don't have to go to Panama," he said.

"I do, but it won't change a thing between us," I said.

"All right, I'll change the ticket to fly out of JFK," he said and hung up.

We went to Laurel's and got our stuff. Laurel's mom wanted us to wait, but we couldn't. It was too exciting to hit the road and travel. Tristan and Gabriel stayed in the Land Rover in front of my father's place, while I raced up to get Shadow. He was surrounded by his new books, while Twist was on the floor, relaxing, and Shadow was barking at me.

"I'll call you when we get to Rye," I said. My father glanced up from his book, but said nothing.

"I never would have left you for Panama," I said.

"They will email your flight confirmation to your Smartphone," he said.

"Email, I didn't think you knew mine," I teased.

My father nodded. His emotions were under lock and key, but I knew I could reach him.

"I never would have left you for Panama and her new life. NEVER," I hollered as I headed to the door with Shadow on leash. I heard what I thought sounded like a slight crack in his emotions—but maybe that's what I wanted to hear. I mean if it had been a movie scene, the script would have read: *father cries **loudly***.

Tristan and Gabriel took turns driving us to Rye, NY, while Shadow and I camped out in the back seat. He's a big dog, but he knows how to curl up next to me. I watched Tristan and Gabriel talking, laughing, and sharing coffee, Red Bull, and stories, just to stay awake.

Before I knew it, we entered Rye, NY. "Hello Rye," I shouted. It's old fashioned, but not un-hip; it looked like a happy place to me. A place where people who work in Manhattan like to come home to in the evenings or on the weekends.

"Do I have my own room?" Gabriel asked.

"Of course," I said.

The large faded yellow house stood down a gravel driveway. My heart was beating just looking at something that now belonged to me, a home. A house is a home. It really is.

All of us got out of Tristan's Land Rover, and stood in front of it. It had been sitting abandoned for years, but still had character.

"Six bedrooms and three bathrooms," I said.

"Look at all the windows," Tristan said, eyeing all the work that needed to be done.

"I want to pick out my room first," Gabriel said.

"Go for it," I said, as I handed him the house key. He raced ahead of us. I liked having a brother; it felt like what I'd always imagined. Tristan held me back and folded his arms around me.

"Look at it," he said, and I stared up at the old house, my house. It felt so new, the feeling.

"If you share your American house with me, I'll share my UK house with you," he said.

"You mean you have a home?" I asked.

"Yes, I've got a tiny house, just outside London, it's terribly lonely," he said.

I turned and kissed him. He was saying things to me that I had only imagined, you know, in all my larger-than-life movie fantasies—but this was real.

We went in to the smell of a very old house that had been sitting unused for years. There were dusty sheets covering furniture, and the windows had cobwebs on them, but the rooms were small, cozy and perfect.

"Come upstairs," Gabriel shouted.

We raced up the wooden staircase to find that he'd chosen a small bedroom facing the overgrown backyard.

"This is mine," he said.

"It's yours, bro," I said. He nodded, and we left him looking out of the window.

"Let's find ours," Tristan said, and we walked along the hallway peeking into the other bedrooms until we reached the one at the far end, which had a bathroom and a small bedroom near to it.

"We could fix this so the bathroom could connect to only our bedroom, if you wanted to," he said.

I walked around the bedroom. It had a lot of window light funneling in that was beautiful, but the bathroom had not been tiled behind the vintage tub and sink. The floor was pine.

"Can you tile it?" I asked.

"You bet."

The tiny bedroom on the other side looked like it had been a nursery.

"Might need to put a little baby in this room," Tristan said with a wink as he caught me looking into it. Babies? Marriage? Love? Commitment? It all just swirled in my head.

"As you like, luv," I said, in my best fake British accent.

We agreed that Tristan would stay to vacuum and dust while Gabriel and I went out to buy beds, a fridge, and a stove. All I had to do was to get the electricity turned on in my name, and I didn't need the deed to do that.

Gabriel and I walked past stores in Rye (a quaint, friendly looking American town, perfect for shooting a coming-of-age film in) and we bought everything we needed, including loads of gourmet food. I felt spoiled, I could have anything I wanted and yet what I wanted was to live with Tristan and Gabriel for the rest of my life.

"We need to make extra keys, pull over there," I said, and jumped out. I walked up to the key maker. "I need two extra house keys made, please," I said, and watched while he copied my beautiful key into duplicates.

"Here's your house key, bro," I sang out, as I got back into Tristan's Land Rover.

"I'm going back to Harvard this spring," Gabriel said as he started the engine.

"So, you'll be home for the holidays and all summer, right?" I asked.

"Yeah. I might bring a girl back with me, okay?" he asked.

"You'd better. Love is number one, second behind a Harvard degree," I said.

Then while we drove back to the house, he played a singer named Rodriguez singing, *Sugar Man*. I had yet to see the documentary and Gabriel gave me a scolding about that. But, wow, we were both transfixed and I felt that for Gabriel songs said it all—like movies for me.

Once inside we found Tristan examining the furniture with obvious appreciation for the way they were made. He gets high off wood. Go figure. The windows no longer had cobwebs, thanks to Tristan's fast dusting. Shadow was fast asleep after playing in the back yard. We sat in the living room on the hardwood floor eating gourmet food out of containers while we waited for the beds to arrive. I felt almost like I was in the film *Out of Africa*. There's a scene where Streep plays Karen Blixen and Redford plays the role of Denys Finch Hatton and they sit together in her suddenly bare home with a wistful bond between them. I looked at Tristan and Gabriel and my heart swelled. Everything felt cohesive and connected between the three of us. Still, we were all ready for a long nap. I pinched my arm just to remind myself that this was my cool life—it was mine, not some movie flashing by.

# 30

## *CIRCLE*

Tristan drove me to the JFK airport. "Make the most of it and then hurry home where you belong," he said, as I undid my seatbelt and we kissed. My heart started to beat.

"Are you my boyfriend? You know, just in case my mother wants to know," I asked.

"Tell her, you're my girlfriend," he said. I jumped out and waved good-bye.

God, I couldn't wait to go to bed with him. He had decided that we should wait until I came back from Panama, just because he thought it was going to be an intense trip. I didn't have an opinion, but I was dying to do 'it' with him. It was so hard to lie in the same bed, only spooning.

Before I boarded the airplane for Panama with my Louis Vuitton carry-on suitcase, I called Paloma, who was now good friends with the filmmaker's soon-to-be-ex-wife. The film shoot had turned out to be a blast.

"I'm sex starved, I hope I don't dry hump a passenger's leg!"

"Girlfriend, I'm so proud of you for waiting. Because once you do it with Tristan, you won't stop," Paloma said, "Remember Holly Golightly in *Breakfast at Tiffany's*, she ended up divinely happy and that's what you're allowing yourself to have," she added.

"It has started to feel like that," I gushed.

"Shut up and go see your Momma and clean up the past," she said, and then hung up. Paloma doesn't waste a second on bullshit—that's why she's my best friend.

The plane ride was smooth and I didn't hump anyone's leg. I exited the busy airport into bright sunshine, warm weather, and the language of Spanish. I was dressed in my white jeans with the words 'THINKING HEART' on the thighs, a white Marc Jacobs sleeveless blouse, and my black Pradas—from Laurel's wedding. My mother didn't meet me at the airport because she wanted me to meet her in the center of the city. At a location she said was easy to find. It wasn't. And yeah, if I found a taxi driver who spoke English and knew the way then it would be. In my opinion, she got a D- in points for that decision. She said something about not being able to leave her job in time. Okay, whatever, just glad I was only staying for the weekend.

Fortunately a short, stocky, friendly-faced taxi driver hopped out of his taxi, "Miss America, I bring you anywhere, I am Pedro" he said. Eager to practice English, he told me he was fifty-four and the father of five kids. I laughed and gave him the address I had in my Smartphone.

During the whole drive over, I helped with his pronunciation, during a typical tourist conversation.

"Here you are. Have a good day. Thank you for being a nice customer," he said, as he pulled up to the curb in downtown Panama. The city was packed with color, noise, people, and almost every American fast food joint you could name. Ugh. Love my country, but I'm not sure about the food it promotes everywhere else. I mean, I came to visit and experience Panama for Panama, not Panama for America. Oh, well.

"Pedro, your English is good, keep speaking every chance you get," I said and I got out.

I was facing the white stone building, as I paid him adding a handsome tip. I entered the community school and walked along the terra cotta tile hallway until I found the third classroom. It was filled with adults. She was in the middle of the room, wearing a loose, knee length brown cotton dress with large flowers printed all over it, and black cowboy boots. Her light brown hair hung in a braid down her back. She was thinner, and her face was makeup free. She seemed older, but that was natural. What really struck me about her was how much happier she appeared—and I couldn't bullshit my mind about that.

"Mi hija," she said, and everyone in the class clapped.

"My?" she asked them in a teacher's voice.

"Daughter," they all said.

And then one-by-one they introduced themselves to me, and told me using their new English words what a nice mother I had, how blessed I was. I headed up to her and she hugged me. It had been years and years and years. I hugged her, but I felt a mix of sadness—and a lot of stored up anger. She excused her class and instead of talking to me, she walked me around the community school building telling me about the cooperative group that ran it and what was taught in each room. Go figure!

Then we headed out into the Panama sunshine, jumped into her dark red jeep, and headed for the Darien Jungle, where she lived with Santiago, her coffee bean man. Right away I noticed the wedding band on her finger. It was silver, interlaced with turquoise, not the gold ring my father had bought her. He hadn't mentioned their divorce; I guess I just assumed it and this now confirmed it. She smiled, laughed and chatted about Panama, as if she had spent her entire life there. And as if I was any old friend coming to visit. I think she was nervous. I was furious.

The Darien Jungle was like a movie set. The farther we drove, the dustier the unpaved roads became, transforming into farmland with a few scattered tabego shops along the way.

"Your Aunt Helen was my good friend. We never lost our connection," she said.

I thought of her ashes in my Louis Vuitton carry-on suitcase, it felt so surreal.

"I don't think she ever gave up on a friendship," I said, trying to imagine anyone dumping her as a friend. I had lost a bunch of friends from high school, and later after college, but auspiciously Paloma and Laurel had remained, my best, best friends.

The dirt road zigzagged up to their plain one-story wood house, sans paint, and to the left and right coffee bean fields spread out for miles. The aroma of coffee was pungent and robust.

"Do you drink coffee?" she asked.

"You'd know the answer, if you knew me," I said. It just slipped out of my mouth, but I wasn't sorry.

"I've missed you so much," she countered.

"Are you fluent in Spanish?" I asked, since I didn't really know her.

"Oh, yes, and Santiago has gotten stronger in English as well, but we speak Spanish all the time," she said.

"Great," I said, since I wasn't bilingual.

"We won't speak Spanish, while you're here," she added.

She parked behind the house, next to a small dairy cow pasture with a cabin in back of it. We got out of the jeep and walked around to the front door, which was wide open—and there stood Santiago. He was in worn blue jeans, a blue jean shirt, and black cowboy boots, and his black hair was short, his eyes dark, and his teeth white. He didn't remind me of any actor. He wasn't handsome like my father, or as tall.

"Welcome to Panama," he said, extending his right hand to me, and I thought about how he had stolen my mother away from my father, without so much as a second thought. Still I shook his strong coarse hand and then watched as he kissed and hugged my mother. They acted like they hadn't seen each other in weeks.

"Your mother has waited a long time for this moment, and I am honored," he said. I could hear Carol back in Los Feliz at Yoga Vibe saying, "Exhale the bad energy out, inhale calmness" so I inhaled, "Nice to meet you," I said, as I let a deep breath out.

"Come, let me show you your own cabin," she said, and we left Santiago by the front door. I had to laugh as she unlatched the gate to the dairy cow pasture. Six light brown dairy cows were grazing near the unpainted one-room cabin. That looked like a shack. She opened the door and we stepped into a potter's studio with pottery stacked up on wall-to-wall shelves. In the left corner near a single window was a twin bed with a mosquito net over it. There were three hanging lamps and wire hooks for my clothes, and a wooden milk-carton as a night table. The floor around the bed was made from colorful handmade tiles.

"I made the tiles. I started with bowls and cups, but then I just found tile making more enjoyable," she said.

I put my LV suitcase down and hung up my white linen jacket, which I didn't need because of the Panama heat. I looked at my Smartphone—it had no signal.

"My cell phone's dead. Where should I charge it?" I asked anxiously.

"We don't have internet, cable, or TV access, just a landline phone," she said, like it was something she was proud of.

"What?" I asked, suddenly feeling like my oxygen supply was being cut off—and I didn't have anything to save me.

"If you need the phone, just help yourself. We only use the internet when we're in the city during the week," she said.

Oh, God, she wasn't a cell phone or online woman; it was like she had gone back in time.

"No worries," I said, trying to sound as if I could make it through the weekend.

"I'll show you the outhouse, and then our house," she said.

"Outhouse?" I asked full of panic.

"We're used to it. And we've got an outdoor shower, too. But we bathe in the stream behind the coffee fields," she said.

"That's different," I said.

The outhouse was an outhouse—if you've seen one, you've seen them all, even with the colorful tiles. Even with the smell of coffee wafting though the circular window—it was still an outhouse.

Their unpainted house had only two rooms: a kitchen with a round table (like the one on the Charlie Rose show), and a bedroom.

"Do you make enough money?" I asked, because I really wanted to know.

"We sell our coffee to one major company in the U.S. and they sell it under their own label. We own the land on both sides," Santiago said, defensively.

"It's the outhouse," my mother said, winking at him.

"Claro que si!" he said and they both laughed.

"Let's go for our walk. We always go for one around this time," she said, and the three of us headed out to walk the coffee bean fields.

We walked for over an hour from one end of the field to the other. This was how they stayed fit and trim. I acted like it was fun—but this over the Charles River, over Central Park, over walking along Malibu Beach—no thanks!

After that she and I sat in brown corduroy upholstered armchairs while Santiago cooked us a vegetarian meal. They ate no meat; they hadn't since re-locating to Panama. She talked about teaching English once a week and selling her pottery twice a month—the two jobs she did just for extra enjoyment. The main job and bliss was their coffee beans. We ate at the round table.

And then she walked me back through the dairy cow pasture to my cabin.

"I'm fine," I said, not wanting her to come in.

"I'll just set the lights for you," she said, and entered to turn on the lights, which ran on a battery timer, all except the one nearest to the bed.

"You look wonderful," she said.

"This is really what you wanted?" I asked, because I was done deep breathing. I was ready to fight for my father.

"It might not seem glamorous, like a movie to you, but yes this is all I want," she said.

"You broke my father's heart; you left him to question his ability to love anyone besides me."

"It wasn't out of spite."

"You came back, after meeting Santiago in a burrito joint in Porter Square, and you started packing. You told my father, 'I'm not in love with you anymore and I'm leaving,' and that was it. I was there," I said, finally telling her the story from my point of view.

"I can hear your pain, but I chose my beating heart over obligation," she said.

"Obligation? That's what we were to you?" I asked, my hands clenched.

"Not you, but my marriage to your father. Only your Aunt Helen understood, and she told me to go, to follow my heart. I wanted to bring you."

"Go with you? Huh! I wouldn't have left my father for this. For that guy," I said.

I was fuming with rage because she was like a lovesick puppy.

"I knew nothing when I met your father. I was inexperienced, undeveloped; I was just following what people of my generation did. Santiago made my heart beat. I left your father for him; it was my first grown-up choice. I'm sorry I hurt you, I'm sorry I hurt your dad. I never planned on it, but I don't regret my choice," she said.

"You're the most selfish woman I know. I'm nothing like you. You've never come back to the States to check on me once, not for college graduation, not to see my Hollywood life, not for anything," I said.

"I've been too scared to return," she said. Like that was an excuse.

"You're an American, in case you forgot. You should visit your own country."

"I've wanted to see you."

"Action speaks volumes. My father hasn't moved on. How do you feel about that?"

"He's a slow learner—"

"My God, how can you criticize him? While you've been happy here, he's been ALONE," I shouted, interrupting her, hoping for once that she'd get it.

"I'm sorry I missed out on your high school graduation, your college, Los Angeles. Your first time at everything," she said.

"I'm talking about my father," I said, like she didn't understand English.

"I'm sorry I missed out on your life experiences."

"I'm talking about him!"

"No, you," she said.

"You're heartless, and you're wrong," I screamed.

"You've got two choices: forgive me, or hate me forever," she said, as if my aunt had told her to say that to me, and she walked out. I pulled Aunt Helen's box of ashes out of my LV suitcase and I threw it onto the tiled floor.

"You're wrong, you're wrong," I shouted. Then I rushed over to the box (that was now crushed) and I picked it up. I held it and I cried so hard.

The next morning, I didn't get up. When my mother came to see if I wanted breakfast, I told her I was too tired to eat. For most of the day I stayed in bed, I felt so depressed that I just didn't want to get up. How could I forgive her for this? How could I? How could my Aunt Helen want her ashes spread in a circle around my mother's two-room, unpainted house? How could she want to be left far from my father and me? And why near my mother? Why her?

Toward the late, late afternoon, I got up and walked barefoot all over the colorful handmade-tiles my mother had made over the years. I couldn't figure anything out and I was too angry to eat.

Okay, so then I had a *Star Wars* movie moment: I thought about the scene where Luke Skywalker (what a fantastic last name) was being trained by Yoda. And Luke's not certain about the 'Force' so he asks, *"But how do I know the good side from the bad?"* And Yoda says to him, *"You will know when you are calm, at peace, passive. A Jedi uses the force for knowledge and defense, never for attack."* That scene just kept playing in my mind over and over—and then I knew I was about to fully understand it.

I walked over to my LV suitcase figuring I should at least put on clean underwear. And that's when I saw it: the orange post-it. It said *I love you, Tristan.* I smiled. It was so sweet, and so needed. Wow, I had him; I wasn't in the past anymore. I had an old house, and love—that was what I wanted. I was sorry my father hadn't gotten a happily-ever-after, but there was still time for a sequel. I marched over to the potter's wheel and noticed the drawings next to it, designs for future tiles. There were photos of Panama (the coffee beans, flowers, and fruit), and then I spotted a photo of me as a baby sleeping, and one of me standing on a chair with no clothes on at age six. And then there was a photo of me and my father, posing in front of the Alice in Wonderland statue in Central Park when I was twelve. My father's hair was long and he had the beginnings of a professor's beard, and I had my hair in pigtails and was wearing a pink and white dress with white clogs. My mother had a photo of us—not what I expected.

Okay, okay, so my Aunt Helen had wanted me to let go of my past, my disappointment with my mother; she had wanted me to know that life is imperfect most of the time. I looked down at the post-it from Tristan in my right hand. I knew I would frame it. I sighed out loud, a deep sigh, like a breath waiting to get out of me.

After that, I got dressed and headed out to greet the six dairy cows, happy knowing that they wouldn't get slaughtered for a hamburger. I went up to each one and said, "I'm letting go of my past, I'm no longer allowing myself to fill up with rage, or regret, or sadness. I am at peace with my past. I feel goodness all around me."

Then I found my mother lying in a natural twine hammock near her unpainted two room house.

"Did you rest?" she asked, eagerly.

"I did more than rest, I feel 100 percent better!"

"Try the other one," she said, pointing to Santiago's hammock.

"Okay," I said, and I lay in it.

"I made them, sometimes we sleep in them," she said proudly.

"You never knew you were an artist, did you?" I asked.

"I didn't."

"You're who you always wanted to be" I said, and she grinned at me.

After a few minutes of swinging in her handmade hammock, I said, "I'd like to do the ash ceremony right now."

I felt filled with emotions, and ready to honor my aunt—because she had truly had a hand in raising me—in a real, profound way, with one-of-a-kind experiences.

"Let's," she said.

I raced with my empty stomach back through the cow pasture and into the potter's cabin, and I grabbed the smashed box of ashes. My mother was standing by her front door, I raced back to her. Fortunately Santiago was working in the coffee bean fields, which was perfect timing, because the ceremony needed to be just with us.

My mother passed me a letter that Aunt Helen had sent her a few months before.

"This is what she wanted read as part of the ceremony," she said softly.

"You read it, while I make a loop around your house with her ashes" I said, because I was too scared to read it.

My mother read the following: *"Here my ashes shall blend with the earth, the wind and the air. May those whom I've loved, know that I love them forever and ever. And that love in a memory can fill up the moments. Cherish and forget me not."* Over and over she read it, until I had completed the circle and we were once again in front of my mother's front door.

We went inside and ate the meal that she had saved for me, and I felt so un-angry, so un-hurt, and so un-sad. That night, we played checkers, Old Maid and tic-tac-toe, something I hadn't done since I was a kid and it was so much fun.

All Sunday, my mother and I just hung out, talking and eating. She even taught me how to pick coffee beans, and how to throw clay on the potter's wheel. I felt so glad that I had come to meet her again, and so relieved that I had Tristan, Gabriel, my father, Shadow, and Twist to be with stateside.

On Monday morning, I flew back to the United States. Wow! I was in the JFK airport once again, and as I was getting off the plane, my cell phone rang. Hurray, I was mobile. I could surf the web again, and Google for anything.

"I'm going on a date," my father's voice said.

"What?" I asked.

"Seems there are a number of random women seeking me out, accidentally, and nonchalantly."

"Oh," I said. Madge the matchmaker hadn't wasted a second.

"Thanks," he said.

"For what?" I sheepishly asked.

But my father didn't answer. Ha ha, he knew I wasn't done trying to get him a happily-ever-after. Blame it on the movies, it's not my fault—some of my favorite films are the ones that end happily-ever-after.

Tristan was waiting outside the terminal, in front of his Land Rover, wearing dark blue jeans, a black t-shirt and work boots. Can it get any better? No, it can't! I'd come full circle at last. And now it was my *Breakfast at Tiffany's* moment, and I took it. He kissed me, and when our lips parted, I looked into his dark brown eyes and I asked, "Did I tell you how blissfully happy and in love with you, I am?" Okay, so in my own words—but I said it more or less like Audrey Hepburn had as Holly Golightly in the movie, and I meant it.

## THE END

*As in my happily-ever-after!*

 Kristina Shook was born in New York City into a wonderful, struggling, bohemian art community. Photographed 1-18 as a documentary by her mother. A full-scholarship graduate of Sarah Lawrence College (Bronxville, New York). Master's degree in Screenwriting from the American Film Institute (Los Angeles). She dwells in LA & NYC. *This is her 2nd novel, (first novel Donna Day sits on a shelf).

Look out for her 3rd novel Ava Anderson: Case of the Strippers (mystery series). www.kristinashook.com

"Some of us aren't meant to belong. Some of us have to turn the world upside down and shake the hell out of it until we make our own place in it."
— Elizabeth Lowell, *Remember Summer*

*Author photo by photographer Alex Chemerisov*
*Book Cover Designer Christine K*
*Formatted by Polgarus Studio pologarusstudio.com*
*Heartfelt thanks to my editor*
*Huge thanks to actress Jennifer Emmaline for proof reading*